GOD AWAKENED

RAVENS NIGHT SAGA
BOOK TWO

HOLLY MACGREGOR

Hardcover ISBN: 978-1-7381864-5-7

Paperback ISBN: 978-1-7381864-3-3

EBook: 978-1-7381864-2-6

Audio Book ISBN: 9781738186426

978-1-7381864-7-1

WARNING

God Awakened includes content that might not be suitable for some readers. I've included a list of these elements at the end of the book. If you have concerns, please check it out so you can decide whether to continue reading.

PROLOGUE

For the one to see the futures past,
Is thrice blessed to conquer lightfast.
Fire be true,
With leadership firm.
Changing destiny right.

CHAPTER 1

*H*e was such a hypocrite, accusing Harlow of lying to him when he himself was lying to her. As was Rowan. Being a close family, he thought, was not the case. Holding his sister to a standard he couldn't uphold. What had he been thinking? Closing his eyes, he shook his head at himself.

Feeling pathetic, he paced the floor. After storming out on his twin, he had followed through on his word. Going directly to Sally's private rooms. Just thinking about the woman made a shiver run down his spine. He continued to question himself as to why he had agreed to this specific mission. He still did not know what he had been thinking.

Looking around the tiny suite, as he paced. He was grateful to be alone. Trying to be who he needed to be around its resident was just one thing too many right now. He needed to process his many thoughts.

Although he had a feeling, however small. He wouldn't have to continue this facade for much longer. Things were happening. Likely coming to a very messy end. So much like his dear friend Cora.

The very person who had been tasked with this current assignment. One where he needed to get very close and intimate with one person. Someone who the secret society thought had insider information. If: Provided that she didn't, she could still gain access to it. If someone managed to persuade her. Had he known then what he knew now, he would have turned the assignment down. Then perhaps Cora would still be alive. Running his hands through his hair, he gripped the strands.

Wanting to scream out his frustrations, he froze. Biting the inside of his cheek and breathing harshly through his nose. The likelihood of this place being filled with similar listening devices was just too high. Not wanting to play his hand too soon. He still had a job to do, after all.

The information remained crucial for The Ravens Night. It was lucky then his temporary imposed grounding offered him opportunities. Not leading his True Guard team on missions. Allowed him to concentrate on the crucial tasks. Enabling him to focus on gathering any information he could from his alleged 'girlfriend.'

Just thinking of her that way, he shivered and holding back his gag reflex. Wrapping his arms around himself, he continued to pace back and forth. Just as well for recordings. He needed to be agitated, so his repetitive walking wouldn't be unusual. It was just the sleazy woman irked him. His gut was churning for the show, he would have to put on soon.

Portraying the character he was compelled to display made him feel uncomfortable. Too far out of his comfort zone, a laid-back and aloof partner. Just thinking about it sent more shivers down his spine. He never had an issue with such a role in a relationship. Then again, a partner in a relationship had never disgusted him before. Not that she was unclean; it was who she was at her core. A selfish, self-serving woman who shows only the face she wants a person to see. A face she hoped would get her what she wanted from them.

Again, he was grateful she wasn't here. He just wasn't in the mood for the antics. Hopefully, this facade wouldn't last much longer and he could move on to more important things. Like discovering what his sister was doing. Maybe he should go see Sloane, perhaps he might know something. With his decision made, he bent to pick up his bag when he heard the locks disengage on the front door.

How had he not noticed she was here? He was so engrossed in his thoughts; that he was slipping. Not good, not good at all. He needed to stay sharp. Especially around this woman, not knowing her true motives yet made her even more dangerous.

Considering all the time they had been together, he had assumed he would have found out more than he had. Perhaps she was on to him and was simply playing with him. But why, though? Or was she simply to be a diversion to keep him from the truth? He suspected that was the case. Still, while he was keeping her occupied, it kept her away from Harlow, who she liked to torment.

Plastering on a fake smile, he prepared himself for an evening of playing her submissive lover. God, how that thought left a foul taste in his mouth. Not to mention the fact he would have to scrub himself from head to toe afterward. At least her unit had a private wet room, a luxury reserved for command leaders. A luxury he and Harlow grew up with as a standard.

As they grew up, he noticed that he and his sister received luxuries that others did not receive. He had always wondered why. Learning early on it was not wise to ask why. If he and his twin inquired about anything, they would face punishment. Quickly, they learned to keep any questions to themselves.

Sadly, it didn't stop the mistreatment of the others in the compound. It also made the treatment of Harlow and her limp intense. Her lack of 'perfection' stood out like a beacon in a world where everything and anything could be fixed. He hated that for her. There is always an effort to protect her. Even her son protected her from ridicule. He would simply brag about how great she was and her many achievements.

He watched the door open to reveal Sally's squeal of delight. Ending his mental road trip. A trait he seemed to share with his twin. One he tried to hide, with some success. Straightening, he prepared himself as she launched herself towards him. Catching her in his arms as she wrapped her limbs around him. With a grunt, he asked,

"What took you so long? I have been waiting for you."

Her answer was to grab his head, holding tight as she kissed him. Shoving her tongue into his mouth, moaning loudly. Fighting past his gag reflex, he kissed her back. He needed to stay focused and complete this mission.

TAPPING HER FOOT, she waited impatiently for the lock to disengage. Being a member of the True Guard, Honor was accustomed to things happening for her in an instant. They had access to too many of the bonus features in and around the compound in which they all lived. However, those who were not a part of this elite group had to make do without it.

With an exasperated sigh, she placed her hands on her hips. This was ridiculous. It shouldn't take this long. Why were they always doing this to her? She knew full well they hadn't wanted her on their team, but they sure as hell didn't want her on any other team, either. The multiple attempts made to make her life frustrating and force her to quit usually made her chuckle. However, today they were successfully annoying her to no end.

Tampering with the timing of locks engaging or the opening of doors was lame. Even the reprogram to keep the automatic lights off. Whenever her access codes were used. She could usually shrug it off. However, today it was pissing her off.

There was something big happening, she knew. They hadn't included her like always. Only this time, when she made any attempt to find out any information, she would hit a wall of silence. An unusual occurrence. There were a few on their team that would keep her informed of the goings-on. They believed she belonged and treated her like a genuine member of the True Guard. If only in secret and behind closed doors. Especially away from Jasper's knowledge.

Lately, however, they have all been silent. Not acknowledging her at all. It hurt. What had she done to deserve such treatment? Logically, she knew she had done nothing. It was Jasper and his jealousy. Why he felt that way toward her was a mystery to her. She had nothing to be jealous of, no family, no friends, nothing. Other than his sour personality, she was jealous of him. A leader with his own True Guard team, friends, and a family. She'd give anything for the last two.

Even if the last one was a found family, like his. Given his brother was missing and now presumed dead. He had been absent for far too long now.

Finally, the locks released, opening the door wide. Grumbling under her breath, she stomped into the room. Ignoring all the grunts, sighs, and eye rolls to her presence. She developed a thick skin because she knew they didn't want or respect her. Her only value to them was her skills and intelligence.

Making her way through the room to her minuscule desk in the far corner. She would perform her responsibilities like she did every day. Maybe if she pretended to ignore them, they would speak freely and allow her some chance of getting information.

Anything would be better than nothing. At least then she would have something to go on. This treatment only served as a reminder that she desired to be assigned to Caden's team. If she had been there, she knew without a doubt that they would include her as an equal. With a mental head shake, she focused on the items on her desk. Taking inventory of new the tasks for today.

There wasn't much for her to do. Nothing of any great importance. Furthering her internal ire. Well, this would mean she could focus more on her investigation of the twins. Why, they were under suspicion and for what? Finally, devising a way to help them.

Relying only on her intuition was fine, but she suspected this time she needed more concrete information. Following her head and her gut this time, she needed to know a little more before she acted. Trusting both, hoping they wouldn't let her down.

Still, this was hard for her to do, to sit back, wait and listen. Life had always required her to take the bull by the horns, so to speak. She knew her shortcomings and how information was key to knowing what to plan and how. Thus, getting it done.

The last thought made her laugh. Being their archivist, Harlow was always spouting old phrases. She enjoyed hearing them, most were amusing. Some she didn't understand. You likely had to have been there then, to get it. While others were so catchy, they quickly became a part of their vernacular.

She admired the women, regardless of what everyone said about her. Not believing a thing, they said. It was lies all lies. Despite her 'imperfections' not being corrected at birth or later, everyone was still jealous of the woman.

Internally scolding herself, she refocused on her work and got to it. Hoping luck was on her side and the plan would work.

A few hours later, she looked up from her station, noticing most of her teammates were now out of the office. She considered it perfect. Standing, she made her way to their little kitchenette. Along the way, she observed the remaining teammates. Taking the long way around, she looked about, attempting to spy on the empty desks. Hoping for anything she might find useful, left out carelessly.

Finally getting herself a steaming cup of brew. Another thing they could all thank the twins for. Their addiction to this magickal brew allowed them all a taste of it. Well, at least the best simulated version of it. Resources were just too precious to reproduce it, so simulated it was.

She took her time getting back to her desk. Twisting her head side to side as she went, easily concealing her continued attempt at spying. It worked fairly well. Only one of her teammates asked if she was ok.

She raised her mug with a smile and a nod. Happy that they smiled and nodded in return. Work must be intense if she was receiving remarks of concern for a supposed stiff neck. This was good. She could put her plan into motion. The one she had come up with while working on her menial tasks this morning.

. . .

THE MORNING HAD PASSED UNEVENTFULLY. It was just after lunch that her plan paid off. The room filled with chatter as members returned. She went unnoticed. Perfect, she thought.

Happy for once, she was invisible. They openly discussed their feelings on how justified their team leader was in his actions against the Faxons. They deserved what was coming to them. She was shocked and felt a powerful urge to defend them.

Instead, she bit her lip and dug her fingernails into her palms. Reminding herself to stay quiet. Needing them to continue. It was a surprise to her that instead of jealousy; it was hatred towards the family. A family favored by the Overseer and by all accounts, for no reason other than they were orphans. Which made little sense, as many of them were orphans as well, with no special treatment. She could include herself in that group.

The conversation continued with her listening intently. As time passed, she noticed not all of her fellow team members felt the same way. There were a few just going with the flow silently agreeing, while others remained silent and quietly fuming with the topic of choice. Did they feel the same way as her? Could she maybe have some allies within her team? Or had this all been a performance designed solely for her benefit? To ensure that they could bring her up to speed on the inner workings and feelings.

She would have to ponder more on this later. She needed all her concentration to listen and work at the same time. Unfortunately, she had to interrupt her plotting and planning when a time-sensitive matter came across her desk. Thankfully, she could hide what she had been working on easily. This was going to take her the rest of the day.

At least she was gaining information from all the chatter. Learning who was on which side. Who was also wavering between the two. Her suspicion with the more she heard was that the Faxons were a part of something larger than themselves was growing.

Accessing her screen, her fingers flew across the touchpad. Searching for any files on the family, tucking them away onto her private drive. At a glance, she hadn't been able to find any information to support her current theory. Which meant it was likely kept on their team leader's private drive.

A private drive they weren't supposed to have. Funny, because they all did. Multiple ones too. All kinds of mistrust were present within Jasper's team. It was a wonder they operated as a team at all. Hopefully tomorrow she will be more successful in digging through the files to find out more information. The conversation today revealed some good information that she could likely use.

Knowing now whose private files she needed to access, she planned how she could gain entry. She had just enough work left from today that she could use as an excuse to come in early tomorrow. Giving her the much-needed time to get the documents off the private drives.

Satisfied with her plans, she proceeded to tidy her desk. Like always, she was the last one finished for the day. However, today she was going to leave early. Not staying for any extra work and trying to impress.

CHAPTER 2

*G*rateful was the last thing he thought he should be feeling. Getting down to the brass tax and having sex with her usually allowed him to garner little pieces of information. Even unwanted or unrelated to his mission, it all helped in the end. He was glad when her stomach growled so loudly that he laughed at her. Teasing her that the tiger she ate for breakfast wanted its release. She better let it loose for fear of it consuming her.

Watching while she angrily stomped around her little kitchenette, preparing something for them to eat. A task she usually delegated to him. This time, however, she had growled at him, mumbling under her breath unintelligible words, presumably about him.

He must of really pissed her off to have her changing routine. Very likely causing her to reveal more of her true colors. Refreshing as it was, she was still a nasty woman. Really whiny too. How anyone could stand to be around her, let alone work with her? Baffled him.

Her behavior only made him laugh harder and for her face to redden further. He needed to remember he was playing a character and should behave a certain way. In order to stifle the laughter, he bit his lips while trying to inhale through his nose. It was hard and took him a couple of minutes. He failed the first few times, earning him glares from where she worked on their food.

It felt good to laugh. He couldn't remember the last time he had. How sad was that? This mission was screwing with not only his head but his emotions as well. Best it ended soon.

Shaking his head and closing his eyes, he regained his composure and pulled the character he needed into place. The lovesick puppy dog.

Following a quick apology, which surprised him, she accepted. They began conversing about nothing at all. She always surprised him with how she could talk endlessly about anything. How she managed it was a skill he doubted no one else had or wanted. It likely was the only real thing about her he had ever seen. Something she didn't share with everyone, either.

Sitting at her little table and chairs, they ate their meal, continuing to gab throughout. The more they talked, the more relaxed she seemed. Which was strange. Sally always seemed to be wound tighter than any spring. He doubted she realized she was revealing some information, albeit sporadically and unintentionally. Causing him to wonder how she actually gained her position as a True Guard team leader. Internally shaking his head, he focused instead on finishing his meal.

They continued to chat long after lunch, taking the conversation to her sofa. He was thankful for the break in their usual hot and heavy routine. As much as he wanted answers on the mission, he could only take so much. The dealings with this woman have changed him and his desire for a partner.

Thinking about it, he had a gut feeling that tonight would be their last night together. Silently sending out a thanks for it, he was worried about the why. His instincts were telling him he might not like the outcome, causing them to delay the inevitable as long as possible.

Like always, he waited for her subtle cues he needed to be her sexual submissive. Such as she called him, when in reality he was just a human sex toy. A toy giving her all the gratification, not once ever caring about him or his needs. To her, he had none.

At first, that had hurt him. Her view of him and the role of a submissive. Now, however, he understood she was simply selfish. Only caring what she could get for herself. Might as well get this over with so she would fall asleep and he could at least get some rest before the morning. He never could fall asleep with her around. Never trusting what she would do. It was better to rest and simply pretend to sleep.

Watching her stand and crook a finger his way, he slowly rose to follow as her slimy smile spread across her face. The pleasant woman he had been chatting with was now gone, and the wicked witch was back. Time for the show, he thought.

Once in her bedroom, he moved into his usual position on the bed after he disrobed. Watching as her eyes glittered in delight. At least she found him attractive. That had allowed him to get somewhat hard for her. If only she knew the truth of what he thought of her, and everyone else, for that matter.

Telling himself off for allowing his mind to wonder. Now was not the time for that. At least not yet. He needed to pay attention. Saying all the right things, doing all the right things. This had to be believable. He doubted she suspected otherwise. He was safe, at least for now.

From the foot of the bed, she crawled, making her way toward him. Stopping when she reached for his semi-erect cock. Looking at him, she wrapped her icy fingers around him. Smiling with an evil glint in her eye, she bent, wrapping her lips around him, swallowing him whole.

Fisting the pillow, his eyes rolled to the back of his head with pleasure. This was one thing this woman could do well. All he had to do was close his eyes and pretend it was someone else, anyone else.

However, one person always came to mind when this happened. It was always her. Honor.

. . .

HER PLANS WENT DOWN the drain. Everything she had schemed yesterday went to waste. She had received an incoming message that woke her up long before her alarm. There was a change of plans for today. She needed to get up and move pronto. Her daily duties had shifted.

Fucking Jasper and his meddling. It had to him. Which pissed her off. He could never leave well enough alone. That one is always the center of attention. When he wasn't, he threw a tantrum.

Who else could it be? He had forever pulled crap like this. He treated her more like a tool to use than a team member. It made little sense.

Learning they assigned her to watch and monitor the live feed in the archives today pissed her off. What had she done to deserve such a treatment? Had she given herself away yesterday in her efforts to find any and all information about the Faxon twins? That couldn't be possible. She had, however, covered her tracks, knew she had.

Being the one that everyone in the compound always went to, to find out information regarding any tech-related trace within their beloved dome. She knew there was no way any of her team could find out what she had been up to yesterday via a tech search. Her being the tech guru and all. The only other compound member with stills close to hers was Caden.

The reason of why she was chosen to observe the library live remains unclear. They recorded this feed and watched it the next day. It always comprised the same three team members. Each was a member of another True Guard team. The intent was to keep it fair. So they claimed.

How Jasper had gotten the assignment made her wonder. Removing the other team's members, then putting her on it. Scared her. It was clear he had an issue with Caden and Harlow and always had. However, as the years passed, he became more charismatic about his feelings. Hiding them with subtle and polite jabs here and there for those higher up. Usually, the slights went right over their heads. Another thing to inflate his ego. Likely why he believed himself above them all.

Once again, she had no proof of this, only her personal beliefs. Seemed to be a trend as of late. Finding any proof against the Faxons was difficult, if not impossible. She thought she would just have to put her plan in motion based only on her instincts and the menial tidbits she had overheard. It sucked she was being excluded yet again from her team. Likely, something big was about to go down. Her team leader didn't trust her, which made her laugh. He was right; she had picked a side, and it wasn't his.

Placing her here meant she wouldn't gain any knowledge of their comings and goings. Well, they were the ones who would be in for a surprise. She had a live show of Harlow's actions today with the new plan of helping her in any way she could.

She wasted no time in getting ready for the day and her new assignment. Hoping that what she had planned would work. It needed to work. All this crap with Jasper was getting old and inflating his already to big ego. The man was a menace.

Getting to the recording booth early, she set up quickly. Going over every permeable option, just in case. Wanting to be as prepared as possible. With so many curveballs being thrown at her lately, she wanted to avoid making any mistakes.

Watching intently, she waited for Harlow to arrive. She had all the past recordings pulled and was ready to use. She planned to make her newfound friend the invisible lady. All she needed was to see the outfit she had on today and she could pull the appropriate video.

Scanning the other feeds in the compound, she looked for a view of her target. Once she appeared, her fingers flew across the touch screen, doing what she needed for her plan to work.

By the time they noticed today's live feed was a recording, Harlow will have done whatever it is she needs to do. They would notice too, of that she was positive. She had noted there was some tampering with the feeds and cameras. Thankfully, with her arriving extra early, she had reworked the tampering. If just a little.

Hopefully granting them both more time. Allowing them to do all they needed to do. She had crossed her fingers, saying a little prayer just in case it didn't work out.

What baffled her was how she knew today was the day that the Faxons were making their move. She didn't know. Was it her reassignment this morning? Or her gut feelings. They were something she had always trusted. Her gut instincts had never failed her and were eerily accurate. Having kept her safe for all these years, now she would use them to keep others safe. Protect them as best she could from those in the compound who wanted to harm them.

CHAPTER 3

*B*ecoming aware slowly, he cursed himself for falling asleep. It was not a safe thing for him to do at the moment. Sally's suite was an unsafe place. The need to be alert at all times was a necessity here. Soon, he could truly relax and get the much-needed sleep he wanted. He hoped. Only time will tell.

Cautiously, he opened his eyes, scanning the bedroom. Not only was he alone in bed, but the lights were off and the door was closed. Exhaling, the breath he hadn't realized he was holding. He relaxed against the headboard for a moment. Taking the time to center himself with some meditative breathing. Swinging his legs over the edge of the bed, he got out as quietly as he could; making his way to the door.

While staying away from the sensor, not wanting the door to open. He placed his ear near the door. Hearing noises on the other side, it took him a moment to realize what he was hearing. There were people on the other side having noisy sex or someone was killing the other. His bet was on the latter. When Sally finally started begging for more after her grunts, groans, and moans.

Turning up his nose in disgust, he shook with a spine-chilling shiver. The sounds of sex and pleasure with the venomous woman turned his stomach. It sounded like the lovers were enjoying them-selves, at least.

Given the task of seducing the woman for information, this exposed an entirely new side of her. Suspecting that this version of her tea was hearing was the real woman coming through. He could feel the difference vibrating in the air.

This was not the same version of the woman he saw. Him having to always be submissive to her pleasure. The sounds indicated the situation had changed. She was only too happy to please her partner. Intrigued, he pressed his ear firmly to the door, hoping to hear more. Sally was a talker by nature. She would always chatter before, during, and after.

They rewarded him for his patience. When they completed she started her inquiry. Her line of questioning furthered his suspicion as to the identity of her partner. Being rewarded again when he heard Jasper snap at her. He didn't like that she allowed someone else to touch and have her. That she belonged to him and only him. The fact Caden touched her was disgusting.

Her sharp reply was that the reason for a Faxon touching her was because he had ordered it. That he had wanted a spy on the inside with intimate knowledge of them. So he could just shove it. He had to hold back a chuckle, listening to them bicker. So his instincts that they were truly a couple were now confirmed. It was a fact that they had both received the same assignment. He suspected, however, that she hadn't gained the information from him that Jasper wanted.

While he at least gained knowledge of a few things before they had happened and could quickly react to combat. At other times, he had to allow them to happen in order to not reveal his hand. As a result, Harlow took the brunt of their ill-treatment. Further, making him feel guilty. He would make it up to her someday.

Listening further, he learned Jasper's full hatred of them. He had always known that, just not to the full extent. Why such hatred though and not jealousy would have to be a problem for another day. Learning the plan was to act on Harlow, and soon. Hopefully, today if Jasper had his way.

The confirmation that they were after her and not him hurt and scared him. She was not a True Guard member, thus she didn't have the necessary training needed to defend herself.

She couldn't handle an integration. Especially one with Jasper. He would use any and all tactics to gain the information he wanted. Not excluding torture. He would have to break his cover if need be and help his sister. There was no way he was leaving her under the guise of that monster.

So there was no telling what he would do to Harlow. He guessed they weren't using his twin as a pawn to get to him, either. He also strongly suspected that was the true cause of Cora's death. The information they wanted she wouldn't share, and now they thought Harlow had it.

Which made little sense. His sister wasn't a member of Ravens Night. A secret society he knew Jasper suspected existed. So why they were after her and not him was odd? He was the one who was a member. So too was her son. She is completely unaware. What information could she have that they wanted?

All the bread crumbs they within the society had left all led back to him. Not Cora or Harlow. Could Jasper know more than he was letting on? Or was he wanting something else and stinging him along for the ride?

He knew she had received the Ravens Night box. Their sacred box. The one that at one time contained their sacred book. A book they have been searching for, for generations. They feared it was lost forever.

Did Jasper know about the book? Was that why he was after his twin? There was a rumor of a saving grace hidden within the depths of the archive. On multiple occasions, saw people searching the library. They had found nothing to show the truth of the fairy tale. Could the fairy tale and the book be one and the same? If so, how had Jasper learned about it? That was worrisome. His sister could be in real danger.

As a nonmember, his sister did not know of the sacred book. How could she? Ignoring his train of thought, he continued to focus on the chatter in the other room. Needing to learn all he could about their plans for Harlow. The assignment and his plans just changed. As far as he could tell, they didn't suspect him of knowing any of their nefarious plans.

When he heard them in the telltale signs of sex once again, he made for the shower room. His emotions were running high and affecting his judgment. He needed to clear his head in order to think clearly again. Jumping in under the spray, he made quick work of cleaning himself.

When he finished, he was entering the bedroom at the same time as Sally. Her shocked look gave away her otherwise intended enticement. How she could have sex with multiple men, one after the other, baffled him. How they believed they were deceiving him too also baffled him.

Not caring anymore, he greeted her with only a head nod. Turning his back to her, he dressed quickly, pulling items from his bag. Turning again when he finished, he looked at her confused expression.

He said as politely as he could.

"Morning Sally."

Making quick work of grabbing his clothes from yesterday and shoving them into his bag.

Standing, he looked at her, saying.

"I've gotta go. It is necessary for me to stop by the office. I failed to let Sloane know about something before I left."

Let her take that statement for what it is. He needed to see his sister. She was in trouble.

Continuing, he said.

"Then I need to head back home. I need to apologize to Harlow."

Sally stood there, her mouth a gape staring after him as he maneuvered his way around her and exited her suite. He could later hear her repeated shouting as he rounded the corner. This time, he laughed loud and free. He didn't fear how anyone watching on the cameras would receive it. He was free and one step closer to completing this mission.

WATCHING as Harlow went through her normal, boring routine gave her pause. Perhaps she wasn't about to do something that caused her team leader to take a great interest in her. Why else would he assign someone to watch the camera feed live, instead of the usual recordings a day later? Had she mistaken her internal warning? It would be a first.

No, she decided she had to be right. Her insides were still uneasy. Something was definitely about to happen. Looking closely, she saw a slight tremor in the way Harlow moved, handling the books she loved so much. Harlow was nervous. Why, though? What was she planning? She wished she knew.

When she got up from her chair and made her way to the back of the library, she knew this was it. Her instincts were right. Harlow was making her move, now. Thinking on the fly, she wanted to keep her the invisible woman. It was her way of helping. Now, which pathways could she be heading toward? She knew there was a maze of halls not used anymore attached to the rear of the library.

Following her instincts, once again, she allowed her finger to fly across the touchpad, giving this woman all the protection she needed. As a failsafe, she disabled all the motion sensors in the rooms along the hallways. Those rooms contained all the old equipment and supplies needed in the olden days to survive the Wasted land.

Was that where this woman was going? If so, that was worrisome. It took True Guard members many years to learn how to navigate, let alone survive there. It wasn't a tranquil place to be. Why else would they all be living in a specially designed state of art dome? Well, it was at the time of its creation. Now, however, it was falling apart piece by piece.

It was why they were in such a race to find a solution. Not to mention find a way of bringing the planet back to life. If that was even possible anymore. All they had to relay on were rumors and fairytales. Telling of ways in which humanity will persevere.

With her worry increasing at Harlows' direction, her curiosity increased. Why would she need such equipment? What could be out there that she would want or need? When she had all the sensors toggled off and empty hallways playing on a loop, she made quick work of protecting the system setting. Making sure no one could tamper with it or find out what she did. It was important to protect herself as well. As best she could, anyway.

Grabbing her things, she did a quick tidying of the screening room. Double-checking everything looked as it should, she left. Thankfully, she could plan on the fly. Running the potential scenarios around in her mind, she navigated the maze of hallways.

In a rush, it took all her willpower to appear calm and nonchalant. Not wanting to send unnecessary warning Jaspers's way. She stuck to a direct route but one also out of the way of many cameras. Being seen as little as possible was her goal, as it would be better.

Jogging, she needed to warn Caden of Harlow's movements. His twin was about to attempt something very dangerous. A task that took a significant amount of training to do. Not just anyone could put on the gear and head out there past the protective dome. Even if his sister had read all the books about the past world, or what it was like now. It would not help her in the world and all that was out there.

It was a dangerous and unpredictable place. Even with all the training the True Guard went through, you were never fully prepared. It was why you never went out there alone, either. They assigned all members to teams for that reason. Now that it appeared, Harlow planned to enter the Wasted alone. She needed to do something. Screw the consequences.

With her fear growing, she headed toward the office of Caden and his team. Taking a chance that if she couldn't find Caden there. The risk was too great to even attempt to go to his quarters looking for him. If not Caden, at least someone might be there. They could either help her or inform him of his twin's actions.

This plan made her feel better. She no longer cared what would happen to her. Not when Harlow's life was on the line. Not when she could do something, anything, to help her.

CHAPTER 4

*L*ast minute, he changed course and made his way towards his suite of rooms that he shared with his family. It was almost like his limbs had a mind of their own. Knowing something he did not. No matter how hard he tried, he could not change course. So odd. Giving in, he increased his pace. At least he could control that.

Arriving home, he allowed his movements to continue and dictate the where. He found himself moving to a long ago forgotten hiding spot. One in which he and Harlow used to hide all their secret treasures they had as children. Smiling at the fondness he felt at the memory, he wondered. What could she have possibly hidden in here? Once he opened it, he revealed a piece of folded paper.

Frowning, that was it? A piece of paper. That was all she treasures? Last time he had looked in here, it contained an abundance of treasures. Now only a folded paper.

Had his sister emptied it, leaving only the paper just for him? Or had taken all the treasures thus leaving this behind? Perhaps she had meant for him to see this?

Curious, he carefully removed it. This could not be from his sister. She would have left him a secret tech note in the way he had taught her. So who was this from and why? Taking care, he unfolded the paper to reveal a letter written in a beautiful hand script. Emotion quickly clogged his throat. A handwritten letter by someone who preferred the art. Not their tech way of communicating.

This was a safer form of communication if you didn't want a mass of people reading it. However, given how creased the letter was and thin the paper had become. He guessed that wasn't the case. Many people had read this letter countless times. Were those tear stains on the paper? He read the letter.

Dear Harlow,

If you are reading this letter, then you have received my last will, and testament to you. Sister of my heart, I'm truly sorry to have left you so soon. Hopefully, my demise was from natural causes, and not nefarious. But never mind that, someone has already done the deed, regardless of the circumstances.

Just know I love you with all my heart, the sister I never had. Tell Caden the same. I love him as if he were my brother. To Rowan, I love that boy as if he were my own. My heart overflowed with gratitude as I proudly embraced the title of his aunt. That nephew of mine is something special.

Please keep on reading my crazy red-headed girl. I know you love to learn and discover new things. For you never know what wonders the library holds. Just promise me not too many romances. Ok. The pages of the books within hold many wonderful and incredible things to behold. I know you will find many answers but also so many more questions too.

So farewell sister of my heart. Take care of our beautiful family.

Yours forever,

Cora Lewis

Was this what was in the box that Harlow had? In stiff movements, he sat on the nearest thing to him, a toilet seat. Unable to think clearly, he read the letter again. This time without the emotions it brought. Now he was reading between the lines. Relying on his knowledge of his sister and Cora. He wasn't the only one on a mission. Cora, their leader of the Ravens Night, had a role for Harlow to play as well. Now he just had to work out exactly what that was.

Then how could he stop her? What she was meddling in was dangerous, even for him. And he was a True Guard leader. Rubbing the back of his neck in frustration. Well, knowing his sister, it would be more like saving her instead. Once she set her mind on something, nothing could deter her. She didn't have the best track record for not getting herself into trouble, either. A magnet for trouble, he always said.

"Shit,"

Standing abruptly, he had forgotten about all the listening devices planted throughout their suite. He continued to curse himself internally, making a ton of noise as he grabbed a few things and left their rooms.

Leaving clues that Rowan too would find this same letter someday soon. If things went south, as he suspected, they would. He was flying by the seat of his pants. Which seemed to happen a lot lately. At least there was someone to continue with the mission.

. . .

DOING as she was told on auto pilot she moved in a stunned daze through the maze of old hallways. The training for all True Guard team members emphasized following orders. Upon arriving at Caden's team's office quarters, Sloane had greeted her with suspicion and intimidation. So doing as he instructed her to, it was a simple task.

He was not the person she had wanted to talk to. At least he was the man's best friend, by all accounts. Having never met this man personally, he terrified her.

The sheer size of him towering over her when he had opened the door made her tremble. She had stared up at him, her mouth a gape unable to speak a single word. He raised an eyebrow while crossing his enormous arms before he demanded in his gruff voice.

"What ya want?"

She continued to stare, opening and closing her mouth, unable to form words.

"Well?"

His sharp demand finally freed her from her muteness. She told him she needed him to warn Caden. At which point he ushered her into the office with such speed she was once again breathless. After catching her breath for a few moments, she explained all of her suspicions. Going into detail about her team leader and his hatred for the Faxons, along with a few other members of the team. How some grand scheme was about to play out, and the twins were in the middle of it.

He gently grabbed her elbow at that moment and led her to a small seating area. Encouraging her to sit, he waited till she sat before he sat opposite her. Before a small nod toward her, to continue. Closing her eyes and taking a deep breath, she told him about her suspicions and the research she had completed. Which sadly didn't add up too much, if anything at all.

Smiling to herself, it was at this point he had awkwardly reached out, placing his massive hand on her knee for a gentle and short pat of reassurance. As odd as it seemed, his compassion toward her helped.

Never in all her life had anyone shown her an ounce of caring. Humbled by his act of kindness, she continued.

Informing him she had received the assignment to watch the archive cameras live feed this morning. At first, she was furious. They had always recorded and watch these cameras feeds later. Why had she been separated out from her team to perform the task in real-time? The more she pondered on it, the more she wondered if they had any suspicions about her true feelings. Was she given this task because of those feelings?

Could there possibly be others on her team who felt the same way? Was she given the task of watching out for Harlow? With her skill set, she definitely could. Though she couldn't be too sure. Even so, she had protected the woman, anyway.

She explained further how she had used old footage of Harlow, replacing the live feed with it instead. As for the back closed-off hallways, she killed them completely. Since there were no recent recordings. She had attempted a loop recording, but decide this was better in the end. Once she had completed the task; she had rushed here as fast as she could.

Her guess was Harlow was about to enter the Wasted. She did not know for what task and why. Her worry was even with all the training the True Guard had, there were still some that severely suffered in the Wasted. Under no circumstances did she want that for Miss Faxon, nor did she deserve it. Then there was the added measure of the fact that Jasper had it out for getting even with her. Why, she did not know.

It was at this point she had reached out, grabbing Sloan's arm and digging her nails into his flesh. Begging, well, more like demanding he tell Caden. He needed to protect his sister and himself as well. There was a slight chance Rowan would need protection, too. So far though, no one had ever mentioned him by name. So again, she wasn't so sure. It would be best if he could protect them all.

Remembering how she had felt drained after pleading her case in front of Sloan and had slumped into the back of her chair, leaning her head back and sighing in relief. She had done it. Now what?

Famous last words, eh! No sooner had she thought of them than

Sloan was giving her a new mission. One that would help, not only Harlow but Caden, Rowan and herself as well.

Snapping herself out of her, reminiscing about the conversation. She had arrived at the door of the first room she needed. Sloane had given her a list of things to collect. Various items she would need.

This room housed the majority of the things listed. Which was good, because the list was huge. She wasn't even sure how she was going to carry it all. He had reassured her it would be fine that she would find everything and then some. Squaring her shoulders; she entered the room.

"Holy Carp!"

Stopping just inside the door, she heard it automatically close as she gazed around. This place was massive. Floor-to-ceiling shelves filled with every type of equipment. Never mind the fact that this stuff was ancient, still looked to be in great condition. Albeit a little dusty. She looked in awe, taking small measured steps.

Remembering her new mission. The one in which Sloane had asked her if she would be willing to help. She went about the room, grabbing everything off her list. Even finding a few extra things here and there that might be of some use. Since she had already been asked to grab certain items, she recognized the value of these additional items as well.

As the pile grew larger, she looked around for something to carry it all in. Finding a backpack sitting by one of the interior doors. She quickly grabbed it. Stuffing everything in. Seeing a little extra space, she did another walk around, picking up a few more things.

The bag was like it was forever expanding on the inside, but not changing on the outside. How strange was that? It meant, however, that she could pack a lot more. Taking advance of such a thing, she further explored the room, adding all kinds of various items.

Finished, she hurried into the next room. Taking stock again of its inventory. All manner of wearable gear for entering the Wasted.

Once again, noticing the quality exceeded everything currently offered to the True Guard. Shaking her head and weaving her way through the many rows of racks, she took her time finding everything she needed in her size. Grabbing a few extra again, just in case. Finding lockers in the back of the room. She searched for an empty one. Upon finding one, she went about the task of changing and suiting up.

As she did, she let her mind wander to the end of her conversation with Sloane. She had agreed to help. If only he promised to inform Caden about his twin and the possibility she was in danger. When he agreed. Reassuring her, he gave his assurance that he would do it and advised her not to worry. She was being sent to help Harlow in the Wasted.

With his set of skills, he could turn her into an invisible woman. No one needed to know she had come to this office. She now too simply followed Harlow in her actions to enter the Wasted.

Grateful for his bending of the truth. No one would ever know for sure the truth. She was going to help Harlow in any way she could. If only to keep her alive so she could do what she needed to do. Regardless of what that was.

It was important. She knew that much. For Sloan had helped her as well. How much did the man really know? More than the two of them. Clearly, because the list he had given her was so detailed. More so than she thought. She had questioned many of the items, taking them regardless. The man knew more than he was telling. So she had decided better be safe than sorry. It was why she had filled the bag with so much extra.

After shoving all her unneeded clothes and other crap into the locker, she slammed it shut. Rotating her neck and shoulders before she picked up the backpack and maneuvered into the last connected room. This one contained an exit into the Wasted.

Nervous butterflies danced in her tummy. What she was about to do was dangerous. Not only because of the land outside. But because she was betraying her team. It didn't matter that they had no like or respect for each other. She was a True Guard member. That was enough.

Within the walls of this room was what you would need to breathe, maneuver, and defend yourself in the Wasted. As quickly as she could, she took everything on the list and some extra. Again. Filling her backpack. It was nearly busting, but still manageable to carry. Finishing the task of gearing herself up, she remembered Sloane's last pep talk.

"You can do this, girl. Never doubt yourself. You have a good heart. Or you wouldn't have risked coming here and warning me."

He placed his massive hand on her shoulder, giving it a light squeeze. With that, he rose from his seat, looking over his shoulder as he walked, expecting her to follow. He then fitted her wrist with a GPS display that he quickly programmed with coordinates. He then jotted her a list of items on his touchpad device and transferred them to her wrist unit.

Shaking head to dislodge the memory. She quickly secured her hair into a braid and tucked it into the hood before placing the goggles over her head. One more check of her pockets, making sure she had enough oxygen fittings. Taking the fitting she had left on the counter in front of her, she placed it to her nose before pulling up the front collar and attaching it to her goggles. Completely covered and ready, she moved toward the exit. Here's hoping, was her last thought.

CHAPTER 5

*C*aden was on his way to his office when he could feel eyes on him. Yes, the hallways had cameras everywhere, but he sensed something different. It felt like daggers. What was going on? Not caring about the implications, he quickened his pace. Continuing to ponder the avenues of Harlow's involvement. Had she found the information they had been searching for? Generations of them have been searching. All of which were unsuccessful.

Uncaring about who was watching him, he decided to hell with it and broke into a run instead. His insides were screaming at him now. Needing to listen to them, he hurried along. He was sure it was a warning about his twin. However, it was possibly something more.

Surprisingly, as he ran through the hallways, they were all empty. Not a soul insight. Strange. The closer he got to his destination, the more his foreboding grew.

When he arrived, he shoved his hand onto the scanner. Cursing inwardly as the thing took its sweet time. He felt an overwhelming sense of impatience wash over him. Which was never a good thing. That was when mistakes happened.

He couldn't afford for any mistakes to happen. This was personal. Very personal. Especially after Cora's death. Who was like family to them. He would allow nothing to happen to his sister if he could help it.

Barging into the room when the door finally opened. He froze a few steps in. What now? He did not know what he should do. Not knowing his sister's movements, there wasn't much he could do. He needed to think before he started acting.

Closing his eyes, he took a deep breath. Rolling his shoulders. Trying anything to achieve a sense of calm. With a few more deep breaths, he opened his eyes. Taking in the empty room, he scanned it, looking for Sloane. Perhaps he might have information that could be helpful. Before he could finish his surveying, he heard Sloane's gruff timber voice.

"Ya gonna just stand there? Or are ya gonna do something?"

Whipping toward his voice, he sneered. For whatever reason, his comment set him on edge. When he calmed enough to see his face finally. He knew he had more knowledge than he did.

"What is it, Sloane? What do you know?"

In a flash, he was standing beside his friend. Again, his worry grew. This seesaw of emotions was tiring him. Why couldn't he stay focused like he did while on scouting missions? Scratching his temple, he attempted again to achieve any sense of calm. Until his friend snapped him from any semblance of calm with his next words.

"Ya need to suit up. Harlow will be in need of ye."

Confused, he squinted at Sloane. Asking.

"What did you say?"

"Your sister has entered the Wasted."

Before he could finish, or even close his mouth. He snapped at him.

"WHAT?"

Shaking his head at his rash reaction, Sloan placed his massive hand on his shoulder.

Looking him in the eyes, he explained how Harlow had come here, to the office, after gearing up. How he had helped her at Cora's request. He should be proud his sister figured out all the clues and not only found the elusive book, but could read it. The longer he listened, the more he seemed to calm. Which was strange, considering what he was hearing.

His twin had geared herself up by way of the old rooms and entered the Wasted. On a mission of her own accord. Thankfully, she had had some help. More than she knew. Cora had secured a promise of aid from Sloane. Whereas Honor had helped her with her sense of what was right and just. No matter where his sister went or what she did, she seemed to inspire loyalty in others. All the while being completely blind to it.

Someday, he hoped she would come to realize and acknowledge the wonderful woman she was. With everything that had happened in her life, she still was a wonderful sister, mother, and friend. An inspiration to all who knew her. Which, sadly, was very few.

Shaking his head, in a failed attempt to sort through all he had just heard.

"You're telling me. Harlow is now geared up and wandering the Wasted. On a mission via Cora. With Honor, close on her tail for support. While the rest of her team and Jasper are potentially suiting up to go after my sister."

He tilted his head, waiting for a reply. Which he got as a head nod from Sloane. With another deep breath, he would deal with the questions he had on Honor later. For now, he had to determine Harlow's destination.

"Ok."

Looking seriously at his friend, he asked.

"Where exactly is Harlow headed, and how much of a head start does she have?"

Sloane nodded in approval of his ability to center himself finally. Answering all his questions while also tossing a bag full of gear in his direction. Continuing to explain how he too needed to enter the old abandoned hallways. Handing him a list of all the things he needed to grab, all the while outfitting himself in the old outer gear. Curious, he glanced at his friend, waiting for further explanation. When none came, he took the list and the gear bag, moving fast to the exit.

It was utter crap out here. Her body clung to the outer wall of the compound dome. The force of the gale winds were wreaking havoc on her senses. It took all her concentration to stay upright. Let alone follow the GPS. Thank goodness the device she wore on her wrist gave indications via vibrations and taps, allowing the wearer to know in which direction to go.

Still, as it was, she would need to find something she could use as a walking stick. She just had to make it around the next bend. Where she could find something, anything, she could turn into a walking aid. If only the gales would let up for just a few minutes.

Knowing there was no point in rushing and acting now, she bided her time glued to the wall. She wondered how Harlow was faring in this environment. Hopefully, much better than she was. Still, she wondered what was out here that was so important to risk her life for. It must be something great, for why would Cora have died for it?

Her death was unnecessary. Extremely sad as well. She never believed the verdict of a suspicious death. It was too convenient. It had to be Jasper or one of his many cronies; she was sure of that. Once again, however, she lacked proof. Which furthered her suspicions. It was a wonder they hadn't done away with her by now. Possibly they just thought of her so insignificant, and not bothered.

This all seemed utterly crazy to her. The primary goal of the compound was to find a solution to the dying of the planet. It was not chasing after people for some imaginary slight. Well, that was how this all looked to her. Why then had a woman died? Could all of this have a connection?

Finally, when the wind lessened, and she could pray herself free. She navigated around the corner with slow and deliberate movements. Moving to the debris field, she picked through items until she found something suitable. Determined to make up for the lost time, she scaled through the many obstacles. Taking protective cover in another debris pile. She took a moment to glance through the GPS. Noticing she was close to her destination, she also saw other blips appear on the screen.

Shocked at this discovery, she was not alone. Worry set in. One she knew was Harlow. She was already at the destination. The others, however, she wasn't so sure. Likely her brother, Caden, for sure. With a sinking feeling, she knew who all the others were. Her team.

How had they been able to suit up and follow Harlow quicker than her? She didn't like where her train of thought was going. Had Jasper been able to tag the woman with a tracking device? Or had he tagged her? The thought made her sick to her stomach.

Shaking her head in disgust and to rid herself of the urge to vomit. This was not a safe place to do such a thing. She needed to get going and help. In any way she could. Scrambling over the terrain, no longer caring about being careful. It was essential she get to the location with speed.

In her haste, she found her wrist caught while she was scaling up a debris pile. When she had reached up to grab hold, her fingers slipped. Grabbing the closest thing meant her hand disappeared into a void. Leaving her momentarily hanging for dear life. With a grunt, she forced herself upward, attempting to pull her hand free.

"Damn it."

She couldn't afford the time lost for this. Balancing her feet cautiously, on jetting out debris, she reached into one of her many pockets. Retrieving a pocket knife, she carefully cut the strap around her wrist. Returning the knife, she sighed in relief. Bracing herself and slowly pulling her hand free, she ignored the shocking pain.

It hurt to leave the GPS behind. The device was handy. Too bad it was the reason her wrist had been stuck. If she had more time, she could have dug it out afterward. Sadly, time was essential. Scrambling over and across the scattered junk, she made her way closer to her destination.

She found it difficult to plan because she didn't know who all the players were. Although she had a fairly good guess. It meant she would have to think on the fly. Something she didn't like to do. It made her nervous.

What she needed to do was calm herself and do it quickly. Harlow needed her help, regardless of whoever was after her. Taking a moment, she closed her eyes for a few deep breaths. Calming her pounding heart. She could do this. She was, after all, a True Guard member. Opening her eyes, she maneuvered herself to the edge of a massive crater opening.

Not seeing anyone else around. It must mean they were all at the bottom. Looking down into the grand hole, she gulped when she couldn't see the floor. Nervously preparing herself mentally for the task, she closed her eyes. After a quick pep talk, she began her descent.

CHAPTER 6

For once when he entered the Wasted, it appeared luck was on his side. Conditions were that he could scale across the terrain with ease. Allowing him to catch up easily with his sister. He could see her in the distance. Struggling through a mountain of debris. It looked as though it had been a building at one time. Which could mean disaster if injured.

Just as the thought crossed his mind. He watched as she took a nasty fall. With concern, he hastened as quickly as the environment allowed him to.

Watching again in horror as she got up and brushed herself off, only to fall as the the ground gave way beneath her feet. Inwardly cursing, he all but ran toward her. After what seemed like forever, he made it to where he last saw her. There was a massive hole. Furthering his belief of a disaster.

Peering into it, he struggled to see anything beyond two feet down. Trying to swallow past the massive lump in his throat. He shouted,

"Harlow."

Waiting for a response that never came. His fear was escalating. Taking a deep breath, he scaled himself down and into the enormous crater before him. Carefully making his way down took skill and time. Time he wasn't sure he had. In his need to rush, he slipped a few times. Ripping and tearing his gloves, leaving a trail of blood behind. God only knew what infections this caused.

Every so often, he would turn and look down. Trying to see if he could get a visual on Harlow. Still, he could not see her. Ignoring the pain in his hands, he continued his descent. Reaching the bottom of the crater, he took a moment to stretch his limbs.

Searching for his sister, he came up empty. The only evidence she had that she had been there was a small bloodstain. Damn it. She wasn't supposed to get hurt. Women were to be protected. Shouting her name as he continued forward, following the small blood trail. Coming to a stop, at a door frame of a stone room bathed in colorful light.

It was beautiful. He'd seen nothing like before. It was calling to him like a blood song. He could feel vibrations throughout his veins. With the compelling draw forward, he looked to see an archway. Beautifully carved with symbols written and Pictish. It all seemed distantly familiar to him. Calling him forward.

After what seemed to be eons. He shook his head, attempting to rid himself of the internal ringing he could hear. Finally, he saw his sister.

"Harlow, what are you doing?"

Seeing her lips move, he could not hear her, however. With his worry escalating, he shouted again.

"You're hurt."

Wanting to help her, he lunged forward. Only to be pulled back. Jerking roughly out of his attacker's grip, he stumped a few steps into the tiny room. Turning, he positioned himself between his sister and whoever was at the bottom of the stairs. Standing firm, he allowed his anger to radiate at the recognition of his rival.

"I see you followed me, Jasper. Where would your other half be then?"

Watching as his fellow True Guard's man suddenly seemed to steam. The man's anger suddenly radiated through the small room. His need for superiority caused a need for laughter to build. Instead, he only allowed his rival to see the smirk on his lips. Further adding pressure to the pot.

Just then, he saw Sally emerge from behind her man. Waltzing her way over toward him, attempting to touch him. He shrugged her off as disgust filled him. Until finally snapping.

"What do you want, Sally?"

Again, she attempted to snuggle close to him. Disgusted with her and her behavior, he rebuffed her. His only consolation was the display of jealousy Jasper wore. Once more, he smiled. As much as he hated his mission to get close to this woman and seduce her for information, he liked the idea of getting under his opponent's skin.

Finally, the callus woman spoke and crossed her arms trying in vain to push up her cleavage. What she had of it, anyway.

"Oh, come on, it wasn't all bad. You liked it."

Again, laughter billowed inside him.

"Enjoyed, ha."

Unable to contain it any longer. He laughed. Actually laughed. Wrapping his arm around his middle, he tried to calm enough to state.

"You really can't tell when it's fake, eh? I was using you like you are using me."

Suddenly angry, he stood erect. Glaring at the couple. Raising his hand, he pointed a finger in their direction. Allowing his anger to fill him, he bellowed.

"But you should have left Harlow out of it."

His concern for his sister allowed him to take his eyes off his rivals and turn to her. Seeing her body growing limp and her eyes unable to focus. He lunged for her to help, but only once more to be pulled back. This time, he struggled against two pairs of hands.

Any attempts to dislodge their hands only caused them to grip him tighter. Still, he kept his gaze glued to his twin as lights of multiple colors filled the room. The energy grew, sending bolts of lightning from within the archway. Horror filled him as his twin, Harlow, shouted his name and the swirling rainbow sucked her backward.

"Caden."

It was only a few moments, however, time seemed to stand still. All three of them stood frozen, watching. Unable to comprehend what they were seeing. That is until he violently bucked his shoulder, allowing him to dislodge Jasper's grip on him. The force of which twisted him and Sally, placing his back to the archway.

Feeling the room close in on him, he sucked in deep breaths. A force was pulling him backward. On instinct, he tightened his grip on Sally. Any attempt naturally to ground himself. Time suddenly was moving in slow motion.

A force knocked him off his feet. Sally sensed the turmoil and gripped him tightly. Being pulled backward while airborne, he saw the worry and concern filling her face.

"Sally. No!"

Looking past her face, he saw a distressed Jasper scrambling to his feet. Clumsily reaching for Sally. After several failed attempts, he grabbed her ankle. Watching as this short but gruff man tried and could not pull backward. The force was simply too strong.

The internal singing increased to a point where it was all he could hear. Growing so loud that he feared his ears would bleed. Using all his strength, he reached up to cover his ears. When he did so, both he and Sally jerked roughly.

As his vision faded, he watched as Sally's eyes filled with pain. She jerked violently, digging her nails into him. Suddenly going limp as her eyes rounded. She released her hold on him. Sucked into a swirling kaleidoscope. The ability to keep his eyes open was growing too difficult. He finally allowed the peaceful lure of blackness to embrace him.

SHE MADE it to the bottom of the great void to hear and see a scuffle unfold. Sally and Jasper were teaming up against Caden. Both were gripping him tightly while he tried to shake them off. Halting his attempt to get to his sister. Just then, a colorful swirl within an archway pulled Harlow backward. Something also prevented her from moving and trying to help. Looking over her shoulder, she saw the rest of her team all standing there. How had she not noticed them?

Scanning their faces, she saw mostly fear, with only a few displaying their hatred. What had the twins done to deserve such feelings? Regardless, she had to do something. Narrowing her eyes at the hand on her shoulder. She looked at its owner, speaking through her teeth.

"Remove. Your. Hand."

Starring him down till he let go. Grunting as she turned just in time to see Caden and Sally flying backward into the archway. At lightning speed, she rushed to grab onto them. In the end, she could only reach for and grab Jasper's ankle. As he took hold of Sally's ankle.

Feeling a tug on her ankle. She turned, looking behind her to see Garth holding on for dear life. Worry and concern in his eyes. Airborne, they all entered the swirling colored lights within the archway one by one.

The archway seemed to be almost angry. As if it were a living entity, it was spitting shards of lightning around and tossing them about. The energy force was intense. So intense, she squeezed her eyes shut while gripping Jasper's ankle tighter. Grabbing it with both hands when she felt his body jerk.

Before she could respond, their bodies collided. Forcing her to release her grip on his ankle and knocking the air from her lungs. Waving her arms, trying to gain some stability, her body went sailing backward into Garth. He quickly wrapped his powerful arms around her, absorbing the collision force with a grunt.

Curious, she opened her eyes. Regretting it immediately. The speed and intensity of swirling colors was too painful. Instantly, nausea swamped her. Followed by stabbing pain throughout her head. Moaning, she fought against the invisible force to hold her head in her hands. Simultaneously, Garth's arms tightened around her, offering her solace.

While she tightly cupped her ears with her hands, she felt jostled about. Any sense of security vanished. They were now moving at an even greater pace than before. Hearing more snapping and crackling of lightning, she knew they must be near an archway. Was it the same one or another? Not having the time to think, let alone prepare. They experienced a sudden upward toss, followed by an immediate free fall.

She screamed at her descent. Only for the sound to die out, as all the air left her lungs. The pressure she felt on her chest was so great. Garth twisted himself to position beneath her during their free fall. Maneuvering so he would take the brunt of their landed impact. All she could do to answer was to shake her head when he tightened his grip on her.

He should have let her go, she thought when they did land. He grunted in pain on impact, immediately barrel-rolling with her tucked safely in his arms. All she could do was hold her breath and protect her head with her arms. Even with all his attempts to protect her, she ended up sailing across the ground. Something large and hard painfully stopped her.

With pain shooting through her side, she took a moment to attempt a deep breath. When her lungs no longer burned, she took a few steady breaths. Cautiously opening her eyes, she wanted to know where she was. Blinding light greeted her, causing a stabbing pain through her head. Slamming her eyes shut in response, and breathing through her gritted teeth.

She waited a few more minutes. When her pain eased slightly, she tried again. Curious still. Slowly her vision cleared until she could make out a blue sky with lots of white fluffy clouds. Whispering.

"Wow."

It was stunning. She had never seen color so vivid before. Well, except for a few moments ago in the beautifully carved archway. Nor had she smelled such clean air, either. Taking a moment to discern what she was resting on. Her mind continued to wander. Time didn't mean a thing to her anymore.

Where were they? Turning to look where she came from, she cried out in pain. The pain was so intense that her vision blurred. Suddenly aware of her body, she hurt everywhere. She felt as though someone had run her through a ringer. Nauseousness overtook her at every movement. Fighting through it, she curled into a ball before allowing the darkness to envelop her.

CHAPTER 7

*H*e noticed the pounding in his head first. Groaning, he reached up to rub his forehead, revealing more aches and pains. He hurt everywhere. What the hell happened? He was trying to rack his brain about what had happened to him. While he was remembering, he heard a gruff voice.

"You are safe, my boy."

Bolting into a sitting position. He regretted it immediately. Nesousness swamped him. Again groaning, he grabbed the sides of his head. Any attempt to stay the endless spinning. Feeling a gentle touch on his shoulder, he sighed as calmness filled him.

"Lay back down. You need a little more rest before you'll be ready for action."

Listening to the words of wisdom, he laid back down. Sighing again at the relief. Where was he? He was not still lying on the turfed ground. He was on a soft bed of some kind. Wanting to know more, he braved opening his eyes to slits. Gratefulness filled him when he realized they were in a dimly lit room. Blinking, it took him a few times to bring everything into focus.

He was lying on a cot within a fabric structure. It was a small space. With only two cots. The one he was on and the one his apparent savior was sitting on. He could hear the ravages of an angry storm outside. The fabric walls and ceiling were dancing to its monstrous tune. Thankfully, it was warm and dry inside.

Turing to view his apparent companion. He was an older man with soft silver hair, very much like a wizard of old. All those stories his sister had read to her son when he was young came rushing back to him. Smiling at the memory of his family. He looked up at the mysterious man's eyes. Eyes that were filled with wisdom and caring. Too many questions filled his mind. Instead, he blurted out.

"Do I know you?"

The reply he got encouraged more questions.

"In time."

In confusion, he squinted, looking closer at the man. He seemed familiar to him. Though he was sure he had never met him before. Tilting his head, he wondered why that was. Someone interrupted him from his musings by asking him a question.

"What's your name, my boy?"

Bringing the man back into focus, he answered.

"Caden. My name is Caden Faxon."

Why was he answering truthfully when he didn't know this man's intentions? Worry filling him, he asked.

"Who are you and where am I?"

The old man smiled and his eye seemed to sparkle. He suddenly felt filled with warmth and comfort again.

"I, my boy, am Cormac. I found you at the edge of the wood, out cold."

He stood, moving to the end of the cot, bending to retrieve something from the floor. Coming toward him, he held what looked like a cup. Still muttering, he said as he moved the cup to him.

"Here my boy. Drink this."

Nodding his acceptance. He rose onto an elbow, reaching out with his other hand, taking the cup. Closing his eyes in pleasure as the smooth, soothing liquid trickled down his throat. Emptying the cup, he held it up for Cormac to take as he laid back down. He murmured his gratitude.

"Thank you."

Cormac again sat on the opposite cot. A small smile spread across his face. One that reached his sparkling eyes.

"You are welcome."

Rolling to his side, he propped his head up with his folded arm. He finally asked his question after a few moments of silence.

"Could you fill me in? Since you apparently know of me. I assume you know what's going on."

Cormac, with a simple nod of his head, explained what he knew. Additionally, he was aware of Caden's connection to Harlow. It was her reaction that had caused him to realize of his arrival. During his explanation, he inquired about his precise connection was to Harlow.

"She is my twin sister."

Again, he wondered why he felt so calm and trusting around this man. He was freely opening up to him and giving him answers to all his questions. It was not something a True Guard member had been trained him to do. However, his instincts said he could trust this man with his life.

Cormac was still talking as his eyelids grew heavy. Eventually, the blackness won, wrapping him in its embrace. As he listened to the fading murmurs.

HONOR WOKE SLOWLY. The faint singing of birds helped soothe her growing anxiety. Despite her best efforts, she couldn't figure out why she was feeling so tightly strung. Taking a moment to take stock of her body. She realized then she was lying on the hard ground. Why was that?

Opening her eyes slowly, she allowed her eyes to scan. Above her was a faint blue sky, being filled with ominous gray clouds. Noticing the increased wind. This was not good.

Cautiously, she sat up. Thankfully, she didn't want to vomit. The pain that coursed through her body was intense, but not overpowering. As her memory flooded back to her, she surveyed around her. Looking for anyone she recognized. She would take stock of where they were later. When they were all safe and accounted for.

Near to her was Garth. Still lying unmoving. Concerned, she scampered over to him. Gently placing her finger to feel for a pulse. Smiling when she felt the strong beating beneath her touch. Glancing at him for any noticeable injuries and satisfied there weren't any, she moved on to looking for the others.

She felt the first of the heavy water droplets hit her when she was a few steps away. Cursing, she turned back to Garth. Picking up the bag near him, she rummaged around in it until she found what she was looking for. Moving as fast as she was able, she went about setting up the portable dome around Garth. Making sure he was ok, she darted out of the dome's protection. Searching for the others. Needing to get them to safety quickly.

With lightning speed, she moved about, checking for a pulse before moving them to the safety of the dome. Her heart hurt for the ones who had not survived the trip. Well, all but one person. She wasn't sad about her, but sad about the outcome her death would cause. God only knew what was about to happen.

Leaving the dead behind. She only brought the surviving members to safety. As she carried the last survivor into the dome, she saw Garth was up and tending to all those within the dome. He had cots all in a row and was placing people onto them. He raised his head and nodded to a cot for her to place their teammate on.

"Thank you, Honor."

She stood upright and froze in place. He was thanking her. No-one had ever done that before. Still in shock, she answered.

"You're welcome. What else can I do?"

Making her way toward him, she saw him shake his head. Before he answered.

"Not a thing, girl. You go and take a seat. You need to rest awhile."

He made quick work of tending to his patients. When he turned, giving her a hard look.

She quickly jumped into motion, sucking in a squeak of pain the movement caused.

"I heard that." He snapped. "Now you rest a little. I'll tend to these before I'll see to you." He said while indicating with a nod of his head to their teammates on all the cots.

As carefully as she could, she sat on the last remaining cot. It was then she realized the extent of her pain. How was she able to forget about it or not feel it? That was odd, for sure. Then there was Garth and his willingness to tend to her. Not that there was anything he could do for her. While conducting a self-assessment, she suspected she had a broken rib or two.

They carried nothing that would aid in the healing of those when on a mission like this one. He could help with all her bumps and scratches. Which would be enough. He may have to help her with a binding, however, to ease the pain in her ribs.

Taking a deep breath, well as deep as she could without pain, she looked around. A storm was raging outside. The lightning display was enough to light up everything. Proudly showing the wind and the dancing rain. Thank goodness for their technology and its abilities. Feeling something touch her foot, she looked down.

Plants were swaying to the music of the storm. Bending carefully, she plucked a few of the leaves. Sitting upright, she placed them beside her. Taking her time, she removed all her headgear. Taking a moment to rub her fingers through her hair. It felt so good.

Easing the zipper of her coverlet, she gently pulled her arms from her sleeves. Taking the leaves from beside her, she placed them over her bruised skin above her broken ribs. Just then, there was a strip of linen shoved into her vision.

"Here. If you're not going to wait for help."

Taking the bandage, she slowly wrapped it around herself. Ignoring the sharp tugs of pain as she went. Hearing a rumbled growl. She looked up to see Garth hovering over her. Without a word, he pushed her hands away and completed the wrap for her. When finished, he helped her slide her arms back into her coverlet.

Looking down at her with his massive arms crossed, he asked.

"Will you rest now?"

His intense stare caused her to gulp. Silently, she nodded her head. He stood there for a few more moments, staring her down. Like he knew she was only nodding to appease him. She had intended to help him. After satisfying himself that she would listen, he turned and went back to work. Tending to the rest of their teammates.

She watched as he moved with efficient speed, tending to everyone. It seemed odd that it was only the two of them awake. What was that? Either way, it was a good thing. They were safe and dry now. Still, she felt bad about leaving the dead behind. But the weather was too intense. She had to care for the living.

Shaking her head at her nonsense, she continued to study her surroundings. They were at the edge of a forest. Lush vegetation surrounded them. It was stunning. The abundance of color was like nothing she had ever witnessed. They were most definitely not at home. The world they left was dying, and any attempt made to save it had failed.

They were now in a thriving and life-filled world. One that had a pulse she could feel flowing through her. With each breath she took, her connection to it grew stronger. It filled a void inside her she never knew existed. It was like waking up and opening your eyes. What it meant, though, she didn't know. Smiling, she lifted her legs up and onto the cut. Wrapping herself with the provided blanket, she closed her eyes. Welcoming the embrace of sleep.

CHAPTER 8

This time, when he woke, it was calm outside and sunny. The brightness was shining through the fabric. Feeling rested, he slowly sat up, swinging his legs over the edge of the cot. Stretching his limbs, he stood, taking stock of his body. He felt great. Rotating his neck, he smiled at how good he felt. It had been a long while since he felt this good and rested.

Taking a deep breath. He stretched one last time. Looking at the other cot and seeing it was empty, he moved to the split in the fabric. Stepping into the sunshine. Closing his eyes, he tilted his head up toward the sun, enjoying the warmth. It felt good. Opening his eyes, he looked for his savior. He found him sitting by a fire a few feet away.

Taking the few steps, sitting across from him, looking into the flames. Finding a sense of comfort in their repeated dance. It was like he could hear their tune. Smiling, he decided he liked it here. Wherever here was. The sound of laughter pulled him from his trance.

Looking at Cormac, he asked.

"What is so funny, old man?"

With a smile on his face, he answered.

"Your sister has a strong connection to fire."

He paused for a moment to think before continuing.

"However, I think you may perhaps dabble with it. I think your affinity may be, shall we say, more electric?"

Confused, he was about to question him when he continued.

"You need to practice all you are able. While keeping your secret. I will be close by whenever you are in need of me. However, we need to get you back to your friends."

He ate quickly at Cormac's encouragement. Helping to clean when they finished. Before they quietly trekked back to where he had come. At his departure, he gave a word of advice.

"Reveal yourself only to either the large healer or the gifted one with a generous heart."

With that, he simply disappeared in a blink of an eye.

Odd, he thought. How did the old man know about Garth or Honor? Clearly not enough to know them by name. Nevertheless, he would follow his directive. He clearly must know something he does not. He knew his sister and assured him people he trusted cared for her.

Using all his training, he moved toward the edge of the forest where Cormac had said he found him. Hidden in position, he watched and waited for the perfect time to reveal himself. Taking the time to think back on to all the conversations he had had with Cora. The more he thought, the more he believed he was home. She always talked about her home and the people she loved and lost over time.

He knew that he and his family were part of a special race of people. Gifted people sworn to take care of those less gifted than them. That they possessed talents, each different and unique to them. That if he should ever find himself here, he should seek their wise visionary.

He suspected he had already met the man in question. Only he had found him instead. Cormac, being a visionary, would go a long way to explaining how he had known to look for him. Plus, exactly who he should reveal himself to.

He practiced as suggested, prepared to wait for a time. Closing his eyes did as he had done so many times before. Taking a deep breath and listening to his instincts. Right away, a connection to the earth felt like an all-consuming knowledge. A thread or force connecting everything and everyone. Opening his eyes, he looked around in awe.

He now understood what Cora had been trying so desperately to explain. It was a wonderful world. He now knew why she always looked so sad and seemed to be missing a piece of herself. How had she continued on? Could this have had something to do with her death? Losing this connection would be massive. Feeling for his friend, he looked closer into himself at the power stirring to life.

The energy force building from somewhere deep inside. Spreading throughout him, till he felt energy pulsing from his fingertips. Watching in awe as sparks flickered from the end of his fingers. Slowly, the sparks spread until they encased his entire being. Wow, this was cool. Smiling as he tried to flex and shape the surrounding sparks. Impressed when he could do so with astonishing ease.

In grossed with his newly discovered skill, he didn't notice when a voice spoke behind him.

"Nice talent you have there."

Surprised, he whirled around to come face to face with Garth. Sighing in relief, he was still angry at himself for losing focus of his situation and not paying attention. He should be aware at all times and not goofing off. Looking at the man in the eyes, he asked.

"What talent?"

As Garth rolled his eyes, he said.

"Your electricity shield."

Nodding his head, he knew the man had more to say. He waited till he continued.

"So you know, I covered for you with Jasper. Telling him you insisted on scouting the area while Honor took care of ensuring the safety of the rest of us inside the makeshift dome."

He shifted his weight from foot to foot.

"She erected the dome and transported every surviving member to safety. Meanwhile, having two broken ribs." Growling, he continued. "The blasted woman never asked for help. Nor did she want to rest and heal. Taking it upon herself to make a compress for her bruised side."

While giving Garth a wide-eyed look, he felt impressed by all Honor had accomplished while also angry she did it alone.

"I know she shouldn't have done it alone. That woman is strong.

Regardless, you need to be careful and watch your way around Jasper. He has a real hard-on for you, man."

This was not news to him, but to hear the confirmation of it from a member of his team did shock him. Not sure of exactly what to say, he replied.

"Ok."

Garth nodded and hesitated to say the last bit. Shaving his hands in his pockets.

"Not everyone survived the trip. We are still unsure of the reason." Pausing again, he seemed to have difficulty with this. "Sally is one of the deceased. So needless to say, Jasper blames you."

Hearing this shocked him. He had never liked the woman, but he never wished her dead. Regardless, he didn't care what Jasper thought. The man could kiss his ass. Squaring his shoulders.

"I am not concerned about Jasper or his opinions."

As Garth rolled his eyes again,

"Alright. Perhaps you should be. If only for what he might do to others. The man is becoming unhinged."

With a nudge of his head behind him, he said.

"Follow me back. I'll fill you in on rest on the way."

The two of them walked along the edge of the forest while Garth continued to tell him how the opinion was becoming divided on Jasper. He also wasn't comfortable leaving Honor for too long. She was next on their team leader's hit list, and he wasn't sure why. Plus, he wasn't sure who he could trust outside of himself or Caden with her safety. Surprised yet again. This man seemed to be quite the chameleon.

The plan so far was to collect the dead and give them a proper burial. He was looking for him in the direction Honor had last seen him. He was enjoying the deception toward Jasper. The more they talked, the more he realized they were on the same page. He enjoyed having an ally.

There was to be a vote tonight for who would lead the group. Jasper insists he's the one and only to lead. Honor quickly pointed out that Caden was also a True Guard leader and had an equal right to lead. Once again, their loyalty to him caught him by surprise. He was a leader, yes, but of another team all together.

He had a shocked look on his face. Cause Garth laughed, saying.

"Don't be so shocked, man. There are many here who will follow you."

Before he could say anything more, the dreaded man himself came into view in the distance. They knew the moment he saw them. His posture hardened as he walked toward them.

"Well, well, well, if it isn't the prodigal son himself." He snapped in his snide little voice.

He had to bite his cheek to keep from laughing at the little man. Both he and Garth towered over Jasper. His rising temper only made him want to blurt out a laugh. If only to see what the small man would do next. Looking at the man beside him, who it seemed when they made eye contact had the same idea.

They both knew that was only asking for more trouble. So they swallowed their laughter and turned back to Jasper. When Garth spoke.

"I found Caden. He had taken refuge deep in the forest during the storm." Directing behind them with a jerk of his thumb. "Sadly, he could not find any locals because of the storm."

The tiny man's face seemed to redden as he listened. If steam could come out of his ears, it would have. Biting his cheek once more, he heard Jasper say through clenched teeth.

"Fine."

Before he stormed off in the direction he came. He and Garth silently followed Jasper back without uttering a word.

SHE WOKE to the sound of voices. Taking a moment, she took a quick inventory. Other than her broken ribs, she felt fine. She was still laying on a cot, feeling the metal bar across her lower back. Wanting to stretch her aching limbs, she refrained, wanting to hear what was clearly an argument.

A whiny voice stammered.

"There is no way that she did all that."

A reply came from a smooth, confident voice.

"She did. I only came to as she was bringing the first of you to the safety of the dome. She had it erected with cots prepared for everyone."

That wasn't entirely true. She wanted to argue, Garth had prepared all the cots and not her. But she was getting the credit for it. Why? Deciding it was better to play possum, she continued to listen in on the conversation. When she heard an irritated Garth say.

"Regardless, it is the truth, and we all owe her. So from now on, give her the respect she deserves."

Hearing some fabric rustle, she assumed someone was leaving. In a quiet, heated huff, apparently. Gradually, she heard them grumbling less and less. Smiling to herself. It pleased her that someone had her back.

"You can open your eyes now. He's gone."

Surprised, she opened her eyes, turning to look at Garth. Curious, she tilted her head and studied him. No one had ever defended her before, let alone lie for her. She wanted to know why, so she asked him.

"Why did you lie to him? You were the one to set up the cots."

Shrugging his shoulders, he said.

"I don't know. He was pissing me off. Plus, you do a lot of work and get no recognition for it. It's about time you did."

He looked down at his feet, seeming unsure of his confidence suddenly. Speaking softly, he continued.

"Regardless of how you were treated in the past, you took the responsibility of saving everyone on this team."

Shocked by his response, she could only reply with a simple.

"Thank you."

Before she choked up.

He moved at lightning speed. Sitting on the cot beside her, with a word of caution.

"No. Don't cry. It's not a safe time, and I don't know what to do with a crying female."

Pausing. He glanced around.

"You need to be on guard. Jasper is distraught over Sally. He blames Caden for her death. Well, in his eyes, murder. Though no one believes that. Not even those who are loyal to him."

His words took her by surprise.

He chuckled.

"Don't look so surprised. Not all of us think so highly of our famous leader as the ass- kissers do. However, the time will come when we reveal ourselves. Just not yet."

Again, he looked around. Seeing they were still alone. He continued, looking sternly into her eyes.

"The story goes like this. Caden left to survey as per protocol. Instructing you to set up a barrier. Then gather everyone together. That is exactly what you did. OK."

Swallowing the growing lump in her throat, she nodded. Whispering.

"Ok."

Taking the hand he offered, he helped her to stand. Hissing through her teeth at the pain in her side, she closed her eyes. Taking a few shallow breaths, she reminded herself to hide the pain. They had work to do. Plus, she didn't want to appear weak.

A few hours into her morning assignment, and she was grateful. Scavenging the surrounding area for necessary items. They were simultaneously making a home base and taking care of their dead. She didn't have it in her to dig the multiple holes for the individual graves. She was the one who had argued against a massive grave. Stating they had all died during their True Guard service and deserved respect. Reluctantly, Jasper had finally agreed. Only after did many of the others side with her.

Near to the location they decided was perfect for a home base creation, there was a forest. Filled with many types of trees and other vegetation. She took her time walking amongst the trees. Breathing in deep the clean earthly smells. Each breath she took gave the impression that she could heal herself. Which, of course, was impossible, right? Still, they had traveled through what could only have been a portal. Was it an opening to a different place or time?

Her gut instinct was they were in the same place, but at a different time. Only Why? That was now the question. One that would have to be dealt with later. She needed to focus on her task.

Her first gathering was of twigs and pine cones for kindling. It amazed her how much all their childhood lessons from days of old were now suddenly very helpful. It was surprisingly easy, too. This place looked like home, but different. It was beautiful and so full of life.

Today's gentle breeze whistled through the leaves. Harmonizing with the multitude of birds chirping and singing. Add to it the dancing beams of sunlight appearing through the trees. She couldn't help herself and moved to the song.

Swaying on the spot, she drifted across the forest floor. Weaving her way in and out of tree trunks. With arms splayed, her fingertips grazed the bark and leaves. Closing her eyes and allowing the energy to build and flow. She was feeling wonderful. Her pain disappearing.

Smiling, she continued to gather anything they might need. Taking her time as she did. There was no rush. Multiple trips back and forth. The others surprised her with their quick work. They had already erected a few housing structures. Working together as a team, instead of against each other, they achieved tasks.

They would determine how much actual teamwork existed. It was likely everyone wanted a safe and secure home base. Still, she remained unconvinced. What were the real motives? The absence of assigned partners for both her and Garth in their tasks was strange. Unlike everyone else, why were they the ones singled out?

As she was about to head back out, she saw an angry-looking Jasper. He was stomping his way back to camp. Followed by Garth and Caden, who looked like they were about to burst into laughter. Smiling, she looked back at her team leader. He had a Napoleon complex. Picturing him in the hat and uniform of the past. She couldn't contain the laughter that followed.

With all eyes on her in shock, she tried to hide her laughter by covering her face. Only Jasper stared at her with a look of what she thought must be hatred. Why he felt that way toward her shocked her. Uncomfortable with his stare, she scanned the other faces.

The more she tried to stop, the harder she laughed. All too soon, others joined in. Which only further enraged their team leader. The harder she laughed, the more her ribs hurt. But it was just too funny. She could not unsee the man in the ridiculous garb. Bending over in laughter, she wrapped her arms around her middle. Allowing the tears to fall.

She heard Jasper sputter and yell obscenities at them. Further proving to her that her opinion of the man was correct. If only they had a plan to do something about it. Before anyone else got hurt or died. They had all traveled through a portal and into another time. All because of this pipsqueak of a man. He was on some sort of mission. For what? She had no clue.

Only that she must find out. Hopefully soon, too. If only to save others that might cross his path.

CHAPTER 9

They had just buried the last of Jasper's team members. He was still in shock at how many had perished. Regardless of their treatment of him and his family, he wished no ill will upon them. Why had they died while the rest of them survived the portal crossing? They still could not answer that question. They only knew they all met their end within the portal itself.

He was further saddened by the fact Jasper had only been present for Sally's burial and mini service. He demanded that the burial and mini-service take place first and separate from all the others. They could have a mass grave and service for all he cared.

Revealing his true colors to his surviving team members. Was it the death of his partner that sent him over the edge? Or could it be something else? He was unraveling more with each moment. He feared he was becoming a ticking time bomb. Action would need to be taken, and sooner rather than later.

It seemed he would have more allies than he thought. Considering the recent actions of their leader. Many were not pleased and would argue over every debate. The fact he was a fellow True Guard team leader seemed to cancel out some of the hatred cast upon him. Their eyes seemed to be suddenly open, as well as their minds. Now thinking for themselves.

Focusing back on the current tasks. He made his way back to their home base. The achievement they had reached this morning surprised him. The compound was coming along nicely. He would make some changes. With the knowledge he had, they needed to take some drastic measures for protection. More for the locals rather than themselves.

If he was right, they had traveled through time. Entering the past. All the technology they had brought here it needed to remain in their hands alone. It was necessary for them to keep the knowledge of it and themselves a secret. This world had not advanced to this point yet.

Thankfully, their tech could make them and their compound invisible. Giving them the freedom to live out their lives. A much happier and healthier one than that of their former one.

He did a quick scan of the area, making sure everyone was making their way back. Also, he confirmed they were alone and there were no locals in sight. They needed to be careful until they had activated all the dome features. Which would have to be done asap.

The tech design provided versatility for multiple levels of usage. Their previous compound had used it to its full capacity. Complete protection and environmental control. It had been the only way humanity had survived. Here, however, they only would need it for invisibility and sound control. He might need to have Honor look and see if she could rewrite some of the inner code. Allowing the dome to give off a feeling of unease to all who came too close. Well, people anyway, but all other life forms would be welcome.

With his decision made, he followed the last of the team members into their new kitchen hall. Now it was time to hold the dreaded meeting. The one where he would actively take leadership of this compound. Laying out all his changes and additional requests.

He hoped Jasper would be an ally. They needed to act together as leaders. This wasn't his team, however, he had knowledge of this time that the others did not. They would be better off if they all worked together. Though he sensed that would not be the case.

He wondered if any of them had noticed the change in themselves. He suspected not. There were no mumblings about it. So if they noticed, they were keeping it to themselves. Upon returning, he had surveyed them while they worked. Many, if not all, had developed superior strength and a growing sense of unity. Now together, working in a unified way.

He also observed that Honor had a task to complete without a partner. Having a ton tossed onto her plate. Still, she managed her tasks without complaint and with great skill. She was faster than the others. Perhaps because she was solo or had she developed more strength and speed than the rest?

He always kept his gaze fixed on her. The inner pull toward her getting stronger by the moment. The way she moved with fluid grace, collecting items from the forest. An area she seemed most comfortable in. Coming alive, dancing amongst the trees to the birdsong. She was pulling him under her spell.

This meeting required him to concentrate, however. It would be best he not dwell on thoughts of Honor. He could contemplate the meaning of his feelings toward her later. Now was best to focus on the well-being of them all.

SHE WAS STILL REELING in shock over the burial ceremonies. Jasper's behavior was also a surprise and not at the same time. Jasper insisted on singling out Sally. Being buried separately and having her own individual service. The others he wanted them all in one mass grave. Jasper argued, "Since they are deceased, they would be oblivious to whether or not we adhere to the code." His statement was harsh and uncaring. Thankfully, everyone had agreed with her to give them the respect they deserved. Each has their graves with a marker stone. Sadly, they were all lumped together in a generic service after his beloved partner's elaborate observance.

When he took off after her long and dedicated service, he left his team members shocked. She was further angry when the reminder only received a few words. Which two of their teammates disregarded the need for respect. They began discussing how Jasper had been right. This was a waste of time and quickly joined their leader. Remembering the angry faces of the men standing around her. Their rigid body posture and their fists clinching at their sides. Everyone unanimously seemed to agree that the dead deserved better respect.

Now they were all seated around a central fire in the newly built kitchen hall. This massive space would seem to be now functioning as a multi-purpose. As high-tech as it was, it was still rather basic and simple. Providing just the essential basic needs to cook, eat, and gather. It still amazed her how their tech could achieve such things. At other times, they were reliant on the primitive.

Now, having gathered together again as per protocol, their meeting was about to start. It was anyone's guess at how crazy this could become. Jasper seemed to be all over the place in his moods and demands. Of course, he was grieving over his partner, as he should be. He should take some time off. They all knew, however, that would never happen. Especially with Caden present.

As he was a fellow True Guard team leader, he had the right to take charge. Based on the reaction of most of her fellow teammates, she would bet they agreed that would be the best course of action. She wasn't sure, however, why they would agree. Was it only because Jasper was being erratic because of his grief and would recover in time? Did they also believe in stripping his title and responsibility?

Time would soon tell. Caden was now calling for everyone's attention to begin the meeting. The difference in leadership was obvious to see right away. Instead of standing apart from the group above them, he was amongst them. Almost like he was an equal. Only you could feel the authority vibrating from him. This man fascinated her. She felt compelled to get closer to him while he spoke. She had a small crush on him, yes. Right now, she experienced a striking sensation, as if lightning had struck her. Shaking her head, she blinked, ridding herself of her wandering mind.

Listening again as he thanked them all for their work today. Commenting on how brave and respectful they all were toward their deceased team members. He was proud of them all. For a man who was not a member of their team, he sure had an exceptional ability to care. For all of them.

She could feel the tears welling in her eyes. Regardless of how those deceased members had treated her, she still hadn't wished them dead. This speech seemed to bring every feeling straight to the surface. For everyone present. Caden had a way with words and with people. The discussion continued and was so different from any they had ever had before.

Caden was insistent on the participation of every member of the team. Wanting their option and suggestions. Further drawing them into his camp. Their willingness to converse surprised her. It was like they were all blooming. It was wonderful. Still, she remained quiet, content to listen. That alone took a lot of concentration on her part. Later, she would ponder the reason for the force drawing her toward her childhood crush.

Looking around, she noticed they were missing three members. The same ones who had all stormed off in disrespect. However, she was grateful now for Caden and his innate talent for bringing out the best in people. It was no wonder he was a True Guard team leader. A very good one too.

What impressed her was his ability to weave into the conversation about his recommendations and requests. The need for secrecy had all of them agreeing whole- heartedly. Not wanting to disturb the locals and the natural order of things. Especially since they still lacked knowledge in both areas.

It was at this moment, while everyone was happily agreeing with each other, that Jasper and his shadows stormed into the hall. Ignoring the fact he was interrupting Caden, he started shouting rude obscenities at him for 'stealing what was rightfully his.' This was his show and team members. All the events leading up to this point were his fault, and he should face consequences.

Honor's jaw dropped in shock at Jasper's ridiculous accusations.

The more he accused, the angrier he got. To the point, he was frothing at the mouth and walking on his tippy toes. Taking a peek at Caden. She was curious about how he would take this outburst of disrespect. He seemed to grow taller suddenly. However, she thought she saw a slight uptick in his lip. Was this funny to him?

As he crossed his enormous arms, she turned back to Jasper. His face was so red with anger he could have had steam coming out of his ears. Before she could stop herself, a laugh blurted out of her mouth.

CHAPTER 10

This man was seriously beginning to piss him off. Was it his mission in life to do just that? Standing to his full height, he had to cross his arm to keep from decking the man. The thought of doing so had him almost smiling. However, giving Jasper any more ammunition, regardless if it was legit, was not a good thing.

What shocked him even more was Honor's outburst of laughter. She had been utterly quiet throughout their earlier chat. Only nodding her head here and there. Sometimes he swore she was looking right through him. She would lean in as if to touch him. Upon closer inspection, he noticed her eyes had a glazed-over look. Still, she seemed to keep up with their discussion.

It was all he could do to stop himself from getting close to her. He found it difficult to resist getting close to her. It was why he began the discussion standing amongst them, rather than in front of them. When he entered the kitchen hall, the need to be close to her was too strong. He had known her for years. Even seeing her in passing.

Sure, it was her eyes he saw when he closed his during his sessions with Sally. But never had he felt this........ he didn't even know what to call it. Perhaps Cormac would know. He would have to ask him the next time he saw him.

Now, sadly, he had to deal with this little pipsqueak of a man,

Jasper. How he ever became a True Guard leader was beyond him. Thankfully, Honor's giggles continued. Even after her eyes rounded and she slapped her hand over her mouth. She couldn't seem to stop. While the rest of their gathering looked on in shock, they too joined in on the laughter. Further adding fuel to the fire.

It was all fun and games until Jasper, in his red-faced anger, flew at Honor. He struck her cheek with such force in a calculated move, causing her to go sailing backward.

At lightning speed, he was at her side. As gently as could be, he cupped her other cheek. Rubbing his thumb along the bone. His heart hurt when saw tears forming in her eyes. Along with the knowledge, she would not let them fall. She would show no weakness. Only he knew crying wasn't a form of weakness. It was brave to display your emotions.

How many times had this young woman experienced hurt? Well, no more. He vowed she was under his protection.

Their momentary spell broke. When Jasper, mouth frothing, he snarled.

"No one laughs at me, you little bitch."

Looking into her eyes, he conveyed his need for her to stay put. With a plead of his own. Standing again to his full height, he turned toward Jasper. At that moment, he noticed that all the team members had gathered around, forming a circle around them. The pipsqueak's shadows were lying on the ground, knocked out. Likely because they tried to help their leader. A leader who was now being restrained.

He didn't seem overly pleased with his team's actions. Well, that was too bad. His actions were horrendous at best. Taking another moment to breathe deeply before he spoke. Looking the man in the eye.

"You disgust me, Jasper."

Loud murmurings of the others in full agreement echoed in the hall.

"That is not the way to treat a woman. Your behavior of late leaves me with no other choice than to hereby strip you of leadership."

Sighs of relief from his conscious team members told him his decision was the right one. Still, this course of action could cause more harm than good. He would have to hope for the good.

Jasper continued to fight the gripping hold on his upper arms as he shouted his venom toward him.

"You have no right to strip my authority. This is my team, not yours, Faxon."

Turning his head, Jasper then attempted to spit in his face.

With his stomach turning in disgust, he was grateful Garth chose at that moment to speak.

"Enough! Caden has every right, and you know it. It's why you're so pissed off. How you've treated Honor, however, you deserve far worse."

More murmurings of agreement spread throughout the hall. It seemed Garth was speaking on behalf of his team. Feeling the gentle touch of fingers on his arm, he looked to see Honor standing not quite behind him, but not beside him, either. Softening his gaze, he reached, wrapping a protective arm around her. Bring her to his side.

Once she was there, he felt her relax and melt into him. Focusing back on Jasper. He attempted to calm the fury in his voice.

"She is under my protection. You hear me, Jasper."

The man's face seemed to bloat in anger and redden even more, if that was possible. He smartly remained silent.

"You and your two cronies." Nudging his head toward the men out cold on the floor.

"Will henceforth reside in our newly constructed restricted living accommodation."

To Jasper's surprise, a unanimous shout of "Yes" echoed from all the men in the room. Not wanting to speak to the man anymore, he tilted his head toward the exit. Knowing those who held Jasper would eagerly lead him away. The unconscious men, like sacks, were slung over the shoulder and carried out behind them.

Turning to Honor, he had to make sure she would be ok. With care, he took her head in his hands. Gently titling her face toward his, he inspected her cheek. To his surprise, it was already beginning to heal. You could hardly see the evidence from Jasper's hand. Amazing.

Her eyes grew with alarm, whispering her concern.

"Is it as bad as that?"

Quick to squash her worry.

"Oh. No. Sorry, I didn't mean to alarm you. You are already healing. I can hardly see a mark."

He watched as her eyes lost their focus before she squeezed them shut. Taking his thumbs, he stroked them under her eyes till she relaxed. He wanted her to look at him again. Her eyes were expressive. Revealing what she was thinking.

Suddenly, a staggering sense of fear overcame him. With his muscles tightening, he went rigid, on alert. Before he could scan their surroundings, he heard the faint whisper of a familiar voice.

"Caden,"

SHE FELT Caden's body go rigid and tense as she opened her eyes. Concerned, she scanned his face, hoping for a clue as to why. Watching his eyes glaze over and fear spread across his strong features. Reaching her hand up to stroke his cheek, she asked.

"Caden, are you okay?"

His only response was to pull away from her. She couldn't help the hurtful gasp that escaped her lips from his actions. Which seemed to bring his eyes back to focus on her. His gaze softened upon seeing her, pleading for her to understand some unspoken message. Squinting in confusion, she opened her mouth to ask what he meant. Only he spoke first while frantically looking around.

"I'm sorry I have to go."

With that statement, he practically flew out of the kitchen hall.

With her jaw still hanging open, she glanced around the room.

This was odd behavior, even for Caden. Right? Looking at everyone else's shocked and confused faces confirmed her suspicions. What had caused such a reaction like that? Had she done something wrong?

Her mind was a jumble of here and there thoughts. Not to mention her jaw and tailbone were still very tender. Jasper had quite a bit of strength. Sending her flying across the room with a slap. Softly, she cradled her cheek while rotating her jaw. Taking note, it did not feel as bad as it did when the strike happened. Was she healing as fast as Caden had claimed?

Confused, she looked to the doorway he had left through as if the answers were there. Thinking back, she had noticed a few odd things happen in the past little bit. Like how did Japer suddenly have that amount of strength? He had taken her completely off guard with his actions. They all seemed to appear to have increased strength and speed. Though none of them had used it against one another.

What had she done to earn such a treatment from their former leader? She knew he had never liked her, but it was usually the silent treatment after he gave her work to do. Oh, and the tasks none else wanted to do. This place had changed all of them, for sure. Most for the good, from what she could tell. Only Jasper seemed to have gotten far worse. He was a completely different person.

A gentle hand on her shoulder pulled her from her mind's wanderings. Refocusing her gaze, she looked over to see it was Garth's hand. Concern filled his eyes. The need to reassure him filled her. Softening her gaze, she said,

"I'm ok, Garth."

He tilted his head with a stern look in question. He didn't believe her. Quick to reassure him, she stated again.

"Really Garth. I'm ok."

She could see from his look he still didn't believe her. All the same, he replied with a head nod. Before saying.

"If you insist. Please make one of your compresses, though, and apply it to your cheek. Okay?"

With that, he carefully took her elbow and guided her over to where they had stored the ingredients. With more encouragement, he had her teaching him how to make and apply her magick stuff. It amazed her he was genuinely curious and willing to learn. Asking how she knew all this stuff. She had no answer. It was unclear to herself how she knew all the information. The know how was just there. He acknowledged with a simple head nod.

His serene acceptance shocked her. This place was really getting to her. It was wonderful in a good way. Even with the bit of bad. She was usually the one on the outside looking in. Here and now, she was in the opposite position. She rather liked it, even if she wasn't sure how to act.

No one seemed to mind, though. Garth again took her elbow, leading her to a chair. Guiding her to sit, he looked toward their fellow team members, saying.

"Look after her. Make sure she rests and eats a little something."

He left when they all either nodded or voiced their agreement. Well, it would seem Garth has labeled himself Caden's second. She was further surprised by the other's care and gentle treatment of her. They sat with her, talking, sharing, and even laughing. Apologizing when she cringed in pain. Her cheek was still tender. Together, they all enjoyed a meal that some of them had prepared. The taste was amazing. Experiencing care felt absolutely nice.

CHAPTER 11

*H*e knew his sister's voice. That was her calling to him. He just couldn't figure out how he heard it in his head. At first, he thought she was in the kitchen hall with them. It was why he had looked around frantically. Thinking then she had been there and left, he ran after her. It was only after he realized he was chasing air that he had heard her voice in his head.

Now he was on a mission to find Cormac. He needed some answers. Like why could he hear his twin's voice in his head? Why could he feel her utter terrifying fear? He knew things were different here, but this was just over the top. What else could he be likely to expect? At this point, it seemed like anything and everything could be possible.

In record time, he made it to the area where the temporary tent had been. Only it was gone and in its place was a small wooded house. Odd.

Cautiously, he made his way up the porch steps to the door. Before he could even blink, the front door swung open and Cormac stood on the other side. An enormous smile spread across his face.

"Welcome my boy." With a wave of his hand, he asked. "What do you think?" With another hand gesture, he indicated he follow him in. All the while, he continued talking. "Nice isn't it? I just can't stand not having the comforts of home surrounding me. So Tada. I recreated home."

Dumfounded, he simply sat where the old man showed, nodding his head on impulse. It took too much thought to fathom how he had created this in such a short amount of time. Mutely, he watched as the man scurried around the place, before ultimately sitting across from him.

It was then he noticed what he had been doing. A small feast sat in front of them. His stomach took the time to growl loudly in response.

"I thought you might be hungry. A large man like yourself needs to eat plenty."

They both dug into the food. Which tasted wonderful to him. This place was just getting better and better. It was that thought that reminded him of why he had come here in the first place. Clearing his throat before asking.

"Why can I hear my sister in my head?"

Cormac froze. Slowly, he sat back in his chair and studied Caden. Before he asked a question of his own.

"Has she spoken to you?"

Not willing to speak for fear of blurting out another question, he nodded his head.

Cormac rubbed his chin while repeating,

"Interesting. Very interesting indeed."

Finally, after a long moment of silence, he asked a question.

"What does it mean? Am I going crazy?"

His emotions were all over the place. He wasn't entirely sure they were all his, either.

Making it even harder for him to think rationally. Still, Cormac was rubbing his chin in thought. Frustrated, he blurted.

"Oh, just spit it out already."

All Cormac did in response was to raise a brow at him before he chuckled.

"No, my boy, you're not crazy. I do, however, need to ask you this. How is your sibling relationship constructed?"

That was an odd way to ask. Still, he answered.

"Harlow and I are twins, if that's what you mean. How does that have anything to do with this?"

He watched as multiple expressions crossed over the old man's face. Finally, he said,

"Well, that answers a multitude of questions."

Confused by his answer, he was about to ask him what he meant when he continued.

"The reason you can hear her, my boy, is because you are twins. Simple as that."

Well, at least he answered the question. He just didn't understand what it meant. It didn't seem he was going to get any answers of comprehension right now. So instead, he steered the conversation toward the fear factor. He explained the overwhelming sense of fear he felt right before he heard her call his name.

"Is she in trouble, Cormac? You assured me she was safe. Now I'm not so sure."

Once again, the old man was rubbing his chin deep in thought.

"I will have to do some digging to find out for sure. What I want you to do is try as hard as you might to stay calm. If only for her sake."

When he attempted to argue, he was met with a raised finger and a shaking of the head.

"Trust me. When she calls to you again, I want you to listen. Really listen to her. Gain all the information you can. Then come to me."

Cormac stared him down, filling the room with a heavy weight of energy. Finally, he nodded his agreement. He possessed the capability to fulfill the task. Even if it went against his instincts. This was his sister. It was his job to protect her. The need to go rushing in and be the hero was strong, even if it was a stupid choice. He could feel the wisdom in the old man and knew he was speaking the truth.

Cormac stood, babbling as he ushered him out of his 'home away from home.'

"Right then. Off you go, my boy. You take care of the tasks at hand."

Hearing the click of the door behind him, he realized there was more he wanted to ask. Like the connection he felt toward Honor and what that meant. Why it was growing stronger with every minute?

He found himself attracted to her. She had a stunning body with curves in all the right places. Her hair it was lush, shiny and full. He wanted to run his fingers through her hair. Gripping it tight in his palm so he could tilt her head to just the right angle. So he could devour her sinful mouth in a kiss.

For all her external beauty, she had an inner beauty that shone. A heart full of gold and a need to help all those in need. Added to all of that, there was his deep desire to have his way with her. Whenever and wherever he liked. Just thinking about now made him hard.

All the dirty things he wanted to do to her and with her. Groaning, he reached down and adjusted himself. His pants were awfully tight. Visualizing her naked. He really wanted to see that.

Groaning, he rubbed a hand down his face. He needed to stop. To think of something else. Anything at all. Taking a deep breath to relax, he closed his eyes, pondering.

What was the reason for this strong magnetic pull towards her? What is the reason for here and now? He never felt this at the compound. What was the reason behind his desire to rip into Jasper for touching and hurting her?

As he turned to enter the cottage and ask his slew of questions, he found the door locked and the lights turned off. Odd. He also had the sudden awareness that Cormac was no longer home. Strange how he knew that.

The questions sadly would have to wait till another time. For now, he would have to wait patiently for his sister to reach out to him. Hopefully, she was ok. Concern twisted in his gut. Still, he tried to take Cormac's advice and calm himself.

SHE WAS HAVING the most wonderful dream. Caden had his arms wrapped around her, and he was kissing her. Dominating her with his mouth. Groaning, she leaned in closer. Wanting more, needing more. She couldn't get enough of him. Digging her nails into his shoulders, she pulled herself up, wrapping her legs around him.

He growled at her inflicted pain. Driving her insatiable need for him higher. As he deepened the kiss, he took hold of her head, angling it just right. He plunged his tongue into her mouth, mimicking what he wanted to do to another part of her.

Moaning, she grabbed fists full of his hair. She couldn't get enough of him. She wanted more. The need to be closer was overwhelming. He was an addiction.

As he tightened his grip on her ass, sparks of desire rippled through her. She couldn't help but grind herself against him. It felt too good. Her reaction seemed to spur him on even more. He growled while squeezing her cheeks and bringing her in closer to him. Aiding her movements up and down. Getting just enough friction.

She was on the verge of exploding when she was suddenly startled awake. Groaning in frustration, she took a moment to scan her tiny room. What had woken her from such a climatic dream? Well, almost climatic anyway.

Not seeing anything amiss, she took a moment to listen. Perhaps it was something outside that had wakened her? Which was strange. Since arriving here, the nights had been utterly peaceful. Blinking stars and a shining moon filled the sky. Other times, clouds filled the sky with gently falling rain. The only sounds were those of animals and birds. Occasionally, the wind would also sing a song across the land. Like it was breathing life into everything it touched.

It was magickal to her. So full of life. She felt invigorated. Feeling a connection to it all, almost like she was a part of it. It was strange.

Taking a deep inhale; she knew she was alone in her room. Also, there was no one right outside her door. So what had awoken her?

Sitting upright, she swung her legs over the edge of the bed. Shaking her head at her silliness, regardless, she would investigate. It was better to err on the side of caution. Quickly, she changed from her sleeping clothes and into her tack gear. She was just finishing with her boots when she heard a light tap at her door.

That was odd. She was so sure there had been no one out there. But then why was she suiting up to check? Sighing to herself, she moved cautiously toward the door. How could she be sure there hadn't been anyone there in the first place? There were no camera feeds in here to show her. A person couldn't just sense things like that? Or could they?

Reaching the door, she peered through the tiny peephole. Gasping in shock at who she saw standing there. She couldn't help but blush scarlet as spoke.

"Caden. What are you doing here? Is everything alright?"

He was fidgeting as he stood there. Ultimately demanding.

"Honor, let me in."

The tone of his voice sent shivers down her spine. She wasn't sure if he heard her whispered reply over the lock disengaging and the door opening.

"Ok."

Moving like the wind, he glided into her space. No sooner had she closed the door and reengaged the locks than she was in his arms. Opening her mouth to question him, only for her to be rendered mute upon looking into his eyes. The most intense heat and desire filled them.

"Honor."

Was all he said before he bent his head toward her. Locking his lips to hers and devouring her mouth like he had in her dream. Not a few minutes ago. A fiery flame lit her up within at his touch. The confidence with which he ate at her mouth filled her tummy with butterflies. He knew what he liked and how he liked it. Or her, for that matter.

Moaning, she sank into his embrace. Allowing him to direct the intensity of the kiss. She loved how he explored her mouth with his tongue. The way he titled her head for better access. His responding growls of pleasure when she did as he demanded.

Like in her dream, she grabbed fists full of his hair. Before she hopped up to wrap her legs around him. His reaction was to squeeze and mold her ass into his massive hands. Causing both of them to moan in unison. Feeling the same liquid fire spreading throughout out her limbs, she ground herself against him.

Only unlike her dream, he pulled his mouth from hers. He ignored her whining.

"No."

Shaking his head, he tightened his grip on her ass and increased her tempo and pressure. Staring into her eyes, he said.

"You look at me when you come. I want to see it in your eyes. I want to see you come apart for me."

Sucking in her shocked gasp. She could only nod her head in a vigorous yes. Her response seemed to please him. The fire in his gaze intensified.

"That's my girl. Now grind yourself on me. Hard."

Lost in her desire for him, she was all too willing to do as he demanded. With his help, she found it easy to rub against him and generate enough friction. The heat of his body combined with his powerful presence was doing wonders in aiding the experience. This man was like no other.

Before she knew it, she was on the precipice of coming. She could feel the starting tingle. Her eyes fluttered closed when she heard.

"Eyes, Honor."

Feeling the ball in her tummy tighten with desire at his command, she locked her gaze with his. She was pleased when he said.

"That's my girl. Your eyes are mine when you come. Just like your orgasms are."

Despite his crazy statement, it filled her with pride. Being his girl made her feel warm and fuzzy. If all her orgasms were his, if they were all like this one, was amping up to be, then sure. Why not? He could have them all.

With a glint in his eye, as if he somehow knew what she had been thinking, and had decided. He smiled. It lit up his entire face. She had pleased him. She liked that. Liked it a lot.

Moaning in pleasure as he leaned in to nibble on her lips. He pulled back, tugging her bottom lip while whispering.

"Good girl."

Dreamily, she smiled at him. He was driving her crazy. She wanted to come now. He seemed to know exactly what she was thinking. Pressing in close to him, he simply demanded.

"Come. Come for me, Honor. Come Now."

That was all she needed. She screamed, coming apart in his arms. Her vision blurred, and she lost all awareness except for her intense orgasm. This was bliss.

She wasn't sure how long she had been unaware. Or the fact she had willingly allowed herself to become so. It was too dangerous for her. Tensing, she quickly heard shhing and felt a hand rubbing her back. Relaxing, she looked at Caden.

He bent, kissing the tip of her nose.

"That was amazing, Honor. Thank you."

Blush filled her cheeks. She had just humped him till she came, and he was thanking her. Hesitantly, she asked.

"What about you?"

Looking at his lap where she could see he was as turned on as she had been. He displayed his hard evidence laying there beside her. When had they moved onto her bed? He must have moved them while she was in the throes of her orgasm.

Feeling a finger under her chin, she looked up at Caden. He was smiling at her.

"Tonight was about you. No need to worry about me."

When she opened her mouth to protest, he shook his head.

"I am very pleased, Honor. It was amazing to watch you come."

She didn't think she could blush even harder. Her cheeks must be scarlet. As if to prove her point, he chuckled as he stroked her cheek.

"So beautiful."

Lost in his gaze, she found herself smiling into his eyes.

Before she could ponder further on tonight's events, he wrapped in his arms covering them in her blanket.

"Sleep, my girl. Tomorrow, it will be time for questions and answers."

Deciding he was right. Plus, her foggy brain and contented body agreed. It could wait till tomorrow. She was snuggling in Caden's arms in her bed. Feeling content, and burrowed her nose into his chest, finding comfort in his scent as she drifted off to sleep.

CHAPTER 12

*H*e allowed himself to wake slowly. This place, with its fresh air, singing birds, and the rising sun, made mornings that much more enjoyable. The need to stretch his aching limbs was intense. However, he didn't want to disturb the precious bundle curled into him.

Turning his head, he looked down to where Honor lay next to him. She looked so peaceful. Even though they squeezed into her minuscule bed. She was truly an amazing person. It was truly remarkable for her to be as kind and caring as she was, despite the treatment she had received in the past. Her beauty shone inside and out.

However, she was still a knockout of a girl, with that girl's next door quality about her. He would love to gaze at her for hours. Taking her all in. From her rich, thick and wavy hair. Which, as of late, seemed to want to curl even more. Like it had a life of its own.

Her eyes. Man, they bewitched him every time. Every emotion she had shone in them. With crystal clear blue clarity.

He loved her smaller size compared to his own. Delicate yet strong. Watching her as she slumbered, he twirled a finger in one of her curls.

Wondering how she had pulled him into her dream last night. It was a mystery to him. When he had realized it was her creation and not his, he had broken the connection. Needing to get to her, and fast. Thankfully, his rooms were right beside hers, so it had taken him no time at all to get to her.

Her arousal hit him as soon as she opened the door, and he couldn't resist. On autopilot, he went about recreating her dream. Only he added a hint of his genuine desires into it. The need to dominate her during sex was so strong. As too was his need to cherish her. He would see to all her needs. Sexual and otherwise.

Unable to resist any longer, he ran a finger down her cheek. Her skin was so soft. She mumbled something unintelligible in her sleep while leaning into his touch. Boosting his ego just a bit more that her subconscious trusted him and recognized him. Smiling, he ran his fingers through her hair, at her scalp. Repeating the motion as she slowly woke.

He watched as she blinked rapidly, trying to better focus her vision. Seeing the moment, she finally recognized him. Her beautiful face lit up with a smile that reached her eyes.

"Good morning, my girl."

Bending, he kissed the top of her head. Her responding moan of contentment filled him with pride. He liked he could comfort her. Knowing where they came from, and how they grew up. He doubted she had much of that in her life. She had been one of the many orphans like Harlow and himself. However, unlike them, she grew up alongside all the other children collectively.

As far as he was aware, she didn't have any extended family to go to on holidays and weekends. Not that they celebrated those much. That time had long since passed. However, things were different during this time.

She brought him out of his mind wandering with her whispered.

"Good morning."

It seemed she took a bit of time to wake up. Unlike him, once he opened his eyes, he was up and ready to go. He also never needed an alarm, either. Naturally waking at the same time every day.

As she sat up to stretch, he did as well. Groaning as he rotated his neck. If he was going to be sleeping with her every night, he had to convince her to move over to his pod. It was spacious compared to hers. Plus, the bed was larger and softer.

Turning toward her, he lifted her chin with his finger. Inspecting her face for any signs of residual bruising. His smile grew when saw her skin had healed. There was no trace of Japer's handy work. Well, at least not physically, mentally however that would take some time. For all of them.

"It has healed Caden. Though I'm not sure how it did that so fast."

He watched her as she shook her head, as if that action would reveal the answer. She glanced back at him after a few moments. Realization on her face.

"It's this place. Isn't it?"

Sighing. He wasn't sure what or how to explain. So he simply said. "Yes, and no."

All she did was scrunch her brows together in response. It was only a matter of time before she would figure things out. This woman was intelligent and used to figuring things out on her own. It was just he had some knowledge, but not all. Cora had left some things out when she has shared her stories. While Cormac seemed happy with only giving information when he saw fit.

He had been hoping they could continue more of last night's actions. It would seem they would discuss things instead. How she would take what he had to tell her was anyone's guess. So he waited till she again made eye contact with him.

When she did, she stated shockingly.

"It was me. I healed myself."

His only reply was a head nod before she continued.

"I healed myself from our entry here, too. But how and why could I do that so quickly?"

She reached out and squeezed his hand. Giving her reassurance and support. He smiled loving at her before he answered.

"Yes, it was you. Part of it is this time and place as well as you."

Taking a deep breath, he explained that, in this time, everything was as it should be. He had some knowledge, though not all. What he knew had come from Cora.

SHOCKED WASN'T the best word to describe how she was feeling right now. She had had the best sleep of her life last night and woke in Caden's arms. It was amazing. Better than anything she had ever imagined. She suspected they would continue their bed acrobats, but she had blurted out questions instead. She was kicking herself for doing it, but she wanted answers, too.

Nevertheless, she wasn't ready for the answers. On some level, she suspected, but she had trouble wrapping her mind around it. She had firsthand experience with healing lately. After her injuries healed rapidly from her journey here. She told herself they had not been as bad as she remembered. There was no way for a person to heal that fast.

How did she suddenly know about mixing ingredients to form things like healing compresses, teas, and more? Then there was her increased strength and speed. Her ability to connect to the earth like they were old friends and simply chatting. It all felt so natural and foreign at the same time.

To say she was ill-prepared to hear Caden say his knowledge all stemmed from Cora. That she had been the one to confide in him. Her genetic lineage traces back to a race of Gods. So to do his and Harlows lineage. And therefore Rowan as well. It was why they had done so well at the upper level, with responsibilities back at the other compound. Only they had kept the information from Harlow, as she was not a member of the True Guard. Also to protect her, since she had already suffered so much early in life.

With her being physically different because of her limp. The fact that all the Faxon's were the only ones with ginger hair. Moreover, they had an unconventional upbringing compared to others. All these reasons made Harlow a target for relentless teasing and bullying. She thought they were all stupid reasons, anyway.

Cora had told many stories over the years. He was finding she had left out some information, and now he was scrambling to figure it all out. Her tales were helping him navigate this environment and engage in some self-discovery. Based on his knowledge, he guessed that, like him; she was some kind of magickal creature.

All magickal beings were descendants of the gods somehow. The result of the War of the Gods. A battle that saw the race of Gods divided into three. One that remained to govern and dictate. Wanting all nonmagickal to worship them. They, sadly, ultimately, all died off when they could no longer reproduce.

A second group who vowed to protect all magick and nonmagick alike. They treasured life, vowing it was their mission to ensure its survival. This was the group he was a descendant of. The last and the third group intermingled with nonmagickal beings, creating many different creatures. They like the second group treasure life. Deciding to enjoy it and live it instead. Sadly, they disappeared as well, over time.

Hearing this news, her mind wanted to go down the rabbit hole of possibilities. It took a significant amount of effort to concentrate on Caden's words. He suspected that everyone in their camp also possessed the gift of being a descendant of a magickal creature. The more she thought about it, the more she agreed with him.

"That would make sense. I mean, how else would Jasper have sent me flying across the room with a simple slap?"

Remembering the pain, she touched her cheek. At least she could heal herself quickly. Focusing back on Caden, she saw remorse and sorrow in his eyes. Wanting to comfort him, she raised her hand to cup his cheek while reassuring him.

"It is not your fault, Caden. All the blame lies with Jasper."

Frowning, he nodded his head in agreement.

"I know that. Still, I should have been able to protect you."

Silly man, she thought.

"You were there, Caden, along with everyone else. There was no warning about his actions. You couldn't have prevented it. Just like the others couldn't."

Rubbing her thumb along his cheek. She smiled at him.

"Besides, now, everyone knows his true colors. In the end, you defended me along with the others."

Wanting a closer connection, she crawled onto his lap, wrapping her arms around his neck.

"What's done is done. Let's move on."

Reluctantly, he agreed, hugging her tight.

"I know you're right. I should have protected you, though. You're mine."

Feeling him vibrate with his last statement, she pulled back to study him.

"What do you mean, yours?" Tilting her head in thought, she continued. "Are you talking about the magnetic pull between us? What is that about, anyway? Each day it grows stronger."

He licked his lower lip before responding. That action alone sent a zing right to her core. Causing her to take a sharp breath.

"Yes, Honor."

He didn't explain further, though she sensed there was more. Raising her brow, she silently asked him to continue.

Instead, he shook his head while wrapping his massive hand around the back of her neck. A sparkle lit in his eyes as he brought her in closer for a seductive kiss. An incredibly enticing kiss. His other hand moved to her lower back, changing the angle of her pelvis. This new position had her moaning in pleasure.

He was quick to increase the pressure on her lower back. Growling with delight when she began grinding herself against him. Tightening her arms around him as she moved. She couldn't get enough of him. Wanting more. Closing her eyes, she savored the tingling of her clit. Moaning into his mouth.

Caden pulled back from their kiss to rest his forehead against hers. Demanding.

"Eyes Honor."

Snapping her eyes open. She gazed into him, seeing the heat reflected in them. She forgot about his demand from before. With a whisper, she moaned.

"Sorry."

His returning smirk was answer enough. Even so, he said.

"No need to be sorry. You look at me when you come."

As soon as he said the last word, she exploded. Screaming his name. Watching the fire in his eyes shift to molten had her coming a second time. The knowing and prideful smirk that spread across his face had her giving him a smirk of her own.

If he could make her this wanton for him. Then she was betting she could bring him to his knees. Her smile grew just thinking about it.

CHAPTER 13

*H*e was still reeling from the events of the past twenty-four hours. The most treasured was the time spent with Honor and making her come. Deciding it was something he wanted to do each and every morning. That realization made him smile and filled him with warmth. He couldn't wait to broach the topic with her.

After her screaming orgasm, he had cradled her in his arms till she came back to herself. Offering her, his warmth and comfort filled something deep inside him. He wanted the chance to be the only one to give her that.

With a mental head shake; he focused on their surroundings. As much as he wanted to reminisce, he needed to be in the moment with her. Even if he was secretly planning to move her in with him. How she would take his news was anyone's guess and had him hesitating.

They were sitting together in the kitchen hall, enjoying a tasty morning meal. While walking over here, Honor appeared to become more reserved. Was she worried about them walking in together? He doubted that was it. Or could it be that she was worried about what had happened here yesterday with Jasper?

How could he and the others help her deal with it? This was her home too, and she should feel safe here. Violation from a team leader was a powerful hit to a person's sense of security. He was thinking of how he could get everyone on board with helping her when she walked in front of him into the hall. His eyes zeroed in on her spectacular ass, and his focus vanished. On autopilot, he followed her like a puppy and went through the motions.

Hence the spiral of his thoughts. After yet another mental headshake, he chimed into the conversation. They were all sitting around the central fire. Discussing things they had noticed happening to them since coming here. All of them experienced an increase in their strength, speed, and senses. They took turns sharing events when they noticed a sensitive sense of smell, increased hearing, and sharpened sight. Also, their intention seemed to always be communicating.

Each person expressed how, at first, they were hesitant to share their experiences. Now, however, that didn't bother them, because they noticed from time to time other team members doing remarkable things. So now seemed as good a time as any to share. They also began discussing how, since their first experiences of change, more gifts started emerging.

It amazed him how different this group had become. The shared events have changed them, it seemed, for the better. Bringing them closer together. He wanted to say it was almost like a family. Smiling at his internal realization, he waited for a lull in the conversation.

"I would like to share with you what I know of this place."

All heads turned in his direction. They all sat calmly, waiting. He would not share with them about him being a member of a secret society. Or that Cora had been their leader and the mission he had been on. He would, however, share the stories she had shared with him, leaving out the source.

He didn't fully trust them yet. Heeding Cormac's advice, he had been truthful with Honor and planned to be with Garth. Everyone else he would wait and see.

"My genetic lineage traces back to a race of Gods."

One of the group exclaimed.

"No shit."

Chuckling, he replied with.

"No shit indeed. My guess is if that is true of me, it is likely then true of all of you."

They all agreed in response, nodding their heads. Instead of cleaning up, the story time continued. He regaled them with tales he had heard. Which seemed to further build their unity of each other. He wasn't able to tell all the tales when talk moved toward their new home and how to better protect the compound and time itself.

It was a unanimous decision that the portal they had traveled through had brought them to the past. Till they knew when in the past, they had to be careful. It was then that a question whether Harlow, who went through first, was in this time, too. Since she had been the archivist and loved books, history and more. Her knowledge would be extremely useful.

He froze. When all eyes turned on him. He knew she was she was here in the same time they were. He could sense her here. Their twin bond and magick connected them, allowing them to communicate mentally. Knowing she was in trouble, however, had him hesitating whether or not to share. Cormac had instructed, only to confide in and trust Garth and Honor. Perhaps things might be changing, though. Possibly in his favor.

It being his twin, he wouldn't mind having the extra help. Still, he hesitated. Thankfully, they seemed to think his reaction was out of the same fear and hope. Not whether he trusted them. They had no way of knowing his new talent, of being so connected with his sister.

He didn't fully understand their connection yet himself. So how could he share it with others? Then there was the point he hadn't confided in Honor about his talent yet. He should tell her first while they were alone.

That connection to his twin had been the reason he had stormed from the kitchen hall yesterday. Leaving Honor in the care of Garth. He regretted that. It should have been him protecting her and comforting her.

In time, he would have to reveal all his talents. Unlike the others, who had each snuck away for self-discovery and practice. He had only practiced and discovered his newfound talents en route between here and Cormac's. He was another person who he hadn't shared the existence of. The need to keep him and Harlow a secret was a gut feeling. He wasn't sure if it was for protection or something else.

However, after this morning's meal and discussion, his feelings towards this group were changing. They all had an innate goodness to them. A need to protect and nurture. As well as providing a united front. It was why he had felt alright leaving Honor in Garth's care. Not knowing all the events surrounding his sister, talking to Cormac first about his newfound feelings toward this group would be wise. He had a feeling they were going to need all the help they could get.

That they all had special gifts in this time was an added bonus. Being True Guard members, they all had established training and knowledge. Now, like him, they needed to work on developing their new talents.

He did like that he could manipulate an electrical current. Last night, he used his newfound talent as he approached Honor's pod. It was an interesting experiment. The gift could render him invisible to all their tech. He wondered what other possibilities it held. It seemed the sky was the limit.

What else was he capable of? There were more things within himself he had yet to uncover. It was a knowledge he possessed deep within. Sometimes, the innate knowing scared him more. Questioning how it was possible to have all this inner knowledge. Where had it come from and how? Was it because of his genealogy or something else? Having so many questions and not enough answers was frustrating.

The feeling he had was that everything was expanding. A new question would arise for every answer, and a fresh problem would pop up for every solution. Then there was a matter of finding time to discover all his new and expanding talents. No matter how he planned out his time, something always came up. In the end, he accepted he would unearth these expanded gifts in real-time.

He wanted to spend his time with Honor. She was like a drug. He couldn't get enough of her. The more he was with her, the more he wanted to be.

THEY HAD BARELY MADE it through her door when she dropped to her knees and made quick work of unfastening his pants. Her fast action left him speechless and momentarily frozen. Grinning as she looked up into his eyes and gripped him firmly in her hand. She could tell by the sternness of his gaze he was not happy with the rash behavior. This man, her man, liked to be in charge. Well, that was too bad.

She wanted him and wanted this. Darting out her tongue. She swirled it around the head of his penis. He tasted slightly salty and earthy. When his eyes rolled back in his head, she pulled back, chuckling.

"Eyes Caden. I want your eyes."

It was only fair, right? Demanding the same of him as he does of her.

Maintaining eye contact, she opened her mouth further, wrapping her lips around him. Goodness, the man was enormous. As she moved, Caden grabbed a fist full of her hair, guiding her movements. She couldn't help the moan that escaped with his actions. Enjoying too the salty pre-come that landed on her tongue.

She liked it when Caden took charge of her. As if he sensed her thoughts, he said.

"My girl likes me in charge."

It was hard with him in her mouth, but she smiled at him the best she could. Nodding slightly. Using his other hand, he cupped her chin and rubbed his thumb along her cheek. Then tilting her head back, allowing him more access to her mouth.

"That's my good girl. I want deeper. I want you to stay nice and still for me."

She nodded her head as best could in this new position. Wanting to please him. To drive him as crazy as he made her.

His eyes softened with pride at her acceptance. Before an inferno engulfed them. With that, he moved, fucking her mouth. Slowly at first, building up the tempo.

Moaning, she sucked on harder. Seeing his desire for her and knowing she was feeding his pleasure had her feeling all tingly. Her need was growing.

Caden could read her so well.

"That's it, my girl. I want you to grab your breasts. Massage them."

Instantly, her hands were on her breasts, squeezing.

"Yesss."

His hips were slowly increasing their tempo.

"That's it. Good. Now I want you to pinch and pull your nipples for me."

She followed his direction. Moaning in pleasure.

"That's it. Good girl. You like playing with your nipples. Yes."

He tilted his head back slightly while still maintaining eye contact.

"Mmmmmm. You are so good at this. Your mouth feels amazing around my dick."

He went silent but for a few moans and grunts of pleasure before he continued directing and fucking her mouth. With added praise.

"So good. When next I hit the back of your throat, I want you to swallow Honor."

Nervously, she blinked her response. She wanted very much to please him. He, in turn, rubbed his thumb along her cheek.

Feeling him at her throat, she swallowed and felt him surge forward. He kept going. Worryingly, her hands flew to his thighs as fear filled her eyes. She could feel his balls rest on her chin.

"Shh, pretty girl. You got this. Breath through your nose."

Following his instructions, she breathed through her nose. Her fear dissipated. She could feel him deep in her throat. It felt foreign and yet like she held a lot of power. Instinctively, she swallowed again. To her amazement, Caden went weak in the knees.

"Shit girl. What you do to me."

Smiling around his enormous cock, she swallowed again. This time, she felt him come. He tightened his grip on her head as he emptied himself down her throat.

When he pulled back and slumped against the door, he ran a hand down his face.

"Damn girl. Where the hell did you learn that?"

She felt proud that she not only pleased him but also made him come. Also, she had achieved her goal, making him weak in the knees. Quit literarily too. Smiling up at him, she shook her head. Before she could reply, however, he had bent down, placing his hands under her arms and lifting her. With a squeak of surprise and excitement, she wrapped her legs around him.

"My turn."

Confused by his statement, she pulled back to look at him. Didn't he just have his turn?

Opening her mouth to ask what he meant, when he placed his finger there. Shaking his head with what she thought was a disapproving look in his eye. Before he tossed her onto the bed. With speed she had never seen before, he removed all her clothes and gear. Leaving her naked before him.

When she opened her mouth again to question him, he shook his head. Grabbing her ankles, he pulled her to the edge of the bed. Tossing her legs over his shoulders before gently running a finger through her folds.

Causing her to suck in a breath before exclaiming.

"Oh, my god."

Chuckling, he replied.

"Well, yes, I am a God. But you are too, my dear. I am Caden when you come."

Whatever he was doing. It felt so good. He smiled at her mischievously while saying.

"My girl likes. She is nice and wet for me."

With that, he used both hands to pull her lower lips apart before bending and thrusting his tongue in deep. This was good, so good. Moaning, she allowed herself to fall back on the bed and simply enjoy the man's tongue.

He kept changing the rhythm as he fucked her with his tongue.

When he circled her clit with his thumb, her hips shot upward. Caden pulled back, and she moaned in frustration.

Verbalizing her displeasure.

"No."

He merely chuckled, while placing his other hand on her lower abdomen, holding her down. Bending, he again took a slow lick of her pussy, from bottom to top.

"Mmmmm, you are delicious, Honor."

This time, he zeroed in on her, tasting and teasing her clit. While simultaneously fucking her with first one finger. Then two fingers, and so on. When he found that place inside her that only she thought she knew about, she was grateful he was holding her down. Positive she would have jumped off the bed.

This seemed to spur him on and increase his efforts. He strengthened the suction and pressure of his tongue while increasing the speed of his fingers. Her hips rose, while she was moaning with pleasure, wanting more.

It was too much and not enough. She needed something and was not sure what it was. Caden knew, though. As she was about to voice her thoughts, she felt a sharp slap on her ass. The sting was enough to send her over into bliss.

She came screaming his name.

"CADEN."

This was a fantastic way to end the day. Especially after the day they had today. Everyone worked together on the finishing touches of their new compound. She had activated the final tweaks and now they were the invisible little town. They had designed so that they could grow in the future if need be. Having access to the forest, water, and agriculture. This new home was a tiny paradise.

She had jokingly called it their Atlantis. To her surprise, the others had liked it and were now calling this place Atlantis, too.

Their evening meal in the hall had been short but sweet. Everyone was tired, having rushed to complete their tasks. They had to finish all the little tedious things that were left from before. Now they could relax enough and get a good night's sleep.

In her and Caden's case, they got to have a little bit of erotic fun before a much- needed night's rest. She fell asleep with a smile, thinking of their oral skills. Something they needed to repeat often.

CHAPTER 14

*H*e paced back and forth. It was all he could do in this piece of shit pod. Tugging at the ends of his hair, he let out a roar of anger. He didn't deserve this. He was a member of the True Guard and a leader. The only rightful leader. He deserved better treatment than this.

How could they do this to him? They had relegated him to one pod with no windows, the highest security door, and ultra tiny. So small he could barely turn around.

"DAMN IT."

Slamming his fist against the wall. All he had done was take out his frustrations on that stupid little woman. He had been forced to take her as a member of his team. She thought she was so much better than everyone else. He had encouraged his team to make life difficult and unwelcoming for her. Hoping she would quit. Luck wasn't on his side there either. She had stuck it out. It pissed him off.

Just because she had a talent didn't mean a thing. It was his job to bring her down a peg or two. That was his right as a leader. Wasn't it? So he handled her how he saw fit. There had never any complaints before. So why start now? Putting him here in this jail pod was below him.

He shouldn't be in here, he should be in his pod. A pod that was the lap of luxury. With a bedroom, a living area, a massive wet room, and a kitchenette. It even boasted a temperature control unit. The best of the best was always his. He had rightfully earned it.

Just like everyone else, he had paid his dues. He has always been working his way to the top. He was so close now. It was just beyond his grasp, too. All that was standing in his way were those dreaded Faxons and their groupies. But now he was stuck in here.

These pods he had designed for the likes of Caden. The scum. Anger filled him again, thinking of the man. Pounding his fist into the metal wall, imagining it was the other man's face. Ya, that was more like it. Smirking, he continued to pummel the wall.

He could feel the skin on his knuckles spiting and pulling away. The blood smeared on the wall, dripping to the floor. Pulling his hand back, he looked at the damage. Fascinated, he didn't feel the pain. Without looking, he bent, taking a piece of the bedding and wrapping it around his knuckles.

He sat on the bed against the wall, emitting an angry sigh. Bringing up a leg, he wrapped an arm around it before resting his chin on his kneecap. How had this happened to him?

He was the leader of this team. It was his time to rule this place. Why else would they have come here? It was their destiny. With him in charge. Arg, he could feel the anger burning inside. He had always known he was a leader. Everything was to be his. Even Sally had known it was true.

Then Caden had to take her from him. The cock sucker. How she could let that man touch her? Shivers racked his body just imagining it. Yuck. Now she was gone from him forever. That man had killed her. The asshole.

That Faxon scum should be in here and not him. He was doing only what a leader should be doing. Punishing his team members and keeping them in their rightful place below him. Whereas Caden had filled their heads with lies. Now they follow him like puppy dogs. It was disgusting.

Shaking his head, he needed to clear his thoughts. They only seemed to fuel his anger. That would not serve him at the moment. Right now, he needed a plan for how to get himself out of here. To do so would require some creative thought. Later, he could think about finally killing Faxon and gaining his rightful place as ruler.

It seemed the only option left. The emotional battle he had waged against the man had seen him end up here. Not Caden. All his hard work down the drain.

He was the better man, after all. He had deserved to be raised in the grand house. Not Caden. The man was scum. Why he and his family got the grand treatment, he didn't know. He only knew they hadn't earned it.

Two of his team members, at least, had stayed loyal to him. He would make sure to reward them handsomely for their efforts. If only he could get word to them, he could rely on them to help him now. The question was how? Grinning to himself, he knew soon he would show everyone what he was made of. His time was now.

Dropping his leg, he started to plan in more detail. Hoping it was possible to lure back some of the rest of his team. If only for a little while. Their back-and-forth allegiance could be an excellent distraction. Yes, this was good. It was wonderful when things came together nicely, and they would, he would make sure of it. He just needed a sign to show him when to put his plane into action.

CHAPTER 15

The sunlight was warm on his skin. Turning slightly, he saw it was high in the sky already. They had slept through the morning. Not something they had ever done before. When they had lived in the compound, life had run like clockwork.

They only knew what the sun had looked like through movies and pictures. Their world had comprised many shades of gray. Many layers of clouds and pollution blanketed the planet's surface. It was perpetual gloom.

Even what little vegetation they had managed to save perpetually looked ashen. Not the vibrant colors they saw now. The only thing he could compare it to was they had lived in a black and white. Only to be projected into a full technicolor film.

At least their ancestors had the foresight to create the dome they lived within. Not only had it sustained life, for further generations, it redacted to create the illusion of natural light. However, this time and place were by far the superior. Was this the answer to the rumored saving grace? Was this the reason for Cora's death? Questions were filling his head.

Though he didn't want to dwell on them now. Right now, he wanted to live in the moment and enjoy. They all wanted to enjoy this new world and all it offered them.

Rolling, he pulled Honor in closer. Bending, he sniffed the top of her head. Closing his eyes, he smiled. She smelled good. Like sweet vanilla. It was quickly becoming his favorite scent.

Honor murmured as she woke.

"Are you smelling me?"

Laughing, he said.

"Yes."

Inhaling again.

"You smell good. Like vanilla."

She shook her head while wrapping her arms around him.

"If you say so."

Chuckling softly, she buried her nose to his chest, inhaling his scent.

"Mmm. You smell like woods and man."

Squinting his brow, he looked at the top of her head.

"Like woods and man, eh!"

Feeling her rub her cheek along his chest, he sighed in contentment.

"If you say so."

Slowly, he ran his fingers through her hair with one hand. This time, she sighed in her contentment. Their bond seemed to grow stronger the more time they spent together. That made sense. However, it was also different somehow. It was like a physical force pulling them together. Shortening the distance between them quicker than they were perhaps ready for.

Still, he would not argue. I felt right to him. Right, on far too many levels to ever question it. He just hoped he didn't mess this up. He still hadn't broached the subject of Harlow being here in the same time as them. Or about Cormac and his cryptic words and ways. How a local man could have such knowledge of the future and understand it baffled him.

He had wondered at one point if he had come through the portal like them. Just from a different future than theirs. However, after a while, he dismissed the thought. The man fit far too well here. So he was thinking instead, that perhaps he had a power of knowledge or something. Sitting the man down to ask his many questions had been impossible so far. Hopefully soon though.

Honor pulled him from his thoughts as she started drawing circles on his chest with her fingers and asking.

"What are you thinking about?"

Deciding now was as good a time as any. He told her about Cormac. That upon entering through the portal, he landed at the edge of the woods, unconscious. He later woke in the old man's tent. It was fortuitous he had found him when he did and nursed him back to health. How the old man had known he would be there, he had yet to learn.

It amazed him how he knew things before they would happen. Also informing him who he could trust out of the newcomers to this time. It had taken him aback, but in the end, he listened and was grateful he had done so.

He smiled into her upturned face.

"You have bewitching eyes, Honor."

His blurted statement sounded more like a whispered seduction. It had Honor melting further into him and looking at him with softening eyes. They forgot their previous chatter. With their eyes locked onto each other, she swung her leg over him, slowly crawling up his body. Placing a hand on either side of his head, she bent, taking his mouth in a lazy kiss.

Allowing her a few moments of power before he wrapped his arms around her and flipped them so he was above her. He quickly swallowed her surprised gasp by deepening the kiss. Coaxing her lips apart, he dove in to explore her mouth with his tongue. Both of them moaned.

Sliding his hand beneath her neck, he angled her head slightly. Allowing him to deepen the kiss more. Honor melted into the mattress with his control, moaning with her pleasure. Before they could continue, there was a pounding at the door.

Pulling back, has saw panic flash in her eyes. Gently cupping her cheek, he bent kissing her forehead.

"Never fear, Honor."

She briefly closed her eyes before looking at him and nodding. Smiling at her, he said.

"That's my girl. Stay here. I'll answer the door."

Standing, he quickly dressed as did she, before sitting on the edge of the bed. The pounding on the door only increased.

"I'm coming and I hear you. Let me get dressed."

He said the last while winking at Honor. There was no point in hiding their relationship.

He wanted to scream to everyone that she was his woman. Not that they didn't know already. He had made sure they could all smell him on her yesterday. Fueling his perpetual need to mark her. Smiling, he liked the idea. If only he would have the time to do that again. Although based on the urgent knocking, he doubted that was an option today.

He approached the door. When he unlocked it, he found Garth standing there, which didn't surprise him. He was, however, surprised by the look on his face. It was a blend of murderous rage and regret.

ONCE AGAIN, she woke in Caden's arms. She enjoyed waking in his arms. They were strong, firm, and safe. Just like the rest of him. She was falling for this man. Regardless of the magnetic pull between them, which to her was an entity, all its own. He was kind, caring, and intelligent.

The way he cared for his family and his team members was old school. Or so some say. She just thought he was being a decent human being. Respecting and treating others as best as humanly possible.

She wanted to be included in his inner circle. That was how her initial crush on him had started. As time passed and hormones became involved, she wanted more. Her attraction grew. Till she was sure everyone knew. Snickering behind her back. The genius, awkward girl with a silly crush.

He was a Faxon living in the grand house in the compound. The Overseer being the only other person to live there. Nobody knew how the Faxon twins were also granted to live there. Even Harlow's son, Caden's nephew, was allowed to live there. Many have speculated why over the years. However, no one knew the true reason. Not even the Faxon's themselves knew.

That much was clear. To them, it was simply home. When others questioned, they couldn't answer. Punishment awaited those who questioned. The Faxons included. So they all stopped asking why. Instead, teasing and ridicule of the twins ensued. It was sad really, children could be so cruel.

Now she was living her dream. She was waking in his arms, warm, content, and secure. Something she wanted to repeat again and again. She even enjoyed the lazy talking in bed. It was nice. It felt normal. Like she belonged.

They were both orphans, yes. Caden, however, had his sister, nephew, and his team members. While she had had no one. It was very lonely. As much as she was used to it, it was starting to hurt. Her chest would feel heavy whenever she would think about it.

Coming through the portal had changed things. In a much larger way than what she had expected. For not only were her teammates kind and caring toward her. So too was Caden. He genuinely seemed to like her and care for her. Smiling, she liked how she was learning his little quirks.

He always woke before her. If only a few minutes. He also liked to share in the mornings. That was when he seemed the most talkative. Sharing with her stories and information he had learned. Like this morning telling her about Cormac, the local old man who had saved him. Who also seemed to share the ability to have powers of some kind. The specifics of which were to be determined.

Before he could go into more detail, she succumbed to her inner urges. Crawling up his body for a kiss. Sure, she could have just leaned up toward him, but that had been more fun. Not to mention arousing. Their bodies touching skin to skin.

She could feel him getting harder between them. Causing her to get wetter. When he flipped them, it surprised her for sure. The turn-on factor of him being in control had her gushing moisture. Her tentative kiss was nothing compared to his panty-melting devouring of her mouth. She wanted more. Everything.

The extreme pounding at her door, however, instantly killed the mood and terrified her. Why she was so afraid when she was a trained True Guard member, she didn't know. Dressing quickly, she sat on the edge of the bed, waiting as Caden had directed. Seeing Garth's large frame standing there when the door opened, she could relax a little. As soon as he entered her pod, she froze. Something was wrong, very wrong. Anger contorted his face, and she could feel it radiating from him.

Had she done something wrong? Was he mad at her? She quickly ran through all the previous events that she could remember to see if she had done anything to him. Coming up blank, she looked up at his face as a small tear fell down her cheek. Before she could ask, his face instantly changed to one of concern, and had Caden spinning around and kneeling in front of her.

His finger touched her cheek, gently swiping the tear away.

"Shh Honor. There is no need to fear. Garth is not mad at you or anything you did."

Searching Caden's face, she knew he spoke the truth. Taking his offered hand, she stood. Tilting her head, she looked at Garth.

"Why are you mad?"

She watched as this large man relaxed and softened his stance and expression. He was the living embodiment of the saying, 'Looks can be deceiving.' She could still feel his anger pulsating within him. This look of calm he displayed was simply an illusion. Tilting her head, she continued to study him while waiting for a reply.

"I'm sorry if I scared you, Honor. That was not my intent."

Closing his eyes, he inhaled before continuing.

"We have a situation."

He looked directly at Caden.

"One that is not all like it seems to be."

He explained how someone discovered a body late this morning. He had yet to investigate why someone informed him first, and not

Caden. Although he suspected it was because they had wanted to give the two of them some alone time. Seeing the shock on both their faces, Garth rushed to say the team both respected and cared for the two of them.

Wanting to give back to them what they could, and that was time together. The team felt it was the least they could do after Jasper's foul treatment of the two of them lately. Which was sweet. She liked this development of a family.

The victim they found was Seth. He was one of Jasper's faithful followers. One of the two men who had been imprisoned for supporting Jasper after his attack on Honor. The problem was, everyone had an alibi. Or so it would seem they did.

The perpetrator who they suspected to be either Jasper or Cory. They had made the scene appear as if one of the free team members had committed the deed.

Confused, she tilted her head, thinking hard. Why?

"Are they playing a game? Or is it to deceive?"

"I believe they are trying to deceive."

Crossing her arms, she leaned into Caden's embrace when he wrapped his arm around her. Listening as Garth explained further. Everyone agreed that his cellmate Cory was the actual killer. Jasper wasn't that skilled. He had braun, yes, for a little fucker. The man, however, didn't enjoy getting his hands dirty.

Either this death was purposeful in the event he was switching sides? Or he is being used as a hopeful distraction? Possibly even both. Quite possibly, he had outlived his usefulness. Which was an even scarier thought.

He was putting his so-called money on the latter. Kill two birds with one stone. Well, they could hope anyway. Jasper wasn't as smart as he thought he was. Cory was even worse. Plus, there was the fact that all of them had now developed gifts, as they liked to call them. Talents apart from all of them now having increased speed, sight, and hearing.

If this were the lengths Jasper and his cronies will go to gain the upper hand. Then they were all in trouble.

Obviously, Jasper was planning something and using these two to do it. Only now there was Just Cory and Jasper left. When they both looked concerned at each other, then at Garth, he assured them they were both still locked up tight.

That was the issue they were having. How did Seth's body get to the location where it was found? Did Cory, or even Jasper, had a talent we weren't aware of? The prison pods still have both men securely locked up. No data can be found of foul play either.

They were going to need a different strategy while allowing the two men to believe everyone fell for their plan. Caden agreed. Also recommending that everyone should continue to wear their active gear. Just in case. At Garth's questioning look. He said.

"Gut feeling."

To which Garth nodded in acceptance. Then told them everyone that could was already gathered in the hall and waiting for them. There was to be an official meeting. As was protocol. Though they all agreed that things needed to change.

CHAPTER 16

*H*is head was spinning. It seemed like things were happening so fast that he couldn't keep track, let alone keep up. This True Guard team was Jasper's, which had once had a chip on its shoulder regarding him. Now it would seem it was now unanimously his. Well, except for the two members housed in the prison pods.

Not only was everyone working together now. They also looked to and respected his guidance. When they had arrived at the kitchen hall hours earlier, all chatter immediately ceased. It felt strange and foreign to him. This was behavior that was drilled into them at training school. Never like it, he rarely ran his team like that. He preferred a family-like environment. Where everyone considered each other as valuable members and took their input seriously.

Instead of immediately getting to task, he had discussed how things would run in the future. He would inform them when perfect protocol was needed or expected. Otherwise, they could be themselves.

They thanked him and agreed. However, he had a feeling things would not be as informal as he preferred them to be. It was like they had put him up on some pedestal. The way they spoke and regarded him. They were just about to round up their discussion when he felt an overwhelming pain radiate throughout his body. Stumbling back a few steps, he grabbed his middle as the urge to vomit rose. Groaning against the urge, he bent over, sighing in pain.

Rough hands touched his shoulders and moved him to sit. Still trying not to vomit, he spoke through clenched teeth.

"Thanks."

In his peripheral vision, he saw Honor kneeling at his side. When she reached out and touched him, the pain instantly eased.

She whispered in concern.

"Are you ok? What happened Caden?"

Closing his eyes, he slowly sat up. He opened his eyes with deep, slow breaths. Everyone's concerned faces stared back at him, which shocked him as he looked around. Not worried about keeping his secret any longer, he said.

"I think it's Harlow."

All he could hear in response was a unanimous inhale of shock. Followed by looks of concern. Till Honor finally broke the silence and asked.

"How?"

Before he could reply, however, he heard a whisper.

"Caden."

He wanted to ease his sister's pain and give her a hug. He missed her dearly. She was his twin, after all. His eyes grew larger when he realized when he thought about hugging her, he felt the embrace.

When Garth asked what was going on, he quickly shushed him. Needing to concentrate. He was dimly aware of Honor talking.

"I think he's talking with her. Or she's talking with him."

He tilted his head and smiled at her. For she was right. Only he suspected Harlow was talking aloud. For every time she spoke, there was an echo.

"Caden?"

"Harlow."

He could feel his sister becoming more aware.

"How Caden?"

"In you head Harlow. Just think, your questions. I can hear you."

Unfocusing his gaze, he concentrated on his mental conversation.

"Wow. Caden. But how?"

Wanting to lighten the mood, he said.

"I have no idea, sis. What trouble have you gotten yourself into now?"

Smiling when he heard an internal grunt from her. At least her sense of humor remained intact. That was good, right?

Hearing her snarky comeback made him chuckle.

"I didn't get myself into this."

Her next statement wiped the smile from his face.

"Some creepy guy took me. He's got me in some kind of prison cell. There is only a slit for a window nearer the ceiling and a wall of thick bars."

Suddenly, an image popped into his head of the cell she was describing. The visual meant she had no means of escape. Along with numbness firing through his limbs. She was likely injured as well. Shocked by the overwhelming pain, his concern grew.

"What's wrong, sis?"

Hearing her internal monologue to herself about being honest with him, he agreed by saying.

"Yes, you should. Now tell me."

"I have my arms tied behind my back and secured to the floor. My shoulders hurt, and I've lost all feeling in my fingers."

Unable to refrain, he growled in anger. Who would treat a woman like that? Well, who would treat anyone like that, for that matter?

Upon noticing his behavior change, he realized that everyone who was watching him had also changed. Like they were in sync with him.

He knew she was leaving something out. So he asked.

"What else Harlow? No lies, remember, only the truth."

He had to concentrate on her reply. She was suddenly silent.

"I have something he believes is his, and if I want my suffering to end, I have to give him what he wants."

He could feel her mind getting somewhat foggy.

"I also deserve all I have coming to me for inconveniencing him."

Rage filled him. Once again, he couldn't contain the growl for escaping.

"That's bullshit, Harlow. You don't deserve any of this."

Looking up, all he saw was red. He was furious. Who the hell would treat his sister this way? He had to do something. Standing and growling in anger when bodies surrounded him. Preventing him from moving. Whipping his head to the side, he saw Garth. Through gritted teeth, he demanded.

"MOVE."

Slowly, the massive man shook his head.

"No Caden."

Maintaining eye contact, Garth said.

"Breathe in through your nose and think. You need to calm. This is not the way to help your sister."

Confused, he squinted, deep in thought. How could he have forgotten about Harlow so fast? It was like the rage on her behalf had completely taken over. Closing his eyes, he took a couple of deep breaths and exhaled. Anything to center himself again.

Opening his eyes, he took in the surrounding scene. It wasn't just two men holding him back, but five. Glancing back at Garth in question.

"You're a powerful man. Much stronger than the rest of us."

Strange, he thought. So he asked.

"Really? I am?"

With an uptick quirk of his upper lip, Garth said.

"Oh, ya man. You even had glowing red eyes."

Looking at the others in the room when they chuckled in agreement.

"That's odd. Why would my eyes change?"

With a straight face. Garth said.

"I have no idea, man. But something with your sister set you off."

He paused before he continued and used his head to point at everyone in the room.

"We all could feel the anger radiating from you. It was like a living thing."

This all sounded so crazy. But it was real, and he had just lived it. Taking another deep breath, he nodded.

"Thanks for stopping me."

Hearing an echo of unanimous 'no problem' had him smiling in relief. These people were trustworthy. So perhaps they could help him in saving Harlow.

WATCHING Caden talk to his sister mentally was shocking. As long as she kept physical contact with him, she had been able to get a sense of the issue. Someone had imprisoned Harlow somewhere. She had got that much and could convey it to everyone.

Which filled them all with multiple emotions. Many were either swearing in shock or anger. Others stood and paced the floor, muttering to themselves. It was like everyone was feeding off each other. The energy in the hall was growing stronger by the minute. Worried, she had looked over at Garth to see his reaction. However, he was watching everything play out in the room.

His face was serious. Like he was studying each individual. Learning how they ticked. The more she thought about it, the more she liked the idea. It was smart. Seeing as he was now Caden's right-hand man. Before she too could study the group, Caden jerked. Causing her to lose her balance and lose the contact she had with him.

She instantly felt a wave of fierce anger knock her in the chest. Unable to breathe, she placed her hand on her chest. Attempting to block the force. Falling to the ground, she finally could take a few shallow breaths. When suddenly there was a flurry of men all reaching for Caden. It took five of them to stop him.

Standing, she rubbed her bottom. She had landed on her tailbone. That hurt. Stomping toward Caden, an arm flew out in front of her, stopping her in her tracks. Looking up, she saw Garth shaking his head.

"No Honor. Wait till he calms down."

Annoyed, she said.

"I can help."

Placing her hands on her hips for effect.

"No, little one."

That was the only response she got. Huffing out a breath in annoyance. With her arms crossed in front of her, she waited.

She knew she could calm him. Before that, she had been doing just that; she realized. It was when he had jerked and she lost contact that he became like this. Though she had never seen him like this before. This was new. He was so much stronger than the rest of them.

Why was that?

Leaving that question for later. She focused on the chatter they were having with him now. He was thanking them for stopping him. Giving him the time to cool down and think. After a chorus of no problems, he whipped around to face her.

Once she met his eyes, she knew he needed her. Uncaring about who saw, she threw herself at him. Wrapping him up in her limbs and holding on tight. Burrowing her head in his neck, she inhaled deep. Loving his scent, her tongue darted out, as if it had a mind of its own and taking a taste. Sighing in pleasure, he tasted salty with a hint of woodsy.

Her actions seemed to change his mood. He quickly moved his arms so one hand was gripping her ass with a firm squeeze. The other went to the back of her neck, encouraging her exploration.

Lathering attention on his neck. She went from licking to sucking. The instinct to mark him was so strong that she didn't want to deny it. Feeling the rumble of his growl before she heard it turned her on even more. Unable to stop herself, she ground herself against him. When he tightened his grip on her ass and aided her movements, she groaned in pleasure.

With her moan, his hand on the back of her neck tightened and pushed her into his skin. Causing her to bite down. His hiss of a,

"Yess,"

Set her off into a colorful orgasm. One that had her sinking her teeth further into his neck. Anything to keep from screaming his name. She remembered then that they weren't alone and in the kitchen hall, too.

Holy crap! What had she just done? Embarrassed, she kept her head buried in Caden's neck. Not wanting to face anyone. She should have been comforting him, not getting herself off like some teenager. As if knowing she heard him whisper.

"Don't worry, my girl. They all know you're mine."

Arg. That wasn't the point.

"I know that Caden. It's just. This should be private. Ours. You know?"

Chuckling softly in her ear, he said.

"I know what you mean, my girl. I will, however, give you what you need."

When she was about to argue, he said.

"Nah uh. I know you felt rebuffed during my chat with Harlow when I shook you off. Believe me, it was not intentional. You needed to be selfish for once and get what you wanted from me. Nothing wrong with that. Plus it was hot."

Pulling back, he cradled her head, touching their foreheads together. His eyes sparkled as he studied her.

"I love you marked me. I will wear it with pride. Everyone will be jealous."

His smirk grew when she giggled.

"That's better. You have a beautiful laugh."

Garth's deep voice agreed from behind Caden.

"She does. You need to make her laugh more often, man."

She noticed then that Caden had turned them, concealing her from the view of the others. Giving some privacy at least. While Garth seemed to stand guard. Still, she couldn't understand why she had to laugh more. Tilting her head, she looked from one to the other and back again. When both men rolled their eyes, she gave up. Pushing to free herself from Caden's hold, he released her. When she turned to walk away, he swatted her butt with a loud slap.

"Ouch."

Whirling toward him, she rubbed her offended cheek. Gasping.

"What was that for?"

Glancing around when she heard a few snickers. Apparently, this was funny. It wasn't so funny to her. It stung.

His smile seemed to grow as he said.

"Because I can."

Reaching out, he grabbed her hand, locking their fingers together. Giving a slight tug, she followed him to the back of the kitchen hall.

When he arranged her to sit on his lap the way he wanted, she turned asking.

"What now?"

Tucking a strand of hair behind her ear, he said.

"Now we discuss my chat with Harlow and how to help. Plus a few other things."

That was how their evening went. Talking and more talking.

CHAPTER 17

He couldn't believe his luck. Those idiots thought they could hold him prisoner. Ha, not a chance. Not with Cory's new talent. That was simply brilliant. Yet another reason that proved all he had been working toward and wanted was rightfully his.

It had been all too easy pointing the finger at Caden. Laughing to himself, he smiled, giving himself a mental pat on the back for a job well done. It was only a matter of time now and he would be free.

Soon he would be back in his luxurious pod and enjoying all its finery. While that scum Faxon was in here, suffering as he should be. Rightfully accused of murder. He could just imagine it all. It made him smile.

There would be even more opportunities to make that man pay for all the injustices he has faced. Power that was rightfully his, and not Caden's. He could picture it all now. The images that it conjured left that warm, fuzzy feeling in his gut. He liked it. It was about time things started going his way.

It was sheer dumb luck that, during his last planning session, Cory should pop in. Literally, in fact. Seeing the other man's new talents had him tossing most of his pre- made plans out the window. This was all the better. So much better.

The grin that had spread across his face had Cory raising an eyebrow. The man knew his place and did not question him. Still, he had wanted to know.

So he instead asked the man if his gift would allow him to travel with someone else in tow. Unsure if it was possible, Cory had disappeared back to his pod. After a few moments' wait, he had popped back with Seth in tow. It was amazing. In the blink of an eye, they could appear, and then disappear.

Grinning, he liked the idea a lot. It had so much potential. Just to be sure for his safety, he made the men repeat the process long into the night.

It was the wee hours of the morning when Cory popped back in alone. Claiming Seth couldn't take it anymore. The man was throwing up all over the place. Not wanting to wear it, he had left him behind. That's when he got another idea.

He told Cory that since the other man couldn't hack it, they might as well be rid of him. It would be better for them if he served another purpose. The evil grin that spread across his face matched his own. This was the reason he enjoyed having this man around. He wasn't afraid to get his hands dirty.

They spent the next few minutes quickly planning. It had to be believable. All fingers needed to point toward Caden. So if or when those idiots did figure it out, they would be long gone.

Deep down, he knew they would eventually figure it out. There was no way for Caden to be a team leader for as long as he had without knowing a thing or two. At least as they tried to piece it together, the two of them could find a new home base.

So he waited. As Cory got all the things they needed. Setting up small care packages for them to use once they left. He had skillfully found a hidden location close to their current compound.

Stashing everything they would need there. So after they escaped, they could easily take it and be on their way. Allowing them time to scout for a better location or perhaps locals they could sway toward their cause.

Licking his lips, he couldn't help but think. It would be easy peasy. Caden liked rules and would follow protocol. If there was one rule, he always followed himself, it was know thine enemy. Boy, did he ever.

Laughing again, he was proud of himself. He couldn't wait to see the look on the man's face when he came charging back and taking what was rightfully his.

Yes, he thought he liked that idea. Seeing Caden on his knees, begging for the compound, he stole. Well, he would steal it back from him. That's all. It was only a matter of time.

He was suddenly aware he was no longer alone in his pod. Pretending aloof, he waited. It wouldn't do for Cory to see him excited. Until hearing a whisper,

"Sir, it's time."

CHAPTER 18

*A*fter everyone had turned in for the night, he had asked Garth to come with Honor and himself back to his pod. He could feel her unease as they traveled closer to it. Raising their joined hands, he cupped hers between his, kissing her knuckles.

"It'll be alright Honor. The pod was scrubbed before I ever took it over."

Behind him, he heard Garth say.

"It's true Honor. It has been done on multiple occasions. Jasper was a snake. We take the protection of Caden seriously."

That was news to him. He met the other man's eyes in question. The response he got surprised him again.

"You're our True Leader Caden. The task is performed on the daily. Regardless."

Meaning they knew he had been with Honor every night. Never once staying in Jasper's pod. Well, now, his pod. Turning his attention back on her, he asked,

"What if we start anew and make it ours?"

He watched as her jaw dropped in awe before closing and her brows drew together, deep in thought, before she nodded her head. Smiling, he gently squeezed her hand before relaxing and continuing on their walk.

He hadn't really stayed here either. The men of the team had insisted he take it over immediately after Jasper's imprisonment. Reluctantly, he did. Only Honor's erotic dream had pulled him from his dream. From then on, he had stayed with her. Only coming here for clothes and the like.

Upon reaching the pod, he noticed a guard standing outside of the door. Turning, he looked back at Garth in question.

The man simply rolled his eyes before saying.

"You always have one."

As they drew nearer, the guard greeted him with a dip of his head.

"Sir."

When they were close enough, he stepped aside. Making eye contact with Garth, he said.

"Nothing Sir. Been all clear."

Garth said nothing, only nodded.

He couldn't help but think this was all rather odd as they entered. This was not True Guard protocol. It was, however, behavior similar to ruling elites in the multitude of stories in their history books. Come to think of it, The Overseer did also have a contingent of guards himself.

Was that what was happening here? Did they now view him as their Overseer? There were, however, more important things that needed their attention though. They took precedence over everything else. Making his way to the sitting area, he promoted Honor to sit. Turning, he intended to do the same to Garth, but the man shook his head.

"In a moment."

He reached into his pocket and pulled out a small device. One he had used not that long ago to scan his and Harlow's quarters back home. Were they back playing at such childlike games? Still, better to be safe than sorry, he guessed.

Turning, Garth scanned the entirety of the pod. What was happening to his brain? He should have thought to do the same. Even if it seemed like overkill in this place and time. It was something he had always done back home.

He should be thinking of Honor's safety. Shaking his head, he made quick work of making them some drinks. The idea occurred to him they might need the boost they offered.

He was going to divulge more information to them. Hoping that they would understand his reasons for secrecy.

Just as he was pouring the last drink, Garth entered the room again, saying.

"All's clear."

He crossed the room, taking the drink Caden offered him before sitting. Raising the glass, he said.

"Thanks."

He offered the man a nod of welcome before picking up his and Honor's drinks. Crossing the room and sitting beside her. He offered her the drink and watched as she took a sip.

"Good?"

Her gentle nod let them know she was tired. At least she liked the drink. This was Jasper's beverage of choice. Still, they shouldn't waste it. It is helpful on occasions like this. Garth interrupted his thoughts.

"So boss man, what's the big secret?"

Hearing his words, Honor let out a startled gasp.

Turning to gaze at her, he wondered where the firecracker of a woman went. Had the incident with Jasper done more damage than he thought? Using the back of his finger, he stroked her cheek.

"It's all right, my girl."

Bending, he kissed the tip of her nose before wrapping his arm around her. When she rested her head on his shoulder, he kissed the top of her head.

Focusing back on Garth, he explained about Cormac, as well as how the man had found him. How he had nursed him back to health. Or rather encouraged his own body to do it for him. How he had instructed him to trust only the two of them. Although he didn't know their names, he described quite well.

Also, how today was not the first time he had heard Harlow. The first time had been the day Jasper had attacked Honor. Now, however, he felt it necessary that the three of them seek out Cormac and his guidance. The man had so much knowledge. Perhaps he would know how to help.

Garth's easy agreement shocked him. So he asked,

"Why do you believe me so easily?"

The man swirled the last of the liquid in his glass for a time before answering.

"There are many reasons. I'll share only one."

Raising his gaze from the swirling liquid and staring at Caden, he continued.

"I can tell when someone is lying, and you never have. Not once."

Simple and blunt, he thought. Nodding his head, he replied,

"Well, ok then. That makes sense."

It was only fair that the man share one of his new talents. Since he wasn't sharing all of his. This being the most well-kept secret was both funny and sad. The nature of all their extra gifts and talents. They seemed to develop almost daily. It was anyone's could guess what new talents could develop and by whom. They were in unfamiliar territory.

Cora had shared some stories of talents and gifts, but nothing like this. It amazed and scared him at the same time. Was there a limit to what a person could do? The thought scared him.

Broaching his next question filled him with a sense of fear. It was his talent. He felt the need to keep it secret for his protection. In the end, he knew he could trust them both. So he asked,

"Will you both come with me this evening to meet Cormac?"

His inquiry seemed to perk Honor right up. She was jumping up and down in her seat. She reminded him of Rowan when he was little and excited over something new and shiny. Smiling, he bent kissing the tip of her nose.

"I take that a yes from you, my girl?"

Nodding her head vigorously.

"Oh yes. It's a definite yes for me."

She turned toward Garth and asked,

"How about you, Garth? Yes?"

He smiled and nodded at Honor.

"I'm definitely game. How are we going to get there discreetly?

Tilting his head, he studied Caden.

"I take it you don't want anyone else knowing about this man or where he is?

So how are we going to get there undiscovered?"

Nodding, he agreed with Garth.

"You are correct. I have our stealth covered."

Allowing a smirk to spread across his face, he heard Honor giggle.

"He's got some talents of his own, Garth."

Rolling his eyes, he wondered if she intended the double meaning.

Garth tilted his head back and roared in laughter. He couldn't seem to stop wrapping his arm around his middle as tears breached his eyes. It was contagious. He couldn't help but join in. Soon Honor joined in, laughing till tears were falling down her cheeks.

IT HAD FELT good to laugh like they had at Caden's pod. She couldn't remember the last time she had laughed. An almost foreign feeling. There wasn't much to laugh about growing up and living in the compound. Here, however, it seemed like everyone was coming out of their shell and blossoming into their true selves.

It was an amazing thing to see and to experience. Every day they became closer, more like a family unit. Similar to how Caden and his True Guard team were at the old compound. At least from her point of view. The only family she ever witnessed was Caden and Harlow. Their society had done away with that traditional way ages ago.

This felt far more natural, though. They seemed to grow for the better. If it was this good now, what would the future hold she wondered? She had trouble imagining anything better. Her instincts were telling her it was possible. She smiled, liking the idea.

She and Caden were now back at her pod, getting all their gear on.

If someone saw them coming back here to stay the night, it wouldn't be odd. It was where they had stayed every night since. After getting ready, they were going to make their way to Garth's pod to collect him for their gurney.

She wasn't sure how they would travel incognito. However, Caden had assured them both not to worry. That he had it handled. No one would know they had left the compound. The idea intrigued her. How would he achieve such a thing? She couldn't wait to find out. Her excitement had her hands shaking to such a degree she needed help to fasten some of the gear.

Her excitement had quickly shifted to arousal with Caden's help. He took things slowly. Gentle caresses here and a lingering touch there. Her breathing became heavy and her mouth dry. The butterflies in her stomach grew with the continued, lust-filled looks he was giving her. Moaning when he fastened the last buckle, she closed her eyes, savoring his touch.

All she could do was moan his name.

"Caden."

Wrapping his fingers around the back of her neck, he drew her in closer.

"Soon my girl. Soon."

Looking into his eyes, she saw the same fire reflected at her. In a trance, she watched as he lowered his head. Moaning when his lips touched hers. She melted into his embrace. Surrendering to her passion for him and his ravishing of her mouth.

All too soon, he pulled back. Groaning in his disappointment. Resting his forehead against hers, he continued to breathe deeply.

"Wow. You taste delectable, my girl."

Grinning, she loved it when he called her that. With a lust-filled sigh, she said.

"I like it when you call me that."

Stroking her cheek with his thumb, he smiled a panty-melting smile. One he reserved only for her.

"We need to leave. We'll revisit this later. Ok?"

Nodding her agreement, she took his offered hand. Allowing him to lead the way. They made it to Garth's pod with no issues. He was already waiting for them, just outside his door. Fiddling with something on the outside wall. She presumed it was all an act to give credence to changing the behavior of his routine.

They came to stand beside him. She couldn't hear the whispered words they shared. Garth took her other hand after a few touches on the touch screen and shutting his door. Caden shared a look with them both, showing the need to be quiet.

Following his lead, they made their way through the compound. Exiting was also quick and easy. Not one person lingering about this late at night had spared them a glance. It baffled her how they could walk unseen. Caden had said he had them covered in that department, but they had yet to tell them how he was going to accomplish it.

It was evident he had a gift for such a thing. They had walked past fellow members without so much as a blink. What he was doing and how he was doing it had her curious.

They continued to travel as they were entering the forest. Holding each other's hands while remaining silent. She didn't care too much for it. It was strange and awkward.

The deeper they went into the woods, the more it felt like a maze. It was thick with trees and branches. Making it necessary to duck and twist your way through. There was no way she could find her way back to the compound without help.

Even while performing her collection tasks, she had never traveled this deep into the trees. It was feeling too close for her liking. Even though their pods were small, the lack of light here and the touching braces felt as if it were encroaching into her space. She didn't like it.

Feeling each of her hands squeezed simultaneously had her looking between Caden and Garth. Each of them remained silent while offering her a reassuring smile of understanding. She could do this. They were there for her. Smiling in return, she nodded. Silently thanking them for their support.

After her little freakout. It felt odd making their trek while she held both their hands. She had to almost run to keep up with their steady pace. Her height only brought her to their shoulders. They would often swing her up off the ground over an obstacle on the ground, making her feel like a child. She didn't like it. When she tried to voice her objection, she received two stern looks. As well as the reminder that their continued contact was necessary.

Hopefully, when they arrived at their destination, she would learn Cadens' secret. Understanding the why always helped her to accomplish her tasks. Otherwise, her mind seemed to wander over all the possibilities over and over. Proving to be a major distraction. Having all the facts was beneficial. Plus, she enjoyed knowing.

Maybe that was why she had been so drawn toward the tech side of things back home. It was a simple platform with rules of black and white. Easy for her to manipulate, to get all the info she required. The self-realization came at a strange moment. Still, it was good to understand herself a little better.

They finally came upon a small clearing, just big enough for the tiny cabin nestled in it. It was cute. It reminded her of those described in children's stories. Smiling, she wanted to see more.

As they all stepped into the clearing, she felt a great gust of wind followed by her ears popping. Releasing their joined hands, she quickly covered her ears.

Almost shouting, she asked.

"What was that?."

Caden and Garth both looked at her with odd expressions. When they said in unison,

"What was what?"

Shaking her head and rotating her jaw. She said.

"You know, the wind gusting and ear popping."

When neither of their expressions changed, she asked.

"Did neither of you feel that?"

Both men shook their heads. Well, that was odd. Titling her head, she studied them for a moment. They did not know what she was talking about. Maybe Cormac, the owner of the cabin, might know.

Pointing to the smoke coming from the rooftop chimney.

"Well, let's go on then. I assume he's in."

Turning, all three of them made their way up to the front door. Which opened before either of them could knock.

CHAPTER 19

*A*llowing his grin to spread across his face as triumph filled him. Cory's new talent for transport was coming in handy. They had popped out of the pod multiple times. First, to set up a secure location not far from the compound where they could store their needed supplies. It had been all too easy. So easy, in fact, they could take more than they had planned.

Cory blinked back multiple times, easily grabbing extra gear and tech. Not to mention all the food and medical supplies he had already taken and stored.

They had even got a solid few hours of sleep. This hiding spot had been perfect. Now they were gearing up. Preparing to leave this area for greener pastures. There was a settlement near to where they had set up a home base. The plan was to recruit some locals.

For now, they had to establish themselves within the small town. Giving them time to see who would be a likely fit to enroll in their cause. There was a good chance that some individuals would have gifts as well, which would be even better.

Just imagining the possibilities sent tingles through his body. Someday soon, he would have all that he had worked so hard for.

Flexing his muscles, he rotated his head. Loosening up and trying hard to contain his excitement. This plan they had concocted was running smoothly. So much so he might get all he wanted much sooner than he thought.

After they left last night, there wasn't even a sound of alarm blaring. Those idiots didn't even realize that he and Cory had left. They were so stupid; he thought. It was a good thing he was now rid of all of them. His right-hand man had become very useful. Proving luck was once again on his side.

Deep down, he had always known he was better than everyone else. That one day he would be the leader of them all. Sad that his former team no longer shared his vision. They would pay the price for their treachery. Along with Caden and Honor. That little bitch.

Just thinking about her betrayal irked him. One day soon she would see justice served to her. He would make sure of it. It was easy enough.

He would take care of her first in front of Faxon. Allowing him to feel the same pain he had inflicted on him when he had killed his precious Sally. The man deserved to suffer. He would see that he did, too.

With his hands on his hips, he stood waiting impatiently, tapping his foot. Waiting for Cory to dismantle their temporary pod tech was taking too long. Regardless of if they might need it later. Time was of the essence right now. He hoped to distance himself further from the compound. A sinking feeling was gripping his gut suddenly. Wanting to leave, he demanded,

"Hurry it up! We need to leave now."

When Cory whipped his head toward him and growled like an animal, he held up his hands in mock surrender. He said.

"Hey, man."

Watching in annoyed silence as Cory clicked one last button before picking up the tech and placing it in his pack. He stood walking past him, growling,

"Let's go Boss."

Whatever had crawled up his ass to die was not his problem. They were on a mission. One that would get him what he so rightfully deserved and belonged to him.

Just thinking about it made him giddy. He could almost feel the power at his fingertips. If what he suspected was true about the locals, then he would have an even greater army with his rule than he had hoped.

Rubbing his hands together as they walked, he couldn't help the smile that spread across his face. Soon, very soon, he would have his dream.

Once they were a few minutes away from where they had set up the temporary pod, they prepared to blink travel. It is how Cory had described it. All he had to do was think of where he wanted to go and blink to get there. Amazing, really.

This meant they would have the advantage. Still, they had wanted to lead a false trail, just in case. They were dealing with trained True Guard members, after all. So they set up their camp away from the compound, on the opposite side of the settlement. Hopefully, sending there would be hunters out into the unknown territory.

They had blinked into the small town, gearing up to recruit anyone and everyone willing to join their cause. This would be an easy victory for him. He had no doubt.

Blending in shouldn't be a problem either. While scouting the area, they had taken footage of the settlement and the people within it. They had made all the tech look like identical housing. He hated they were using the work crafted by Honor. She was good at that sort of thing. Better at it than Caden was. Still, he hated the woman.

It was just as well that it was her designs and modifications were assisting him in his goals. Giving him all the means by which to make her and Caden suffer before ending them. It was just too bad he couldn't do the same to Harlow and Rowan.

He frowned, thinking of the plans he had had for them. Now, though, he wouldn't get the chance to bring them to fruition. It was sad, really. They would have been so much fun.

That was his last thought before he joined hands with Cory, nodding that he was ready. Watching as he clenched his jaw and blinked. Taking them to the edge of the settlement.

CHAPTER 20

*H*e was nervous. So much so that he was pacing. Honor's concern for him and come and gone. She was now giggling and teasing him. Which Garth even thought funny. Frustrated, he ran his fingers through his hair. This was not a funny matter. His sister was in serious need of some help. She was a prisoner to an unknown foe. The plan had to work. It must.

Yes, like everyone else, she possessed gifted talents. Through their shared connection, he knew she was too frightened to even realize she had them. They were just too new to become an established habit for her. He had been trying to no avail to gain communication with her again.

Stomping in frustration, he realized the talent of the connection must be hers and not his. Why else couldn't he make contact? Deep in his gut, he didn't believe that to be true. Ever since coming here, he had to work on retraining his brain on what is truth. He needed to learn new logic.

Garth's deep-bellied laugh pulled him from his inner thoughts. Snapping his head up to look at him, he asked.

"What's so funny, big man?"

The man couldn't stop laughing as he gripped his middle, saying.

"You are. Stopping around like a toddler."

Staring him down. He relaxed a little when Garth stopped laughing and raised his hands in surrender.

"Look I'm sorry, man. I know you're worried about your sister. It's just funny seeing a grown man stomp around having a tantrum."

Rubbing his hand down his face, he continued.

"We have a plan. A good one too. Let's just pray that Harlow remembers her gifts and uses them. Whatever they are. She has to have some juice, being she's your twin."

Allowing his words to sink in. He nodded in agreement.

"You're right. I can't seem to gain control of my emotions."

Honor stood and walked toward him with a look of concern. When she wrapped her arms around him, he felt instantly at peace. Smiling, he bent and placed a kiss on the top of her head.

"Thank you, my girl."

It was then he realized not only was she a calming influence, but she was physically calming him down.

"Holy shit Honor."

Pulling back to look in her eyes, he rested his hands on her shoulders.

"When you touch me, you can instantly calm me."

Her smile was gentle as she nodded her agreement.

Tilting his head, he was curious.

"Can you do this with anyone else? Or is it just me?"

Her answer was a whisper.

"Only with you Caden."

Somehow, her answer filled him with a sense of pride and satisfaction. His internal voice was suddenly screaming, MINE! The shift of his feelings had him wanting to take her here and now. But it wasn't the right time. They were waiting for Cormac's signal.

The old man had flown into action when he heard the conversation he had had with his twin. He summoned a man out of thin air with a grand wave of his arm. Giving him instructions with a message to give.

"Tell them they are to come. To be ready, for the Raven must fly tonight. Then all will be as it should be."

Watching as the stranger nodded his understanding, then disappeared again.

He was back at scurrying around in his tiny cabin, grabbing this and that. Placing it all on his small table, he gave instructions to Honor for the herbs, spices, and plants. Multiple recipes for spells, potions, and compresses.

Regarding himself and Garth, he informed them about the plans and provided instructions on where they should meet him. He had to gather some others together if we were to be successful.

Which is exactly where they were now waiting. Hidden by their tech. They could make out a massive, stone-built structure in the distance. Was this where Hollow was being kept? They didn't know.

Even when he had tried to reach out and sense her, he couldn't. She was indeed being blocked or protected by some serious magick. He didn't like it.

Instructions from Cormac were that they were to wait for his signal. Only then could they act on his instructions. Which he didn't like either. Being a True Guard team leader, he was used to giving orders. Taking them was not what he was used to. At least not since his training days. He had been one of the lucky ones, gaining leadership and a team right out of training school. It had happened before in the past, but so rarely. He felt a sense of honor being included in such a prestigious few.

The old man's parting words before he, too, disappeared in a blink. 'Hopefully, you'll not be needed.' What did he mean by that?

So here is where they have been waiting. Waiting on a signal. No longer wanting to get stuck in his head, he asked.

"So what do you think of Cormac?"

. . .

EVEN SHE WAS NOW TOO restless. The need to do something, anything, was growing by the second. She couldn't imagine how Caden was feeling. It was his twin sister in danger. They shared and strong connection to one another. If she had to guess, he was feeling some of his twin's fears as well as his own.

It would explain so much. Lately, he just wasn't himself. The sporadic nature of his emotions and behaviors. It was likely his sister coming through because of their shared link. Only he had yet to realize it. Once he did, she was sure he could balance it all out.

It differed from the link they shared together. Theirs felt more like a magnetic pull to her. And yet not all. Almost like they were missing something. She couldn't put her finger on it. If she wasn't in constant contact with him, she felt edgy, almost frantic. It was how she knew she could calm him when she touched him. Having witnessed it several times already in practice.

He had realized that phenomenon on his own. So she knew he would figure this out as well. It was just a matter of when. The poor man was on the edge of emotion over load, his, hers and his sisters.

She and Garth really shouldn't have tried to lighten his mood by laughing at him. That hadn't been fair. It was funny seeing him pace and stomp around. He had looked like a child throwing a tantrum. Just like Garth had accused before.

So instead, she went to him, wrapping her arms around him. Watching him realize her effect on him filled her with warmth. Being able to ease his pain made her proud. Helping her man. She liked that thought. Her man. He was hers, just as much as she was his. She also could have sworn she heard him shout MINE inside her head.

What a strange sensation that was. The echo of his voice. It was creepy. While also welcoming at the same time. Closing her eyes, she took a deep breath to clear her thoughts.

Suddenly, Caden stiffened in her arms. His face draining of color. Fear filled her.

"What is it, Caden? What's wrong?"

Garth quickly rose and was standing beside them. He too asked.

"What is it? What's wrong?"

Stiffly, Caden looked between the two of them and said.

"They have Rowan too."

Shocked, she couldn't contain her gasp of fear.

"No,"

Was all she could voice.

They had his nephew. He was only a young man. Still a child, really. Why would they hurt him? To get to his mother? She really hoped not. How was Rowan even here?

Looking at Garth, she mouthed, 'This is bad.' He gave her a small nod. The look they shared, however, was one of promise. A promise to be there for Caden, Harlow, and Rowan, then to take revenge on those who have harmed them. Garth placed his hand atop theirs in a reassuring motion.

Time seemed to be suspended for them. Like they were in a dreamlike state. Ranges of emotions flowed around all around them. Containing them in a bubble. Constantly cycling back and forth. It was as if on some level they were one mind, or connected somehow.

It felt odd, but in a comforting way. A closeness of understanding, being, and familiarity. The air was shifting around them, whispering a voice of caution.

Lights and sparks were joining the flow of the wind before settling on their layered hands. Odd, she thought. They had intended to offer support to Caden. His hand was resting atop her shoulder. She had placed hers on his, then Garth on hers in a caring gesture.

She could feel the heat rising among their hands. What was happening? That thought echoed among them. Singing its question repeatedly until it felt like a branding iron was searing their palms. All three of them screamed a silent scream of pain.

With a loud crack, thunder echoed, amounts them forcing them apart. Sending them flying in different directions. When she landed with a thud, the impact forced all the air from her lungs. A furious shout had her breathing quick.

"What have you done?"

Turning toward the voice, she saw a fuming Cormac. He was much taller than she remembered and she had only met the man yesterday. The energy flowing around him fluctuated. Filled with trepidation, she stood. Brushing the dirt off herself. Crying out in pain when her right palm brushed along her leg.

Pulling her hand back. She cradled it with her other to look. Gasping in shock at what she saw. A circle with an interwoven vine of thorns. Still holding her wrist, she looked up when she heard footsteps come toward her.

Cormac stood inches from her. Reaching out, he grabbed her hand. Investigating her palm. When he made eye contact with her, he growled.

"You shouldn't have."

Confused, she furrowed her brow.

Exasperated, he huffed and turned, giving her his back.

"What shouldn't I have done?"

Shaking his head, he made his way over to where each Caden and Garth lay. They were out cold. He took his time inspecting their palms as well.

Wanting answers, she demanded.

"Cormac, what shouldn't I have done?"

Standing tall, he turned, making eye contact with her. Shaking his head once again. Arg, what a frustrating man.

"Why won't you tell me?"

Closing his eyes, he took a deep breath. It looks as though he was counting down the way his lips were moving. Was he calming himself? What had she done that was so bad? She wasn't aware of doing anything at all.

When he snapped his eyes open, he locked them on her.

"I will only say it once. So it'll wait till they wake."

The force of energy that came her way with his statement pushed her back a step. Wow! This man had some serious power.

Unable to stay away any longer. She went to Caden's side. Kneeling, she brushed back the hair from his face. He looked like he was in pain. Looking behind her, she studied Garth's face as well. He, too, looked like he was in pain. Looking back at Cormac, she asked,

"Why are they still out cold? Are they in pain?"

When all he did was stare. She knew the answer. 'He will only say it once.' Damn it, men could be so frustrating.

Well, if she had to wait, she might as be comfortable while she did. Laying down beside Caden, she wrapped herself around him. Closing her eyes, she sighed in comfort. If he was still sleeping, what could it hurt for her to catch a little shuteye herself?

With Cormac standing nearby, they would be safe.

CHAPTER 21

*W*ell, this was just great. Pacing, he continued to mumble. Fighting the urge to tug at his hair, he instead clinched his hands into fists. His frustrations growing. How the hell had she done it? Let alone figure it out the complicated spell.

It had taken him years to learn such a thing. Could it be she was more powerful than he? Or was there a real credence to instinct?

He couldn't help but wonder? Looking over to where Honor now slept, beside Caden, her fated Mate. Shaking his head, those two really should have completed the deed by now.

He had hoped that his silence on the matter would have resulted in the two of them acting on their lustful feelings. Doing what came naturally.

Sex was a requirement for the ceremony, of course. As well as bloodletting and speaking the ancient language. Achieving those last two requirements could be as simple as a drop of blood from a love bite and their souls speaking to each other.

It wasn't necessary to have a priestess conduct a ceremony like Kieran and Harlow had. However, their circumstances were different. Theirs was a destiny for more.

Maybe, if he had intervened, he could have prevented this. Now he had to figure out how to convince these two to perform the act, and fast. Should he go for the direct approach or subtle? Perhaps he should take his cues from them and go from there.

He missed the era when, once you had met your True Mate, there was no waiting. The deed was done and life continued. Now, however, with all the tales of deception on the issue and the two in question before him. They didn't know what was happening to them. So how could he have expected them to perform the ritual? Perhaps a little story time was in order.

Perhaps he was losing his marbles, as they say. If he expected so much from others. Maybe he had become too complacent in allowing things to simply be. Following the entire Neera fiasco.

Now was the time for action and interaction. He needed to guide all three of them through this magick hail storm. However, his insides told him that teaching would have to wait till after Rowan's change.

"Arg!"

Reaching up, he weft his fingers through his hair and giving a good tug. Despite his efforts, he could never break the bad habit of tugging at his hair when he was pent up with frustration. He was at war with himself. Partial blame for the situation these three found themselves in rested with him. Had he given them more instruction, this might not have happened?

His mind and gut were fighting over this. Knowledge was power tight? All three of them could benefit from some tutelage. But from what he could see, it would not happen anytime soon. They would, however, have to learn through experience and reaction.

Stomping his foot. He couldn't stand to look at them any longer. All he saw when doing so was a tangled mess. Further building his internal tsunami. There was also a haze of a black cloud that followed the two of them. Someone he wasn't sure who had it out for them.

Another magick from the looks of things. With this third person now present in their corner, it would seem that the cloud has lessened. Still, he did not like the lingering black cloudiness.

Deep in thought, he paced again. Pondering the reason for their actions. It had been a very long time since he had been the same age. However, he had grown up in this world. He had all the teaching, and the lessons drilled into him at an early age. Also becoming so reliant on the images he saw. It was time to be creative.

These three were from an apocalyptic time. So used to reacting rather than planning. Could that, by chance, be the reason logic had vanished in this situation? He still doubted this was intentional. They were new to this time, and not aware of all ins and outs. Which was why they all needed some training. Something that he sadly suspected would have to wait till all the chaos was over with.

Although, if he could convince them to complete their bonding in a timely manner. Perhaps he could do a mini thriving session with them. Show them how to trust their internal knowing. Allowing them to gain their confidence and abilities along the way.

The more he thought about it, the more it brought a sense of calm. Well, he did his best to stay calm, given the circumstances. This had not been intentional. It was likely a gut reaction.

Now what should he do? The web of possibilities was endless. He needed to find the avenue with the greatest result. To do so, he would need them to be safe in their slumber. What he had to accomplish would take a bit of time. Not to mention he liked to work in peaceful silence.

That was not something that he could get around here. With his decision made, he nodded his head. Walking toward the sleeping trio, he closed his eyes, thinking of his newest tiny cabin. Summoning the power needed, he held his breath, waving his arm in the air.

Unaware, however, someone saw him from a distance before they disappeared with a small popping sound.

HE WAS IN LUCK. His massive furry companion had grabbed him and they escaped the carnage. It was a good thing too. The prisoners weren't ready to give up just yet. However, he had a feeling they would be soon. Smiling, he liked that thought.

Soon he would have what he wanted. There was also the chance that this current girl possessed enough power to grant all his desires. He would have to play her a little differently, though. She was a tough nut to crack. Not like the others he so frequently chose.

As a side benefit, he now would have another furry companion. Perhaps this new member could be used to sway the girl. She had seemed to form a strong attachment to him. Rather quickly, too, it seemed.

He smiled, liking the idea a lot. He was a master at getting others to do everything he wanted. Rightly so. He was a magick, after all. It was his birthright to rule over all nonmagicks. After all, they created them for that purpose. To worship and do all the bidding of any magick being.

All his hard work had led him to this point. This was the closest he had ever been. He couldn't fail now. Pride filled him. This was his time. His chance to show all those who had doubted him. Well, those that were still alive, that is. Most were now long gone. Only a few remained.

Smiling again as he pictured the looks on all their faces when they recognized him for who was. The magick born without gifts and now the most powerful one of all. He couldn't wait for that day. He would show them all just how powerful he could be. Taking all that was his.

Still, at least this big brute was useful, even if he hated being carried around like a small child. A necessity because of his weak state. It was likely the reason everyone assumed he was dead now. Little did they know. He would show them. Show them all. He was better than them all.

He saw movement out of the corner of his eye. Strange, he thought. The attack had come from the other side of the building. Which is why they had left from this side. All the people had gathered over there.

It was a minor setback losing this grand place. It had its uses, that was for sure. However, it was a pain to run. There were never enough servants around at any given time. So getting things done took forever.

Not to mention the guard dogs and their endless barking and howling were getting on his nerves. It was a good thing to be rid of them. They were a dime a dozen, and he was positive the brute carrying him would be all too pleased to create more such creatures. He had perfected the task.

Squinting, he tried to study the figure. Who was it and why were they on this side? Not to mention waving their arm in the air as if they wanted to gain attention. Suddenly, they all disappeared with a soft popping sound. Clearly another magick. But who? Were they a part of the attacking party? Or were they simply in the wrong place at the wrong time?

Wanting to find out more. He shouted to his big brute.

"Head over there. I want to inspect."

He pointed to where the magick being had been. A grunt was his only reply as he turned and headed that way. A grunt followed with each stomp. Looking at his carrier's face, he could see the sweat beginning to form. His shifter friend was struggling with the shift.

Feeling a small bit of compassion, he said.

"Set me just here and you can shift back to your human-like form while I investigate."

He pointed to the place where he saw the magick disappear. Sitting on the ground, he looked around to see if he could find any visual clues as to who was there. Closing his eyes, he saw nothing of significance. He took a moment. The remnants of power left behind were familiar.

He had been born a magick with no gifts, but over the years he had learned and picked up a few things. So he wasn't without some talent. It was just not enough for him. He deserved more.

He knew this he should know this person. They were someone from his past. But who? He couldn't remember. Frowning, he inhaled deeply. Trying in vain to jog his memory.

It frustrated him. It was just outside of his reach. Even his brain was weak, just like the rest of him. However, he made sure to protect his greatest asset. So this person in question must not have been of any significance. Otherwise, he would remember them.

They possibly have developed into someone of consequence. Potentially a person he needs to watch out for. Possibly even investigate. But later. Right now, he had things to do. Important things.

Turning to look at his shifter companion to see how he fared. He was back in his human form, standing and waiting patiently. With his thick arms crossed, he grunted his question.

"You ready?"

Nodding his head, he cursed his need to be carried around. At least he could reserve his strength this way. Even Briggs, when in his human form, was faster and stronger than any nonmagick. He also didn't need to tell the brute where to go. Just like any other dog, they will always go back home.

Ozel better have everything asked for prepared. He would be in much need of an energy boost.

CHAPTER 22

God, his bones ached. What the hell had happened? When he attempted to move, pain filled him, causing him to groan. Deciding to stay still, he tried to remember. Were they in some kind of battle? This felt different from the aftermath of a fight. It felt like something had touched him. The effect was a vice-like embrace.

He elected to be cautious when opening his eyes. Remaining very still, he cracked one eyelid open. Thankfully, the light was low. Opening both his eyes, he scanned his surroundings. The light was candlelight, flicking softly around Cormac's tiny hut.

Exhaling a breath, he hadn't realized he was holding. He was safe. Though how he had got here was a mystery. He was still having trouble remember recent events.

Carefully turning his head, he saw Honor was curled into his side, sound asleep and snoring softly. Needing to touch her and ignoring his pain, he reached over to move a strand of hair from her face.

A smile spread across her face at his gentle touch. Even in sleep, she reconsigned him. Their connection ran deep. He couldn't help the smile that spread across his face. He extracted himself from the cot as cautiously as he could. After rearranging the blanket, he bent and kissed her forehead.

Gingerly, he moved about the cabin. Since there was no evidence of Cormac or Garth, he went outside to search. Once on the other side of the door, he found them both sitting on the steps. Each held a cup of steaming brew in their hands. Sipping while they gazed out and over the surrounding trees.

"Mind if I join you?"

Garth turned, giving him a silent nod before he moved down a step. His expression looked like he was in the same amount of pain as he was himself.

Sitting, he took the offered brew from Cormac.

"Thank you."

The old man nodded his head in acceptance. They all remained this way. Drinking their steaming brews in silence. It was nice to just sit here. Gazing around at all the natural beauty. He couldn't help but wonder what the ancestors had done that had destroyed all of this. Why would they have done it?

Since coming here, he could feel the difference. Not just the magickal difference, but the difference in the land, trees, sky, and all the animals. It was magnificent. What they had been taught as children was that their leaders had attempted to repair the damage at some point. However, as a result, they had made it much worse.

With their compound, like many other around the world, an extremely wealthy man funded the creation of the domed city in which they lived. An attempt to give humanity a chance. Hopefully offering time to find a solution. Sadly, that had not happened. The solution, until now.

When offered a refill of brew, he shook off his thoughts.

He and Garth said in unison.

"Thanks."

They both seemed to be of the same mind. Enjoy the calm and the brew while they can. Things were about to become even more intense than before. A deep inner feeling that spoke rather loudly when he woke up this morning.

He had always been a person to trust in his gut immensely. It had never steered wrong. It looked to him as though Garth was such a man as well. While in the man's presence, he felt a strong and genuine connection. A connection that was to be tested.

He doubted, however, that it would be Honor to test it. She would be more likely to be the one to strengthen it. Just like the knowledge he had, she was the one responsible for how they were feeling at the moment.

He finally remembered. The three of them had been waiting for a signal from Cormac before they went charging in. They were the backup force to rescue his sister and his nephew. Only things hadn't gone according to plan.

All three of them had been standing together regaling over their shock. They were unaware that Rowan had also been kidnapped. Learning that knowledge had sent all three of them spinning.

What Honor did, and how she had done it was still a mystery. He couldn't figure it out. No matter how many times he tried. However, he bet Cormac knew exactly what had happened. Something big happened to them. Why else would they be feeling this sore? Not to mention out cold for hours. Whatever the mystery, not any of them seemed to want to talk about right now. Perhaps it was best to wait till she was awake.

So they sat. Enjoying the signing of the birds as they danced in the sky. The rustle of tree branches and leaves as they joined along. Creatures softly crunching on their scrounging finds from the ground. The forest was alive in every way.

Closing his eyes, he leaned back, allowing the post behind him to support his weight. With a deep inhale, he enjoyed the many scents and fragrances wafting in the breeze. The healing life force flowing through his body brought a smile to his lips.

This new ability was amazing. Plus, it felt good. Like a loving embrace of life. He relaxed, emitting a deep sigh. He rather liked this life.

SHE FELT WARM. Where was she? Last she remembered, they were waiting for Cormac's signal, near a massive stone structure. Why couldn't she remember anything after that? Blinking, she took her time to survey where she was. It looked like the old man's tiny hut. Glancing around, she saw she was alone in the small space.

Where was everyone? Stretching as she sat up, she rotated her neck. It was stiff. How long had she been sleeping for she wondered? Swinging her legs over the edge of the cot, she stood, reaching her arms to the ceiling. It felt wonderful to stretch.

Deciding they all must be outside, she went in search of them. As she guessed, they were out here sitting on the steps to the tiny cabin drinking what might be several cups of brew.

"Have any more of that brew?"

She asked, desire filling her tone.

Cormac stood, nodding his head, while showing her to take his seat. Quickly placing a steaming brew into her hand.

Wrapping her fingers around the cup, she savored the heat. Bending her head, she took her first sip. A moan of pleasure escaped her lips at the taste.

"This is good."

Once again, all she received was a nod. Was no one talking? Why? Curious, she asked.

"Are you's all mad at me? Did I do something wrong?"

All heads turned to look at her. She kept looking from on to the other, waiting. However, it was Cormac who spoke first.

"In a manner of speaking."

Confused, she looked at each of them in turn. Their expression revealed no more clues to his answer. Focusing back on Cormac's face, she waited for him to explain. She didn't have to wait long.

"You, my dear, performed a piece of ancient magick."

Drawing her brows together in concentration, she tilted her head, studying him. He was serious.

Scared, she asked with a wobble in her voice.

"How the hell did I do that? I don't know any magick."

She instantly calmed when Caden pulled her onto his lap and wrapped her in his arms. The secure and loving embrace did wonders for her.

Listening intently as the old man continued to explain. Being a magical race, they possess an inherent ability to access and use all magic as they see fit. As such, the ancestors established rules for when it was being used. What she had done was, in essence, against those rules. However, since she was new to the skill and unaware of what she was doing, they would show leniency.

His words shocked and scared her. She could not withhold the gasp that escaped her lips. In her distress, Caden tightened his hold on her. While Garth shot to his feet while shouting.

"They will not harm her."

His fierce response had the old man softening. A small smile lit his face.

"I did not mean to imply such. I was only explaining. Nothing will happen to her."

He continued to tell them she had inadvertently cast a binding spell. A spell that included all three of them. Until they completed the agreement, they would all wear her mark on their palm. The magickal binding tattoo.

Each of them, now shockingly, looked at their palms. On their right palms was a circle with an interwoven vine of thorns. As strange as it was, the mark was beautiful. How had she been able to do this? Also, what had she bound them to? She couldn't remember. Returning her gaze to Cormac. She waited.

After a few moments, he resumed speaking. Telling how, when there is an identical desire among a group, and there is an Oracle around, is dangerous. Resulting in a perfect condition to perform an unbreakable agreement. All will wear the mark on their palm until they completed the task. Either one of them alone or all three combined.

It was Caden who interrupted the explanation.

"Hey wait. What did you say Honor was?"

He had said she was something? Thinking back on his words. It took her a moment to remember. She was an Oracle. What was that?

In barely a whisper. She said.

"I'm an Oracle. What is that?"

Looking at Cormac. She studied him, tilting her head.

He explained to them in a calm and gentle tone that an Oracle is a powerful and rare magical creature. There hadn't been one in eons. Her capabilities were endless. However, like all magickals, she would be stronger in a specific set of magicks. A master, if you will.

At one time, there used to be a school at which they would learn the craft of all magicks. That time is when the ancients we have today originated from. Sadly, not one of them is an Oracle. They had all died out long ago.

Unable to contain her feelings. She whispered.

"That's sad."

Cormac offered her a small smile. Blinking in agreement, he said.

"That it is my child."

Taking a deep breath. He looked as though he was gathering the courage to continue. Looking around to make sure they were alone. He said.

"I must confess something. None of you must repeat what I am about to say."

Studying each of their faces. He took one more deep breath before saying.

"Like you, Honor, I am an Oracle."

He held up a finger to shush them when all three of them gasped. Continuing to say that he had had to go into hiding. Needing then to assume the life of a Shaman. It had served him well and had kept him and the others safe.

That he had been living this life of deception for long, he was forgetting who he really was. Had he made use of all his talents, he might have foreseen this and been able to stop it. Or at the very least, given them instruction on this time and basic magickal knowledge.

Shaking his head, he refused their apologies. He was at fault just as much as they were, if not more. Being the elder among them. Therefore, he insisted.

He was entrusting them with this secret. Which also meant Honor would need to pay close attention to her abilities. For they will increase. She must practice, while also keeping them and her true identity a secret.

There are those in this world who would seek her out for her power. Wanting it for themselves. He implored Caden and Garth to keep her safe. When she tried to object, Cormac shook his head.

"I know you are capable, my dear. But you must keep your secret for now. Now is not the time to reveal ourselves."

Knowing he was right, she nodded her head in agreement.

Perking up, he clapped his hands together.

"Now Caden, you my son are going to stop dilly-dallying and bind your Mate here. You know what to do. Simply follow all of your instincts."

Nudging his head in Honor's direction.

She could feel the heat rising in her cheeks as Cormac spoke. Then deepening to crimson when Garth burst out laughing. Covering her cheeks with her hands, she closed her eyes. Knowing full well what the old man had mentioned.

When she felt the force of Garth's slap on Caden's back pushing her forward, she turned to look at him. He wore a frozen expression of shock.

As if some light switch clicked on, his gaze locked with hers. Swallowing past the lump rising in her throat at her nerves. His eyes displayed so much desire that, instinctually, she backed away.

With a wicked crook of his lip, he just as quickly wrapped his hand around her middle, tossing her over his shoulder and bounding into the tiny cabin.

When she shouted at him to put her down. His massive palm landed swats to each ass cheek.

"Quiet woman."

When he stopped at the door, he turned.
"Thanks for the advice."
All she could do was groan.

CHAPTER 23

*I*t felt as if a fog had instantly enveloped them. Stepping over the threshold of the tiny cottage, he was able to zero in on her. Only her. Hyperaware of everything. He could hear her breathing increasing, not to mention the smell of her arousal. It was intoxicating to him. Had him salivating to taste her. All of her.

Standing in the middle of the tiny room, he allowed her to slide down the front of his body. Feeling every inch of him. It had taken him a moment to register what Cormac had said. Then, like a movie playing in his head, he had replayed everything with Honor.

He had delayed his ah-ha moment. But it was no less powerful. He finally understood their unique connection. Need had built until he was about to burst. He had to have her and now. No more waiting. It seemed like someone had scattered some pieces of the puzzle before. Now they were about to be put in their rightful place.

He knew what Cormac's cryptic message meant. They were to bond together as a True Mated pair. Trusting their instincts for the how of the magick part.

Using his hands, he cupped her head. Bending, he took her lips in a gentle kiss. She sagged against him. Moaning in pleasure. Pulling back slightly, he traced her lips with his tongue.

Standing to his full height, he chuckled when she continued to lean in for more. Rubbing his thumbs along her cheeks, he smiled.

"You like that, my girl."

Looking at her desire-filled eyes as she nodded her head. He allowed his smile to grow.

"I'm glad."

Bending to take her lips again, this time, he devoured her. He couldn't get enough of her taste. When she dueled her tongue with his, he growled. Securing his hand around the back of her neck, he allowed his other to slide down her back. Reaching her ass, he squeezed till she moaned in pleasure.

Her arms wrapped around his neck and her hands grabbed fists full of hair. The momentum of her jumping up to wrap her legs around him had her tugging on his hair.

Growling he said.

"God woman. What you do to me."

He liked it when she pulled his hair. He wondered if she enjoyed to same. To test his theory, he wrapped her long hair around his hand. With a good tug, he held her head back. Bending, he held eye contact as he feasted on her neck.

Smiling at her intake of breath. He watched as her eyes glazed over and became unfocused. His impulse to mark her was so strong he increased his suction. The growl that formed in his throat, roared when she ground herself against him. Strengthening his hold on her rear, he helped by moving her up and down slightly.

Throwing her head back. She came screaming his name.

"CADEN,"

While she was still riding the high of her orgasm, he divested them of their clothes. Laying her carefully on the bed, he crawled between her splayed legs. Kissing each one back and forth. He couldn't get enough of her.

Her body knowing this familiar tune rose, with a need to be closer to him. Looking up at her body, he saw she was still riding her high, with eyes beautifully glazed. Her chest rising in uneven breaths.

While maintaining eye contact, he used his thumbs to pull her lower lips apart. Darting out his tongue, he took a slow lick. Smiling as this seemed to snap her out of her orgasmic haze and focus on him.

With their gazes still locked, he ate her out with a vengeance. When he fucked her with his tongue, her hips began to rise and fall. Wanting her to stay still, he moved his hand to hold her hips down.

His control over her body had her thrashing her head and moaning. Soon she was begging him for more. He loved it when she begged.

With a breathy sigh.

"Please…… Caden. Please. More."

If his girl wanted more, he'd give her more. Swirling his finger inside her, he collected her juices. Placing his finger at her rear entrance, he pushed into his first knuckle. Holding it there.

Rising, he asked.

"How's that, my girl?"

Her violent head nod had him smiling before returning to his feast. He could do this every day. She was sweet and tangy.

Swirling his tongue around her very extended, hard little clit. He added more fingers inside her. With fingers in both her rear and her delicious pussy, he fucked her hard. The sound of her growing wetness filled to room. Zeroing in on her clit, he sucked hard. Sensing she was close, he pinched her little nub with teeth. Sending her screaming over the edge.

Before she could come down from her high, he rose above her, thrusting into her hard and deep. Holding himself there while she contracted around.

Groaning, he muttered.

"Heaven."

Lowering, he wrapped a hand around the back of her neck. Holding her still, he kissed her. Devouring her mouth. Savoring her taste. When she moaned, wrapping her arms and legs around him, he began to move. Gradually picking up the pace, till he was slamming into her.

When she started begging,

"Harder, Caden, harder. I want you to take me harder."

He pulled out and flipped her over. Grabbing her hips, he pulled her to her knees before surging into her again. Fucking her hard. He was sure his fingers would leave marks. When she turned her face to look at him and smile. He lost it.

Bending, he reached for her. One hand wrapped around the front of her neck, bringing her back to his chest. His other hand reached down, feeling through her pussy lips. Holding himself inside her, he whispered in her ear,

"Mine Honor."

She lulled her head to the side and onto his shoulder with a moan.

"Yes, Caden. Yours."

Holding her firm, he again started fucking her. Rubbing her clit, harder and harder. When she moaned,

"Oh, my God."

He couldn't help the smirk.

"No, just Caden, my girl."

Wanting her lips, he turned her head. Devouring her mouth and swallowing her scream as she came apart in his arms. Her orgasm triggered his. Pulling back from their kiss, he buried his head in her neck. He was bucking into her with an endless release.

Feeling her sink her teeth into his neck sent him into a second release. He, too, succumbed to the urge and bit down into her flesh, sending her over once more.

Empty and drained, with a metallic taste in his mouth, they collapsed in a heap on the cot. Ragged breathing, tangled arms, and legs. Running his hand up and down her back. He calmed her.

He watched as she slowly turned her head. She asked with unfocused eyes and a dreamy smile on her face.

"Can we do that again?"

Loving her, he kissed the tip of her nose. Saying,

"Yes, my girl. We can do that again."

Brushing hair from her cheek, he smiled as she closed her eyes and said.

"MM... K,"

Wrapping his arm around her, he pulled her in close. He fell asleep with a smile on his face.

She woke feeling achy. Caden had an insatiable appetite for her. He had woken her many times through the night. They tried every position possible. The orgasms he gave her were out of this world. Smiling, she couldn't help but remember the many fireworks displays behind her eyes. The man was talented.

Rolling over in the small cot they had shared last night, she knew she was alone. Their connection was stronger than ever before. It was like an awareness. Sitting up, she stretched as she swung her legs over the edge. Closing her eyes, she focused on healing her aches and pains. They really needed a bigger bed for their night time gymnastics.

Realizing she was still naked. She rushed around, gathering her clothes and getting dressed. At the basin, she splashed some water over her face. Grabbing a hair tie from one of her many pockets, she secured her hair.

With a skip in her step, she made her way outside. The sun was so bright today and streaming through the trees; she needed to cover her eyes. As painful as it was, she was grateful for the experience. The warmth of the sunshine always felt so good.

After her eyes had adjusted to the brightness, she could see Caden and Garth sparing in the tiny front yard. Instead of the usual training techniques, they were using their newfound talents. It was amazing to see. They danced as if in a ballet, and their confidence shone. Like they had had these gifts their entire lives. Well, in a way, they have. They were just not accessible in the world they came from.

"Talented aren't they?"

Hearing Cormac speak from behind her startled her. Gasping, she placed her hand over her chest. Turning, she stated.

"Don't sneak up on a girl like that."

His softening smile touched her heart.

"I'm sorry, my dear. I thought you heard me coming up behind you."

He gently took her elbow, helping her to sit on the top step. They continued to watch.

Caden was fast and strong. He is always outmaneuvering his appointment. The only time Garth seemed to have the upper hand was when Caden allowed it. Seemed strange to her why he would do such a thing. Since they were training, it was a good thing they each learned to excel in their skill sets.

She was so engrossed in watching she hadn't noticed Cormac had moved until his arm appeared in front of her with a dish of food.

"Here, my child. Eat up, you're going to need the energy."

Taking the dish, she said her thanks. Turning back to watch her man, she dug into the food. When she had finished Cormac announced it was now her turn to train. The only catch was it would be two against one.

She was about to face off against Caden and Garth with Cormac shouting instructions at her. Nerves filled her. After watching the men spar, she wasn't sure how capable she was. Entering the tiny yard with trepidation, she couldn't help the smile that spread across her face. The men were teasing her, albeit in an encouraging way.

It was nice to have the positive encouragement. A foreign thing for her. She rather liked it. Before they truly began, Caden had run up to her, embracing her. Picking her up off her feet, he twirled her around, making her giggle. His broadening smile had her sharing a smile of her own. He kissed her temple, whispering,

"You can do this, my girl."

Setting her on her feet, he swatted her ass before turning and going to stand beside Garth. Who winked at her before he got into a defensive position.

She could do this. It was like the True Guard training. Those maneuvers were already so ingrained in her that all she had to do was focus on her many new gifts. The only trouble was she didn't know what those were.

So this was how the rest of their day played out. Cormac shouted specific attack formations for the men and her to defend in kind. Then she was to attack them while they defended. They repeated this structure, varying the two against one.

It amazed her how naturally things came to her. Relying on her instincts, and not overthinking, had given the best results.

It was hard for her at first. She had always planned and re-planned. Liking to be prepared for any scenario. These exercises, however, forced her out of that norm. While also teaching her how to trust herself and look within.

They had finished their evening meal and were now working on individually attacking dummies. Following the old man's instructions to a tee. He said he wanted them to become familiar with their gifts. It was necessary that using them and accepting them became as common as breathing.

She understood his point. Usually, things like that level of acceptance took time. What she didn't understand was why he was rushing them. Well, at least to her, it seemed like he was rushing them.

Frustrated with the repetition, she asked,

"Where do you think he had to disappear to this evening?"

The men seemed less bored than her. Having turned this individual practice into some sort of completion. Rolling her eyes at them. Placing her hands on her hips, she said.

"Well?"

They both stopped and turned to look at her. Caden spoke.

"He went to see Harlow and Rowan."

Oh my god, how could she have forgotten them? Worry filled her as she studied her Mate. That was still so strange to comprehend. Her Mate. Through their bond, she knew he wasn't worried about them. Their connection grew with each passing moment.

However, earlier this morning, when they had begun training together, he had taken her aside. Insisting she was to focus only on her training. Not to worry about him or their growing connection. She needed to direct all her attention towards developing her talents.

Realization dawned on her. He had been helping to channel her focus through their bond. She had forgotten about his family. Who was now hers as well? Forgotten about the magickal promise she had created amongst the three of them.

She was the one who was an Oracle. It should be her protecting him and helping him deal with his emotions towards his twin and nephew. What was wrong with her? Why could she no longer multi-task? How could she be so selfish? Thinking only of herself, not her Mate or his family.

With her emotions tumbling out of control, she locked her gaze on Caden.

"I'm so sorry, Caden. I didn't mean to be so selfish."

With concern quickly spreading across his face, he moved at lightning speed. Standing in front of her, he wrapped her in his arms, saying.

"Hush now, my girl. You're speaking nonsense."

Cradling the back of her head, he bent kissing her hair.

"You were not being selfish. Nor have you ever been."

She felt Garth come to stand beside them.

"Honor, you have always put others first. Even when you shouldn't have. Caden was only doing what a true Mate should."

She felt his big and rough hand pat her on the back. Smiling into Caden's neck, she allowed herself to relax. Before she could even broach the next subject, Caden said.

"Don't worry about the unbreakable agreement. It would not have happened if we hadn't all been thinking the same. So do not blame yourself. Magick happens for a reason."

She wasn't sure she completely agreed with that, but she would allow it for now. When he moved to whisper into her ear.

"Magick does happen for a reason."

Not only did a shiver run up her spine, but she had forgotten again about their connection. He knew what she was feeling. Just like she knew his feelings when she remembered to check that is. God, what was wrong with her?

His soft chuckle in her ear tickled.

"Nothing is wrong with you, my girl."

He placed his finger under her chin. Tilting her head back. Seeing the love shining in his eyes took her breath away. Slowly, he bent down, taking her lips in a tender kiss.

CHAPTER 24

*B*lending in had been easier than either of them thought. They also knew that no one from their compound had attempted to follow them. Having left traceable devices in several locations, just to be on the safe side. It was easy to relax and focus on the task at hand.

Already they had garnered an ally in a local family. Having met the man when they came into the small village. He was the perfect candidate for them. He lived on the outer edges of town on a farm with masses amount of land. Easy for them to wander and plan while also practicing all their newfound gifts.

This villager had been all too eager to help them out and offer his home. A large and mundane man, he had divided relationships with the locals. Which would serve their purpose in collecting followers. Creating a cause for these 'nonmagicks' could get behind was a piece of cake.

The fact they were recruiting magicks who were either hiding their gifts, ashamed of them, or didn't have any. All of whom were pretending to be nonmagicks. Just made this that much more funny to him. They were the perfect type to convert to his cause. Wanting so much to belong.

Their host had a large place, where gatherings went unnoticed.

Even the potential for battle practice was vast. He couldn't help the smile that spread across his face. Luck was finally on his side. Giving him every advantage he would need to take down the Faxon clan once and for all. While also making them hurt first.

If only he could get Cory to keep his wandering eye off their host's daughter and wife. What he did with them didn't interest him. The possibility of him getting caught and ruining their chances at getting what was rightfully his was high.

He had come this far. Nothing was going to ruin this for him. Not even his right-hand man. If he needed to, he would take him to hand. It was just he didn't want to. That could get messy and fast.

The man had the ability to blink anywhere, he wanted to go. Why not into another woman's bedroom across town? There were plenty around. He could have a different one each night.

He couldn't see the point. They were simply a distraction. Who needed that? One was pretty much like another. The only reason he had kept Sally for so long was she was great in bed, yes, but that girl had skills at playing people. Getting him whatever he wanted.

He had made sure he had her placed where he wanted her. That way, she was close to him and able to do his bidding. Now that she was gone, still pissed him off. He would have to do the dirty work himself.

Sighing, he continued his way into the small village. Wishing could have used Cory and his talent. It could, however, hurt his cause, just appearing out of thin air in the middle of town. They were posing as nonmagicks after all. It wouldn't do being seen using his gifts.

That would have to come in time with only those he trusted. So far, that only comprised Cory. He was incredibly crazy. Although he seemed to act a little odd since coming to the farm. Well, maybe he should say he was behaving normally.

Other than Cory's need to chase the woman on the farm, he appeared to blend in. He looked and behaved like a local. Far better than his friend was, apparently.

During their morning meal together, they made a suggestion for him to go into town today. His host had said if he wanted to meet the locals, start at the pub. It was possible he could find more like-minded folks there willing to join the cause, like they had been.

It hadn't taken long to arrive at his destination. When he entered, the chatter never waned. He had to weave his way through the throng of people. Finding the only chair left in the place he sat. Taking a moment to survey the crowd. This wasn't what he had expected. Well, he wasn't sure what to expect.

There were so many people all crammed into one tiny space. It appeared that people from all walks of life had gathered here. It would take him a while to discern who would be good potential targets. This might even take a couple of days.

He wasn't fond of that idea. He would rather it have been quick. Still, it was better to get this right. There wasn't time for any more mistakes on this mission. He would ensure that it was done right from here on out.

CHAPTER 25

They were all sitting inside the tiny cabin, discussing how they could explain their absence from the compound for so long. So far, they haven't come up with any great ideas. Sneaking out in the middle of the night had been a great idea at the time. Now, though, they wondered what the others thought.

He hadn't been sure who he could trust implicitly other than Garth and Honor. The need to keep Cormac a secret ran strong in all of them. Yes, the old man was strange and quirky. But his power and knowledge were immense. They now understood why. Both he and Honor were Oracles. Very rare and powerful, coveted magickal creatures.

He was thankful she was his true Mate. Now that he had finally claimed her, at least this way he could offer her some more protection. His scent overpowered hers, announcing to the world who she belonged to. If anyone was in doubt, they each wore the permeant bonding mark. Which only appeared after a successful mating.

Another thing Cormac had forgotten to mention to them. Not that they cared. It was just when they had found it they both had freaked out, thinking that they had created another binding vow. In a way, they had, but not one that would endanger their lives. This mark was like a couple in the future wearing wedding rings.

Learning that, they finally calmed before pride filled them. A tattoo unique to them announcing to the world who they were to each other. However, any magick would know before seeing the tattoo. Just being in their presence, everyone could feel it and smell their connection.

It filled him with a sense of pride knowing he had marked her and she him. He wanted to show off his tattoo. It was beautiful, just like his Mate. His Oracle.

Regardless, his instinct was still to lock her away until everything was safe. She was his to protect. His Mate. However, he knew she would never stay in the background hiding. Like himself, they received training as a True Guard member to protect and defend. However, in their case, the goal was to find a solution for the dying planet. Thus saving all of humanity as well.

In a sense, they had achieved that goal. Somewhat. It all depends on how you look at it. Now was not the time to dwell on where they came from. As far as he knew, there was no way of going back. Not to mention why would any of them want to? The here and now was far superior.

Their dinner table discussion topic shifted toward the unbreakable promise. Because it was open-ended who they were targeting. That left a sour taste in their mouths. It could be one person or many. They needed to identify the persons responsible for attacking Harlow and Rowan.

Only then could they formulate any kind of plan to end the pact. They still had to learn the consequences if they didn't complete it. Also, was there a time line? Until they could visit the ancients and undergo a ritual of some kind. They wouldn't know the specifics of the binding oath they formed.

The ancient five acting as one possessed the strength, knowledge, and power for such a ritual. Yes, Honor was the Oracle who performed the spell, but he and Garth compiled their magick as well. Hence the additions to the markings.

Later, Cormac studied the markings and discovered that they differed from what he had been taught. Therefore, he was wary of intervening himself. Insisting the ancients become involved.

With Cormac arriving to aid Harlow and Rowan, they were sure they could pinpoint some people. Knowing the type of injury his nephew had received, and who inflicted it. They had one target identified. There was also Jasper, who clearly had issues with both himself and Honor. He had even gone after his twin through Sally. That evil bitch. He didn't relish killing another creature, but that woman was nasty to her core.

They were so deep in their conversation that they hadn't heard Cormac return. It wasn't until he spoke that they all looked at him.

"It may take time to reveal the identity of the who."

The old man definitely had a way with words and phrases. He often spoke as if he were from multiple different times in history. At least, being from the future, they had the advantage of watching all the old movies. They spanned a significant time difference. It gave them great insight into language and cultures. They could recognize that he, too, seemed to process the same knowledge.

It was Garth, who finally spoke after our unintentional staring contest.

"We are aware. If what you say is true about us and our long life span. Then we needn't worry about time."

Cormac simply nodded his head in acceptance. Well, that then answered their question about the time allotted for their pact. It was endless. Sort of.

Focusing back on Cormac, he saw the man had more to say, however. He could tell. There was a small tick that appeared on his brow every time he held back. Smiling at his discovery, he made eye contact with the old man to let him know he knew.

Unsurprising he saw shock reflected at him. Followed quickly with gratitude. He would not give the man away. If he had survived eons, with this trait and no one had figured it out, he wouldn't share. It was not his secret to tell.

Whether what he said next was really what he had been keeping secret. He couldn't be sure. His instincts were telling him no, but to look at Cormac, he would have said yes. He showed no signs of any tells.

"I need you all to gear up and ready yourselves."

Confused since their last attempt to do so had ended with them not assisting, then creating an unbreakable promise. It was why they had been training again. Learning as quickly as they could about their gifts and how to use them. It felt strange to be going on a mission.

When they were still looking at him, confused, he reluctantly continued.

"Rowan is stable enough for transport. He is being moved to the shifter kingdom."

Now they stared at him in shock. A shifter kingdom?

Taking pity on them, Cormac decided it was best they had some basic knowledge. He often forgot they didn't know of all the tribes within this world. Since they had all accepted their gifts so readily and learned to use them quickly. He would forget.

So he told how there are many differing tribes of all kinds of magickal creatures. Within each tribe, there is a leader or multiple leaders. All are uniquely individual. They all got along together, mostly. If there was an issue that their leaders couldn't solve. Then the ultimate decision would rest with the leader of the Gods.

Which is what happened when a shifter attacked Rowan. A renegade shifter bit a member of the God race. As this is forbidden, it required immediate attention. Action was, therefore, required at the highest order. Hence, the official meeting of the leaders.

The triad rules the shifter kingdom. Flanna is the alpha shifter for all her bears. Whereas Hakan is the alpha of all his dragon shifters. Aramis is alpha over all his wolf shifters, while also embracing any form of shifter.

Since the matter involves Rowan and the wolves. Aramis traveled to the tribe of the Gods for an official gathering. They placed a price on the renegade's head, and Rowan is required to travel to the shifter kingdom.

There have been complications with his transition. Given the limited knowledge within Kieran's village, Rowan's progress of his healing surprised the healers who accompanied Aramis. There was cause for concern, however, he was still in the thick of it. Usually, once bitten, the conversion only takes a short time. Everyone agreed he will thrive better in the shifter kingdom.

It was clear there were some secrets the shifters weren't willing to share with the Gods. They were, however, in a unanimous agreement it was illegal to bite and transform a magick against their will. Hence the price on the renegades' head. As well as his sentence of death. After interrogation, of course.

After the brief history lesson. They agreed the fact they were True Guard members and Gods would be an asset to Rowan's transportation.

Caden's talent for invisibility would be useful with Rowan's transportation. No one knew about Cormac's plans to have them accompany his nephew from one kingdom to another. They were his hidden secret.

The old man informed them he had agreed to have help waiting at the alpha shifter's court when Harlow was to arrive. They had spread the word she was worried about the health of her cellmate and wanted to help. Keeping it secret that Rowan was, in fact, her son.

Hell, most people believed she was the reincarnated Neera. Brought back for vengeance. Cormac said that was another story for another time. One perhaps Harlow could share herself someday. Right now, they were needed.

HER HEAD WAS SPINNING. It wasn't long after they had geared up and tidied the tiny cabin. Cormac instructed them to all take each other's hands and for her to repeat after him.

All she wanted to do was go back into the cabin with Caden. She couldn't get enough of him. They had only shared one night together as a bonded pair.

Knowing they had an eternity together wasn't enough. Sitting on his lap while they had been discussing various things had been odd and wonderful. She wasn't used to displays of affection. He would trace a finger along her neckline. Or twirl a piece of her hair with his fingers.

When he was so inclined, he brushed her hair aside, inhaling at her neck, placing soft kisses. His actions were driving her crazy. She was so turned on.

It didn't seem to bother him. She did not know what she was to do. Was she to touch him back? Kiss him back? So she sat there frozen in insecurity. Only occasionally adding to the conversation. This wasn't like her at all.

Caden made her feel. She felt beautiful, delicate, and sexy. He was finally hers after having had a crush on him for all those years. Now what was she to do?

Shaking her head, she dispelled her thoughts. She needed to focus and recite a spell. Closing eyes, she took a deep breath. Relying on her instincts. Voicing the words with Cormac. She could feel the energy flowing through them. Swirling faster, engulfing them and taking them away.

When a loud popping sound rang out, she wanted to cover her ears. Tugging on her hands had her glancing between Caden and Garth. Both of whom were shaking their heads. Right, she forgot if she let go, the spell would break.

When the second popping sound occurred, she cried out in pain. It hurt so much. She didn't expect the landing. Falling to her knees, gasping in pain.

Loving arms quickly embraced her. Dulling the pain. Taking a few deep breaths and looking at Caden. She whispered.

"Thank you."

He smiled as he stroked her cheek with the back of his finger.

"I've got you. My girl."

Helping her to stand, he kept his arm wrapped around her shoulders. Looking up at him, she smiled. Telling him with her eyes how much he meant to her. His returning smile warmed her insides.

Everyone seemed to sense to shift in the air. A group was coming. It was time for them to get to work. Caden's nephew was traveling with this group. He needed their protection.

Getting into position, they waited for Caden's command to move. Deciding early on it would be best if they made use of their True Guard training while also implementing their new talents. It meant they could move like clockwork.

They didn't expect any issues because they had scheduled Rowan's move for a different time than what they had advertised. To be on the safe side, however, Cormac had promised the leaders he would see to it there was extra protection. He just hadn't mentioned who the extra protection was.

They reached the alpha shifters' court in no time. The only issue had been when Rowan had flailed about in pain. She and Garth had to hold Caden back from rushing to him. It took only a few moments to calm her Mate. Helping him to see it was safer if they stayed hidden.

She wasn't sure why she knew, but there was more information Cormac had not shared with them. Was it perhaps her link with Caden? Why she knew? It was because of that link she now knew of Cormac's tell. Possibly.

What was so important that he tell them at the right time? Was there ever a right time? Shaking her head, again dispelling her thoughts. She needed to focus on her responsibilities.

It hadn't taken the healers long to calm Rowan and get the group on the move again. It was hard seeing the young man suffer. Only from what she could see, he wasn't so young anymore. How was that possible? When they left, Rowan was a boy of about fifteen. This man they were escorting was at least twenty-five. There was more to that story, for sure.

After safely situating Rowan in his new quarters, they learned that the adjoining rooms would be theirs. Since they were still expecting an attack of some kind, the trio would stay the hidden secret.

They had been further surprised when Aramis himself was the one to lead them to their rooms. They would deliver anything they needed. Assuring them as he left, only he and two of his most trusted staff knew of them.

Leaving her wondering how he could make such a promise, he surprised her by looking at her and only tapping a finger at his temple. Shit, had she been projecting her thoughts? How else could he have known? She didn't know she could do that.

Hearing his laughter as he walked down the hall gave her the answer. She really must get a handle on some of her new powers. Sometimes, though, there were simply too many of them. As soon as she felt she mastered one another would pop up in its place. Then there was the added pressure of not revealing what she was.

Not realizing how much she was stressing out, it surprised her when Caden engulfed her in his arms. He easily swallowed her startled cry with a hungry kiss. Instantly relaxing into his embrace. The man was magick.

When he pulled back, he studied her face.

"Why don't lay down on the bed for a while?"

When she shook her head, he continued.

"We'll take turns, ok, One resting while the other two keep watch."

Reluctantly, she agreed. When he phrased it like that, he was her Mate but also her acting commander.

After he tucked her in, the quickness with which she fell asleep surprised her.

CHAPTER 26

*H*e had his doubts this was a good idea. Ozel, however, swore it would work. The scrawny little man possessed a fair bit of magick just enough to be useful to him. Otherwise, he would have taken what he needed from him instead.

Blood magicks were not an area he was familiar with. They were the darker of the dark magicks. Not that he cared about dark vs. light. He would use either if it served his purpose. Well, to be more accurate, he would use those versed in various forms of light and dark magick. It was all about power.

To him, it was all the same thing, anyway. It was just a means for the elders to use to control those they wanted to keep under them. Light vs dark. The elders favored light. Declaring it the only acceptable form of magicks. He was no longer subjected to that rule.

He always makes his own rules. Power for the sake of power. He would ultimately have it all.

If only he could laugh in their faces and show them how right he was. But alas, he could not. They had all perished ages ago, while he was still among the living. Such as it was.

The search for a never-ending source of life. He was confident now he had found it. Way else was everybody else pursuing her as well. Sadly, she kept slipping through his fingers. Not for long, though.

Soon he would be in possession of something she desired greatly. He smiled, anticipating the look on her face. Rubbing his hands together in delight, he scanned the crowded room.

He was to look for an able and plump body. Preferably a female body. The bigger the better his tiny man had instructed. He could ply her with a drink mixed with Ozel's potion. Then take what he needed.

It wasn't long before an unknowing victim approached him. Her advances he welcomed. He wasn't without his own skills. He could already feel the energy returning. Smiling when the server brought their drinks, he easily slipped the potion into hers. Watching in amazement, as she threw it all back. The magickal haze filled her vision.

Chuckling to himself, he needed to work fast. The drink was meant to be sipped and not guzzled. Hopefully, it wouldn't cause any unwanted damage. For his sake, he didn't want to get caught. The position was only to allow for a transfer of energy or power. From her to him.

As he was getting friendlier, with his prize, he was unaware he was being watched from the other side of the room. When she relaxed enough, he sank his teeth into the flesh of her neck. Piercing her skin, he drank her down. When he had his fill, he pulled back. Pressing a magicked compress to her wound, he quickly gave her the second potion straight. This one would fog her memory of him and their actions.

Wow! He couldn't believe it. Ozel had been right. This blood magic was powerful. He could see and hear with so much clarity it almost hurt. This had been what he had been trying to achieve by obtaining that girl. The one that so resembled Neera. However, this one possessed within her tiny body ten times the power.

He had always relied on that form of magick because he was accustomed to it and knew it was effective. This though worked too. It was a bit messy for him. He wished they could streamline it a bit. That would be better. The results were amazing.

Having an alteration to the plan, he was about to leave when suddenly a gruff, stubby man plopped down across from him.

"Hi there."

Closing his eyes, he curbed his gag reflex. The man's breath stank. How could he keep himself in such a scrawler?

"I think you and I should talk."

Opening his eyes. He did not agree, but what choice did he have? Remaining quiet, he waited for the man to continue.

While his victim slouched beside him, snoring, he pointed and said.

"I saw what you did there."

Not caring for her welfare, he said.

"So."

The man across from him smiled and leaned back in his seat.

"You're a magick aren't you?"

Now he was feeling the concern and annoyance. Still, he remained silent.

The man nodded.

"You are."

He turned and scanned the room before looking back at him. As if checking for something.

"We could use a man like you."

He raised his brows like an invitation. One he didn't take.

"Alright, I get it. You're a tough guy. But I think all these nomagick types deserve what they get. I mean, we are the more powerful ones. We should take what is rightfully ours. Right?"

Cautiously, he nodded. He agreed with this stranger's views. Perhaps this stubby man might be of some use. Tilting his head, he studied the man. There was something different about him. Also, something familiar too. He couldn't put his finger on it just yet. He would, though, he always did figure things out. It was simply a matter of time.

Watching as the man across from him rose, placing his hands on the table. He bent, leaning closer to say.

"If you're interested in our cause, we'd be happy to have you."

When he left, there was a piece of paper where his hand had been. Taking the paper, he read the scratched writing. An address of a farm just outside the city.

Perhaps more fortuitous luck had just dropped itself into his lap.

Smiling, he couldn't help but think this was interesting. Very interesting indeed.

CHAPTER 27

*I*t had been tough sitting in the next room and hearing Rowan struggle through his change. So many things were going on in the poor man's body. It was literally at war with itself. Which is why it was taking so long. At least that is what he thought. Additionally, since he was a bitten shifter, the phases of the moon would affect him more intensely.

Since the full moon was only days away. The poor man was in even more turmoil. All everyone wanted to do was help him. Unfortunately, from here on out, it was all up to him and his body.

There were a few times Garth had to hold him back by placing a hand on his shoulder to remind him to stay away. He didn't enjoy hearing his nephew's moaning and groaning. His instinct was to help him in his unconscious state.

He also knew that they were doing exactly that. They were the hidden secret help. Ready and waiting to pounce, when the time arrived. Thankfully, that time would be soon. Loud footsteps were coming from down the hall.

Whipping his head to look at Garth. They shared a silent conversation of understanding. With Honor still asleep, they didn't want to risk waking her just yet. If someone woke her before she was ready, she would not be quiet.

Prepping themselves as quietly as they could. They continued to listen to the happenings on the other side of the wall.

There was scuffling and thumping, quickly followed by complaining.

"Why is there so much crap in here?"

What crap he wondered? There was only Rowan and the bed he was lying on in that room. What crap is he talking about?

Hearing a hollow slap against flesh.

"You think they would just offer him up to us? Then you're daft. Of course, he's protected by magick."

Ah, now he understood what they meant. Their grouching at each other continued. Back and forth. What he couldn't hear were the continued noises Rowan had been making. Did that mean Rowan was aware of what was going on?

When Garth moved to intercept them, he held up his hand to halt them. Shaking his head, he then tugged on his ear, showing he wanted to listen some more. He was hoping they would reveal information.

Like who they were working for. What their name was. Why do they want Harlow and now Rowan? There were too many unanswered questions.

Hearing a few huffs and puffs, followed by groaning.

"Can't you control him?"

Came a snarl and an accompanying growl.

"No. That mutt is an alpha."

Hearing more struggling, he had to bite his cheek to hold himself back. The time wasn't right to interfere.

Hearing someone shout.

"STOP."

He looked at Garth with growing eyes. It was Harlow's voice. He never should have doubted that she wouldn't rush in and defend her son. Focusing back on the other room, they listened.

"This mutt is mineeee."

Hearing a feminine growl, he knew it came from his twin. Wanting to offer her some comfort and reassurance. He projected to her.

"Stay calm sister dear."

Closing his eyes, he could feel their unique connection. She had heard him. He was realizing their connection was always there, yes.

But it was her gift for their internal conversations. Therefore, she had to open to it.

Hearing Garth's whispered question.

"Are you talking with her?"

Before he could reply, however, Honor whispered.

"Yes. He is. So shh, and listen to next door."

This was good. He knew he could trust them to look out for Rowan while he stayed focused on Harlow.

Suddenly, a whiny voice stated.

"Well, this has worked better than I had hoped it would."

Now the winy voice was boasting.

"Two for the price of one."

His twin fear quickly overwhelmed him, when he felt Honor lay her hand on his back.

He instantly calmed. Turning to look at her. He smiled, mouthing a 'thank you.' Needing more time, he encouraged his sister.

"Stall Harlow. Help is on the way. Get him talking."

They had made it clear that more help was following his sister and her traveling companions. In case anyone intended her harm, they would know she had protection. While also encouraging those who meant her harm to come crawling out of the woodwork. It would seem their plan was working thus far.

It was the fact, however, that their timing sucked and needed work. So hopefully his dear sister could wrangle some much-needed information out of her slimy opponents.

He heard her question.

"What is this, better than you thought?"

Uh oh. He could hear the snakiness in her voice. This version of his sister no one wanted to be on the other side of. She was much smarter and more creative than people gave her credit for. She was prepared to eviscerate you using this voice.

"Do you not hear? Or are you addled in the head?"

Biting his lip, he almost felt sorry for her opponents. Looking between Garth and Honor, who also looked like they were about to burst out laughing. This guy didn't know what he had coming.

"Isn't obvious. We already got the guard dog, and now we have you as well."

So that's what they wanted Rowan for. Was he bitten because of that?

Feeling a rush of anger from his twin. Followed by her sneer.

"Oh, really. Is that so?"

He needed to calm her down. This tended to happen around her when she was angry. Right now, she had every right to be. Her son as well as herself were being threatened.

"That's it, Harlow, almost there."

Hearing her internal monologue of confusion. He knew she was really getting scared. Wanting to reassure her he wasn't a manifestation of her mind. He said.

"It's not."

He could tell she felt frustrated with herself because her mind was wandering. Commotion within the room grew louder. Hearing a frustrated whiny man shout.

"ENOUGH."

Hearing Harlow gasp. The whining continued.

"Make your choice. What's it going to be?"

He could feel the shift in the air. The tides had changed and were not in their favor. He needed to act and act now.

In a rage, he stormed from the room. Smashing into the next. The sight he saw before him had him seeing red. His nephew struggling with a grotesque shifter. In a smooth dance, he wrapped his hand around the shifter's neck. Focusing all his energy toward his electrical abilities, he sent them into his victim's body. Channeling his fury into the twisting of his neck to the side.

An awful cracking sound filled the room, followed by the thuds of falling bodies. The whiny man tried in vain to peddle himself backward. Screaming and demanding fair treatment.

Looking at his sister to make sure she was alright. When he saw her, his sister was frozen in place and in shock. He could tell that her mind was working overtime. Trying to process everything.

He was so focused on her he didn't notice the other man had moved. She wasn't fast enough to dodge the man when shifted behind her. With careful precision, he placed the knife to her throat.

He feared for his sister and froze in front of her. Clinching his teeth. He said.

"I wouldn't if I were you."

He was still speaking when someone burst through the door. Upon seeing her whispered.

"Harlow."

Raising his arm to block the man. He wanted answers. His sister stopped him with a

"NO."

Taking a moment to calm himself, he took a deep breath. In doing so, he could easily sense that this man was Harlow's true Mate. Making eye contact, he willed her to trust him.

"His name is Kieran. He is my husband Caden. Please trust him. He only fears for me and Rowan."

He felt an overwhelming sense of emotions. Hers and his. He understood all too well the meaning of being a true Mate. He could easily sympathize with the man.

"I know who Kieran is. But let's take care of this scum, ok?"

With her Mate close by, he could feel the shift in his twin. Understanding had dawned. With the two of them acting as one, they could easily handle this guy.

With a smirk and a tilt of her brow.

"Ok, brother mine."

He couldn't help the snort that escaped at her term of endearment. She knew he hated it. It was why he also used it on her.

It was then the whiny man tugged her backward. To steady herself, Harlow had to grab his arm. When he started shouting.

"Who is he? What does he want with you?"

This time, his sister snorted before saying,

"Well, I don't know what he wants with me. This gentleman is Caden, my twin brother."

He watched as she attempted to shrug off the knife as the tip penetrated further. Both he and Kieran hissed in response. Then she said.

"Plus, you already met my husband, Kieran."

The whiny man scrunched his face in anger.

"I've had enough."

Knowing this wasn't good, he couldn't keep his growl at bay. Before demanding.

"Release my sister."

Feeling compelled, he made eye contact with his twin. Pulling a card from her deck, he wanted her to know he knew the same game. He gave her a wink.

He watched her work her magick, using her gifts. The blade slowly slipped from the man's fingers. In a swift and rehearsed move, she grabbed her captor, bringing him around. Connecting her heel with his jewels. While he whined in pain, she flipped him.

Understanding her intentions, he was too happy to oblige. Raising his fist, he swung, connecting with the man's face. Rendering him unconscious. Looking at the smiley weasel who dared harm his family. He felt happy knowing justice would be served.

As the thought had crossed his mind, he felt a burning in his palm. Looking down, he saw his promissory tattoo had faded slightly.

It was torture to sit and listen to all the happenings in the next room. How could they treat people like that? They weren't commodities. Luckily, they all heard each other. Even if there were still far too many questions about who, what, and why?

They knew things had escalated quickly when Caden stormed out. She only hoped he could keep calm enough to defuse the situation. It was possible through their shared connection for her to calm him. So far, she had only mastered the skill through physical touch.

The encounter had happened so fast in reality. Even though living through it had felt like an eternity. She couldn't help but laugh that when help had arrived, it was, of course, too late. Well, that hadn't been entirely true. Caden was a help for Rowan and Harlow.

Staring down at her right palm. She still couldn't believe it had faded. So to had Caden's and Garth's tattoo. Her Mate's actions defending Rowan and Harlow were working toward their shared vow. If she had to guess, they had one person left based on the rate of fading. The idea made her feel giddy, but it also caused her concern. They did not know who the other parties were that were involved.

Now, they were all sitting in some grand room in Aramis' court. She sat on her Mate Caden's lap, cuddling. Likewise, Harlow sat on her Mate's lap. Cormac sat with Rowan and Garth. Followed up by Aramis and Kieran's most trusted. When Cora had entered the room, they were all shocked. Until they learned in this time, she went by Corrina, however, in their time she was Cora. She then introduced Aidan and Cillian to them.

Adjusting to this new world of theirs was a challenge. It was information overload. However, the more they all knew, the better off they all would be.

After today's earlier events. They all enjoyed a wonderful celebration meal. Once Cormac and the healers revived everyone from Ozel's magick. They had learned the whiny little man had attempted to save them all from Brigg's hatred by casting a sleeping spell on them. A spell so strong that it simulated death.

He stated killing everyone was pointless since they were only sent to collect their newest creation. So he gave the appearance of a killing curse instead. It helped speed things along for them. However, they had yet to gain a name from him other than the Master. Whoever that was? Ozel refused to reveal his Master's name.

Looking around the room, she couldn't help but see all the similarities there were to the grand ballroom at the original compound. It was like they were all most out of time. Shining and glimmering with ornate details. All the displays of wealth and power.

The official meeting or gathering of information was about to happen. Now that Rowan could join them. She still felt shocked to see that he had aged. He was so much older than when she had last seen him. Which, for her, wasn't that long ago. His age was a topic of conversation to be discussed. As to was his last statement of 'He's Coming.'

It would appear the twins understood his meaning. They weren't sharing, however. Even when she had questioned her Mate in private, he refused to share. She couldn't help herself, she wanted to know. Repeatedly, she had asked him until he finally grew angry. Snapping at her, shouting, Enough.

Allowing her curiosity to get the better of her had ended up upsetting them both. She was feeling horrible when he apologized to her.

Holding her head in his massive hands, he rubbed his thumbs along her cheeks. In a loving whisper,

"I'm sorry, my girl. I should not have snapped at you."

Bending, he kissed the tip of her nose before continuing.

"I can only guess at the meaning of the statement. It is not mine to share. We must all wait for Rowan to hear the truth."

Knowing he was right, she nodded her head in agreement. Though she had a pretty good guess herself who he had meant. It was the how was that possible and the why of it that bothered her the most. Most likely the others as well.

What had surprised her was when Caden had asked her if she noticed a difference in Harlow. He had just sat down, pulling her onto his lap, when he whispered his question in her ear. She watched when his twin moved about the room with her Mate and Aramis talking. It looked to be a serious conversation.

There was, however, something very different about the bonded pair, though. She could feel an enormous wave of power emanating from them. More so than everyone in the room combined. They also looked slightly different. While they too displayed the Mating mark, they wore many more markings. Powerful ones. Markings that shone through their clothing for her.

Sucking in a breath, she had an innate urge to bow to the couple. Unsure why, she just knew that they all should. For they represented all power and all living things.

When she had gasped, Harlow had turned to look at her. Upon studying her, realized what she knew. Unable to stop herself, Honor had lowered her lids as a sign of respect. The other woman nodded slightly while doing the same. Before turning back to the conversation.

As Caden whispered into her ear,

"What is it?"

She attempted to do something she never had.

Turning, she placed her hand on his head, supporting the back of his neck. Closing her eyes, she focused on sending him all her thoughts about the couple. When she heard him suck in a breath, she knew what she was attempting was working.

After she finished, she opened her eyes and looked into his surprised ones. Watching as he turned to look at his twin. No doubt sharing their unique internal conversation. One she knew he believed was all his sisters doing. Only she knew that was not true.

Smiling at her man, and feeling the bond he shared with his twin, warmed her heart. There was never any doubt in her mind that when those two worked together, anything was possible. Throw in all the rest of them here in this room and look out.

This was when Aramis had called an order to get this official meeting started. It was also when two others joined the room with them. She guessed the other shifter leaders Cormac had told them about.

CHAPTER 28

Oh, man, did his brain hurt. His sister and her true Mate were the eternal mother and father overall. He couldn't believe it, while in other ways it made total sense. You just needed to look at her son to see the evidence of how fantastic of a mother she was.

His head was still spinning over Rowan. Who now was a grown man in his own right. He had come through the portal when he was twenty-five. He was only seven years younger than he and his mother were. So strange. The last time he had seen him was when they sent him off to official training school at fifteen.

They had yet to figure out exactly how the portal worked. It did not spit you out in the order you went in. Well, sometimes it did. He and Jasper's team had all arrived at the same time. Then there was why some survived while others did not.

Rubbing his hand over his face, he turned his to look at his slumbering Mate. As soon as they were escorted to their private rooms. She seized him with desire and ravished him. He smiled, remembering how enthusiastic she had been. Not caring who if anyone heard them. Her passion for him filled him with pride.

Now she was snoring softly beside him. While he pondered over all they had just learned. Some changes were happening with the new position of the Gods. They had yet to discover who was after Harlow and Rowan. Did it possibly have something to do with the prophecy, Neera's followers, or both?

They still haven't been able to get any viable information from Ozel. Who they learned was Cillian's sibling. A good man who felt responsible for his brother's actions. Even Kieran had said he found Cillian a good friend. He should not bear the responsibility of his brother's actions.

That's why they assigned him the task of setting up the guild. A guild for the protection detail of the God and Goddess? Cillian displayed great compassion and possessed many skills that would cattier to his new position.

The fact he was also a Ravens Night member was an added bonus. He could sense other members as they had each walked into the room. There were quite a few of them. So if he was in charge of his sister's security, that was alright by him.

While Aiden, his brother-in-law's best friend, and a fellow creator of Ravens Night, was taking the position of clan chief and leader from Kieran. He, too, was an impressive man. One he could see himself getting along with well. Liking him before they had even spoken to each other. This internal knowing was a gift he really liked and was using more often.

Seeing Corrina or Cora, as he knew her, had been quite shocking. To say the least. Learning she was taking responsibility for Ravens Night had not been surprising. She had been doing so in his timeline. He wondered how things differed for Cora in his time to the Corrina in this one.

Was it possible their coming back here changed things for the better? Is this what the prophecy was about? Before he could ponder further, a loud banging on their door pulled him from his thoughts.

Honor shot up with a scream, scanning the room. Sighing, when she realized it was someone at the door, she relaxed, closing her eyes.

She garbled with a yawn. Before saying.

"It's just Garth."

Petting her hair, he leaned in, kissing her forehead.

"I know, my girl. Let's see what is so urgent."

She smiled at him with love shining in her eyes as she nodded.

Speaking in a voice only loud enough, he knew only he could hear with his superior hearing. He said.

"Come on in, Garth."

As he entered, they both sucked in a shocking breath at the overwhelming sense of worry that encompassed the man. How the door had blocked that, he wasn't sure. But was grateful for the tranquil bobble they had shared last night.

Concern filled Honor's voice when she asked.

"What is it, Garth? What's wrong?"

The large man's face only softened slightly at her question. Shaking his head, he only replied.

"I'm not sure exactly. I do know we have to head back to the compound now."

Confused by the man's unusual behavior, he knew his concern was genuine. Something was happening. Events that would require their presence. What those events were was unknown.

What a leader he was turning out to be. A crappy one, for sure. How could he have forgotten about his responsibilities? He had zeroed in on Honor, excluding all else. Well, except his sister and his nephew. Leaving a gap that, thankfully, Garth had the sense to fill.

Feeling the guilt, he rubbed a hand over his face. Staring at Garth, he said.

"I'm sorry, man. I didn't intend for you to carry that burden."

The massive man softened.

"No worries. You found your true Mate. You can repay me when it's my turn."

After sharing a look of understanding, they nodded in agreement.

They made a quick set of plans before Garth left to notify Aramis of their departure. This left them some privacy to get dressed and ready to leave.

He regretted this new devilment meant he would not be seeing more of his twin or his nephew. It also meant they would miss the rest of their meeting. There had been so much to talk about yesterday they had decided to continue on this morning. So Rowan had yet to explain the meaning of 'He's coming.'

Even after he had joined them last night. The conversation revolved heavily around talk of the prophecy. That in itself was something to ponder. Processing it was still causing him trouble. Honor's ability to distract him made him even more grateful.

His Mate's hand on his shoulder startled him, as he was so caught up in his thoughts. Looking into her eyes, he saw her love and compassion reflected in them.

"It'll be ok. Why don't you close your eyes and concentrate? Focus on the message you want to tell Harlow. Then simply send it to her. She will hear you."

Surprise filled him and had him looking at her in awe. She could read him so well. He seemed to flounder all over the place lately. Before he could even thank her, she said.

"It's ok. Now focus."

Nodding his head, he closed his eyes and did as his very intelligent Mate suggested. He couldn't help the chuckle that passed through his lips at his sister's reply.

"Ok, brother mine. Just be careful. If you need any help, let me know."

He could hear the teasing snark of her voice before it shifted to supportive. Realizing then their connection truly went both ways. Finally, he was complete. He had his twin and his Mate.

"Yes, you do, brother mine. Yes, you do."

He felt her warm embrace surround him. Opening his eyes, he saw Honor smiling at him. She knew and was complete, too.

Time he took charge. Grabbing his Mate's hand with a gentle squeeze, he wanted to convey to her his thanks, gratefulness, and readiness to move forward.

THEY WERE BEING ESCORTED by one of Aramis's men. He was taking them to a secure and private place they could instantly travel. How the man seemed to know exactly what they needed baffled her. It had to be Cormac's influence.

They were all three traveling this way at his advice, as well. When Garth informed them of their need for departure, Cormac insisted Honor was the way. It was the fastest way and the safest for them.

Why else would someone grant them precisely all their requirements? She was to keep her true talents and what she was a secret. But how then would someone not figure it all out when all three would simply disappear?

Now wasn't the time to ponder on such worries. She had more important things to freak out about. Like moving the three of them from one location to another all on her own.

This time, she was sorely responsible for their transport. It was all on her. The closer they got to her destination, the more her tummy butterflies fluttered.

What if she said the spell wrong? Or what would happen if she lost contact with one of them? It was an enormous responsibility. Being in charge of others while also transporting them through space.

She was internalizing her worries so much she hadn't noticed when they arrived at the location. Or that they had been given privacy to proceed. It wasn't till Caden squeezed their joined hands did she look around.

Her breathing increased as her self-imposed pressure weighed on her. Panic filled her. What if she messed up like she had before? Creating a binding promise. One that tied together with Garth, Caden, and herself. A spell she had no intention of making. What if she did something like that again?

Caden's kiss quickly snapped her out of her freakout. What a kiss it was, too. She instantly felt a desire and need for her Mate. Moaning into his mouth, she wrapped her arms around his neck. When she fisted her fingers into his hair, his responding growl intensified her growing internal fire.

When he pulled back and rested his forehead on hers, she couldn't help the moan that escaped. Her man was a fantastic kisser. He was also superb at distracting her. Slowing her breathing, she stared into his molten eyes. She couldn't help but smile when she realized their kiss affected him just as much as it did her.

Leaning into his touch, he held her cheek in his palm. She whispered her thanks.

"You're welcome, my girl. I've got you. Now let's get going."

Forming a circle, they held onto each other's hands. With a deep inhale, she closed her eyes and began reciting the spell. Willing with all her might that it worked.

In an ear-popping whoosh, they left Aramis's palace and then were standing in Cormac's tiny cabin.

She did it. Wow! She couldn't believe it. Looking around, she had to convince herself that they were here.

Garth's surprised, Shout.

"Holy Shit!"

Pulled her from her daze. Looking at him, she couldn't help the smile that spread across her face. Matching his grinning smirk.

"Girl, from now on I'm only traveling with you. Not Cormac. That was one smooth ride."

Caden's responding growl caused her to laugh. They all knew he was jesting. Still, the big man threw his arms up in the air in mock surrender.

"Hey, man. I know she's all yours. I only meant she's far better at that blinking travel thing than the old man is. Ok?"

The men shared eye contact till Caden sighed and relaxed. Nodding his head in agreement with Garth.

Rolling her eyes at their caveman's behaviors. Chuckling internally at the knowledge that this was how it was always going to be now. Still, it felt good.

Now they had to figure out what Garth had sensed they needed to be here so badly for. Then a plan of action. While also determining if anyone had noticed their absence.

They had all snuck away in the dead of night. Without a word to anybody. Doubts lingered about whom to trust. However, her internal voice was shifting. More so in a positive light regarding those they had left behind.

Which surprised her. Given the history with most of them. She should be on the cautious side. Was this her tapping into her new abilities? Perhaps.

Suddenly, a plan came to her. A knowing of sorts. Looking from Caden to Garth, she explained what she felt along with what they should do. They readily agreed and put the plan in motion.

It was a simple one. Waltz right back into their encampment. If what she suspected was true. Then they would have a plain explanation for their absence. They went searching for the missing prisoners.

How she knew they were gone, she wasn't sure. But they would claim they went looking and could not find them. Still, needing to keep Cormac a much-guarded secret was an overwhelming feeling. One, all three of them shared.

Also, worrying was how Jasper and his cronies escaped. And the same night they had left, too. Did they process the same gifts as Caden? Surely not. They would have seen or run into them that night. Wouldn't they?

A fail-safe in case her intuition was wrong. They planned to wait on hearing the speculation offered within the camp. Only then would they off up a confirmation.

Regarding the strategy of Seth's death, the plan was to make Jasper believe they had all fallen for his plan. Wanting to know what his actual plan was. It made sense to wait him out. Therefore, it would make sense for the three of them to sneak away in the dead of night and follow the men.

What scared her now was what was he going to do now that he was free? They had no way now of discovering his plans.

This worry filled them all as they trekked through the woods and back to camp. Only time will tell. Unless there was a gifted one among them within the camp that could know.

CHAPTER 29

*H*e couldn't stop the grin from spreading across his face. The view in front of him was too good to be true. A mass of people, double the count of that from the camp compound, were standing before him. All were waiting for his instruction.

Finally, things were going his way. As they rightfully should. Rubbing his hands together at his excitement. He couldn't help but imagine Caden's shocked expression. With this number of followers, he could finally take out that ever-so-smug Honor. Easily hurting Faxon in the process.

That man had taken everything from him, always had. First were the many advancements in classes and the True Guard. He even took his lover from him, too. How Sally could touch the leech he never understood. The last stab in the back was his taking Honor from him. Ultimately, his last betrayal, which he would pay for with his life. After he suffered first, of course.

The man had to pay for his crimes. He couldn't steal and get away with it. It was up to him to make sure all was just. He was a True Guard leader, after all. Finally, on his way to achieving his place as the True Overseer.

He could almost reach out and touch his dream, his birthright. Just thinking about it made him salivate. That and the fact that justice would finally be served. Now, however, work needed to be done.

Knowing the layout of the compound, the tech it possessed, and its weaponry, he had mapped out a plan to teach. These buffoons needed to be brought up to speed. And fast, if they were going to be of any use to him. They needed to know True Guard combat and armament. He would begin with intense drills. Weeding out the week and useless.

There was no time for babysitting. Even if these people were magick and nonmagick, he didn't care. They were here to serve his purpose. Regardless of what he told them. All simple-minded. Sure, he could talk a good game. But they followed him so easily. If only he had more time. He could have increased his numbers.

They only needed training enough to get him to his goal. Caden and Honor. After that, they were expendable. It didn't matter if they lived or died. He would prefer if they all died. If he were being honest, that would be easier. A simple means to an end.

What a glorious end it would be, too. He would have his team back. Well, some of them anyway. The disloyal ones, he would take great pride in, their discipline and eventual demise. Showing everyone what would happen when you weren't loyal.

Yes, things were finally going his way. Now time to get these idiots groomed. Thus, the tedious task of training began.

A two-week program. Filled with combat training and psychological grooming. He wanted to make sure that they maintained a complete focus on the task at hand. It wouldn't do to have any free thinkers among them.

The fact they all believed in him and his cause so readily and followed him here proved to him he could take things further. Making his goal that much easier to obtain in the end.

As the days progressed, he could see his plan was working. Far better than he even expected. Over time, he could distinguish who possessed gifts and who did not among them. Even if everyone claimed to be nonmagickal.

Having abilities was an asset when in combat. That was why he had sought the ones he had. The misfits of society. No one would miss them and he could easily brainwash them. Easily becoming his puppets.

The possibilities this created made him happy. Regardless of the cause, he spewed to get their allegiance. It would aid in his attack against the compound and Caden. If and when he needed to dispose of all members of this group, he could simply turn them on each other in the end. He wouldn't need to get his hands dirty.

That they had all aligned themselves with magick against magick was just comical to him. Further proving to him they were simply stupid. All of them put here for him to use.

It was near the end of the first week when he saw his last recruit. This one he knew was a magick. However, he couldn't get a full read on the guy. Still, like the others, he looked lost and full of anger. Something he could use to his advantage.

In the week that was left, he would easily whip his scrawny butt into shape. Adding one more to the cause.

HE HAD BIDED HIS TIME. Waiting and listening to the rumors. It wouldn't be wise to go rushing into a deal without a little research first.

The magick that had approached him in the bar had seemed legit. Even with his inflated sense of self.

Still, those were the types he liked to work with. They were so singularly focused they ignored all else around them. Including him.

Greedy types worked well for him. As a leech in the magick community. The literalness of that term always troubled him. Not liking how others described him. He couldn't help his requirement to siphon the power he needed constantly. Therefore, these types of being worked well for him.

Since he was a magick being with no magick ability. He could use magick if it was gifted to him. Hence, they referred to him as a leech among their kind. Alining himself with this tiny man would offer him many abilities. Giving him what he had worked so hard for. So much like the one he now set his sights on.

It was funny how alike they were. He had been as strong, viral, and forthcoming once. That was eons ago now. A time he would rather forget. Now, his sole focus was on survival and gaining power. The more the better.

So it wasn't any wonder when the rumors of missing persons running rapidly piqued his curiosity. He knew they weren't missing. At least not all of them. It was the curiosity about the cause and a desire to belong that had them flocking toward the requiter.

Still, the man was a mystery. Suddenly, appearing one day. No one seemed concerned enough to question. People embraced him with open arms. So much so that he and his travel companion were staying at a local farm. Even if its owner was an outcast himself. The village as a whole welcomed the pair.

So now he was trekking his way to the outskirts of town and to this dilapidated farm. A perfect location really for starting and training for a cause. What better place was there to start an army? That was what they were doing. He wasn't sure who their victims were yet.

That gave him cause for concern. Only because he didn't enjoy marching in and didn't know who he was fighting. The why of it never bothered him. He relished a good fight. Knowing one's enemy was key to besting them.

So now he would watch and learn. Hopefully, from a distance. He needed to be careful. Some might recognize him. After recent events, he did not possess enough strength to deal with any more trouble.

At least he would be able to still use the potion and spell power Ozel had left him. Even though it meant drinking the blood of a live victim. It wasn't something he relished doing. The taste of blood was revolting. However, the power boost he received from it was amazing.

It was the most powerful he had ever been. He experienced heightened senses like never before. With increased speed, strength, and magick abilities. If only it were permanent, and he didn't require the spell and potion.

He was running low on the potion. He had gained all the ingredients to make more. Only he could not create the brew. A magick with power had to. The sad kink in his otherwise magickal abilities. Perhaps he could convince his so-called new friend to do it for him?

It was the real reason he was heading to the farm. The one rumor spreading around was the demise of Briggs and Ozel's capture at the court of the shifters.

All of his hard word work was gone in one fell swoop. The years spent researching and recruiting taken. It was likely just as well. Lately Ozel was questioning and thinking for himself.

Neera made too much of an impact on him. Gaining his trust and loyalty away from himself. She took what was rightly his, anyway. She was to be the key to him, gaining all the power he had needed. Only she wasn't the one from the prophecy.

She still served a purpose to him. The true key being discovered and flushed out. It was only a matter of time till he had his hands on her again. This time, he would simply take all he wanted from her.

As he neared the outer edges of the farm, he could hear grunts, groans, and shouts. The sounds of a battle going on. Interesting. Maybe more things were turning in his favor. Not only could he use them to create more potion. He could use them to gain Harlow.

Lucky for him, the back of the farm edged against a dense forest. Standing amongst the perimeter of trees, he watched and planned. He would observe finding those he would target. Liking his smarts, he smiled, unaware he was too was being observed. The willing victim of another plan.

CHAPTER 30

*I*t had been a week since they left Aramis's court. Returning to the compound. Other than their escapees, nothing had changed. People readily accepted their lies about their absence. Which left a foul taste in his mouth. He didn't like lying or that his people accepted it so easily.

Or had they? As the week progressed, it appeared as though they all knew they had told a tale about their whereabouts and accepted it. Why, he wondered, had they done that? Garth had reassured him it was fine.

He was their leader. They all respected and followed him. As such, they only needed to know what he willingly divulged. Which he guessed was true. Only he didn't like running his team like that.

Which again, both Honor and Garth reminded him. He was their leader. There was no longer a True Guard. That was in their past. They were now forging ahead. Into a new future. One in which they hopefully could change the outcome.

There was also why Garth had felt the need to return immediately. He couldn't explain it himself. Only that he had woken up with the undeniable urge to return to the compound and them as well. It was the strangest thing he said. The all-knowing feeling. All he could compare it to was his ability to know lies from truths. It had been similar and completely different at the same time.

Life in the compound had gone on as if all were normal this week. Well, that was not entirely true. They needn't worry about leaving the meetings early and missing out on important information. He had been able to attend, so to speak, through his sister. With their shared connection and other gifts, it was as if he were there.

Their shared connection became even stronger. He could hear, smell, and touch everything in the room. Which still creeped him out. This gift was nice and all, but he didn't enjoy being this close to his twin. Thankfully, they each needed to be open and willing to have that level of communication.

Still, it was yet another thing to get used to. Despite the overwhelming nature of it all, the mating connection he shared with Honor helped ground him. Their daily growing bond helped to discover all how his new abilities grew and developed. They seemed to expand at random. Though he suspected he was finally just accepting of his true self. Why he felt a sense of growing turmoil since arriving here, he was suspecting was yet another gift he possessed. Not an internal war of self.

This internal six sense, as he now liked to call it, had a familiar sense to it. So very much like the connection he shared with Harlow. He knew it was not a link to Rowan. So who then could it possibly be he wondered? The idea baffled him. Other than their mates, it was only the three of them for family.

They learned the answers over time, like most things around here. Which he was grateful they had an abundance of. Not having the stress and worry over the planet's imminent death. They were fortunate not to have the stress and worry of searching for a cure or solution to save what remained of humanity.

As a whole; they agreed they had been sent or had arrived back here to address their plight in the future. Now they took stock of local and current events. Mapping out what could have possibly happened and what they might do about it.

It was all linked. They were now connecting the dots. Which was made even easier with his twin bond. It seemed Ravens Night could finally fulfill the prophecy. The current and future members are all gathered together now. The puzzle pieces were starting to fit together.

Through his twin connection, they had learned of the prophecy and Neera. They found out how Harlow was involved in it all. Her and Rowan's kidnapping. Their escape and how Brigg's bite combined with his nephew's magick ability meant that he, too, was now a shifter.

He was thankful for all Cora had done to prepare him. Her sharing of stories, tales, and memories. They had always resonated with him. Deep down the feeling of connection to magick, magickal creatures and beings. Cementing a sense of truth and understanding. Even if at the time it seemed fanciful and idiotic.

Now he understood the connection between all living things. His Ture Mate, being an Oracle, helped him immensely. Even if she too was discovering how along with him. They realized sadly that in the future, the planet dying meant so too had all their magickal gifts. They were a symbiotic relationship. Neither could survive without the other. Just like a True Mating bond.

Understanding that and practicing it were two different things. So he had insisted all within the compound practice their said gifts regularly while also learning to respect and be thankful for all that surrounded them. Starting now, they all would protect all living things. Very much inspired by the mission set out by the ancestors of their race of Gods.

Everyone resonated with Kieran's brief history of their people, liking some while shocked at others. It had been challenging at first when he connected with Harlow. He didn't expect the experience to be intense. Not to mention the overwhelming feelings he felt at hearing all the stories. Knowing now who they were, and descended from, helped form a sense of pride within the new compound.

A loyalty amongst themselves and to all magickal beings. A desire to protect all life was the foundation and the plan moving forward. The idea of creating a sanctuary was forming. It would serve as a foundation for all governing knowledge as well.

Their first order of business was to assist Aramis and the remaining trifecta of rulers of the shifter kingdom. The aftermath of Brigg's attack on Rowan involved and affected many. While also addressing the creation of another leader, the young Faxon was a predominant Alpha in his own right.

Wherever his nephew roamed, all bowed before him. Sensing his power and strength. He himself had sensed it. During one of the many connections with Harlow, for various meetings, Rowan's entrance into the room packed a power punch. A vibration so powerful, like the one he felt when he had conceited with his sister again for the first time.

She and her True Mate Kieran were now the eternal Goddess and God of all. The aura that surrounded them was stunningly beautiful and extremely powerful. Well deserved, in his opinion. Though he suspected it also had a something to do with who Kieran's father was.

Reading between the lines and watching Cormac's reactions to his brother-in-law's stories. He suspected his hunch was correct. However, that was a mystery to solve another day.

It was now about how to integrate another alpha into the mix. The shifter kingdom already had the leadership of the trifecta. They had no need for another.

He had suggested that his nephew take the rule of those who didn't fit in. The misfits of the shifter community and govern them within Kieran's old kingdom. The one that Aidan now ruled.

To him, it made sense, as that was where most of them ended up, anyway. Welcomed under the protection of the Gods. It was also the home base for Ravens Night and its operations. That he had kept to himself. It is a secret society and all. However, he had felt Harlow's agreement on the latter. Liking the idea of her son being near and having a home. She wanted her family close to her.

The plan for tomorrow was to discuss, finally, the meaning of Rowan's words, "He's Coming." This had been the initial reason for the meeting. However, other things needed to be dealt with first. Plus, they had all decided some backstory was necessary before he broached the meaning of his words.

Hopefully, then the planning process word be easier and quicker. That was the plan, anyway. But when does anything ever go to plan?

SHE COULD TELL her Mate was exhausted. The daily task of connecting with his twin and attending the meeting while also relaying in real time to her and Garth took a toll. One in which every night this week had the two of them going to bed early and falling instantly asleep wrapped in each other's arms.

Waking each morning and performing the same routine. It was hard to be amazed anymore. With so many involved in the meetings, they discussed everything at length. Encouraging everyone always to share their opinions and provide input into various solutions. It was progress for sure. But tedious and boring.

With the dynamics of power shifting, everyone wanted to work together, moving forward. The division they experienced in the past was partially to blame for the events. Perhaps, if they had been more informed and formed an alliance, they could have experienced a different outcome.

They then discussed the formation of a unit that would cater to or function as a go- between. She and Garth had shared a questioning look when Caden had shared that information. He had the oddest look on his face. Plus, she would have sworn she had heard him laugh.

Why he found that funny, she couldn't tell. It was an excellent idea. A group or society with members representing each kingdom and each magickal creature or being. With the responsibility of conveying information to and from each court. While also maintaining a fair and just representation for all magickal and nonmagickal alike.

It sounded very much like they were describing the True Guard. That was the reason for its creation in the beginning. Or at least that was the history written about them. Now, however, the group was the personal policing unit for the Overseer. What sets this group apart is its secrecy, known only to its members and the rulers. The selection would be decided by Harlow and Kieran, rulers of each kingdom.

It was a unanimous decision to proceed with its creation, but had yet Rowan to reveal his meaning and warning of his vogue statement. It was difficult for the poor man to cope with his transition. Thankfully Aramis has taken him under his wing. Teaching him what he knew and giving him ways to deal with all the changes within him.

What surprised her was that he was personally seeing to Rowan's education. The two of them seemed to form a genuine friendship. Her fondness for the ruler was growing. The Faxons deserved to have some good karma come their way. It had to be hard to form proper healthy friendships when you're cast as an outsider by the community. She knew the lesson well herself.

While she now had her true Mate and Harlow had hers. It was great to see that Rowan would have a close bond with someone. If only a good friend. Everyone needed someone.

Her woman's intuition was telling her he would need this friendship going forward. That he too would soon find his true Mate. First, though, he needed to reveal his information. The anticipation of this was building at an enormous rate.

Thankfully, everyone was understanding and caring for the delay. Reassuring he needn't rush his recovery to reveal his information. As time passed, however, human nature meant they all began to speculate. Each tale becoming worse and more out there.

All seemed to center on the Overseer and his nefarious plans. The man had a way of playing people and granting his wishes. It was no wonder he was their number one culprit. They warned against speculating too much. As clearly, Rowan had come through the arch much older than when they had all left him. He had been fifteen and just entered final training for the True Guard.

Shaking off her rememberings, she rolled into her Mate. Burrowing her nose into his chest and inhaling his scent. They deserved to have time for just themselves. She knew he was awake when he tightened his arms around her. The sense of security and his intoxicating smell had her dampening below. This man could make her wet in no time at all.

Most times, all she had to do was look at him or even think of him, and she was instantly moistening her panties. Moaning, she started kissing a trail down his sculpted chest.

In a sexy and groggy timber,

"Good morning. Is my girl hungry?"

Smiling, she looked at his eyes, nodding her head. Watching as they darkened with desire. She slowly made her way down his body, kissing as she went. She could feel his muscles tightening as his breathing quickened.

When she reached his large, and weeping member, she wrapped her fingers around him. Grinning when he swore under his breath. Pleased she could affect him so, she opened her mouth, taking him in. Moaning the moment his salty, manly flavor hit her tongue. Tightening her lips around him and drawing to the back of her throat, she swallowed.

"Christ woman."

He all but shouted, raising his hips and driving himself deeper. His hands went instantly to the back of her head. Holding her there as he gripped her hair. As he ground himself into her, with her chin now resting against him. She had to breathe through her nose.

His total domination of her turned her on. She could feel her wetness dripping down her thighs. Moaning once more, she swallowed around him. The instant she did, he bucked his hips forward, sending himself further down her throat.

Wanting to send him over the edge. She sucked as hard as could before swallowing once more. Looking up at him when he howled his instant release. He was pulling her hair at the roots while she continued to swallow every last drop he gave her.

He startled her by flipping her while she was licking him clean. Before she could blink, her knees were at her chest and his head between her legs. She could not finish his name when he licked her from rosebud to nub before biting down. Her orgasm hit her like a tidal wave.

Reaching around her legs, she grabbed his head like he had hers. Riding out her pleasure. He continued to lick her, holding her lips open. He fucked her with his tongue. Before he moved lower, rimming her back hole.

When he pulled back to look at her, she could only utter a garbled, "No."

A mischievous smirk spread across his face as he placed one hand on her belly, holding her still. With his other, he slowly entered her with his fingers. Two in her rear, two in her core. Pressing heavy with his thumb on her burning nub.

His voice purred as said.

"My girl likes to come for me. Doesn't she?"

While his face was soft and loving, his eyes bored into hers, compelling an answer. Licking her lips, she could only whisper.

"Yes, Caden."

His only reply was a nod of his head before he held her firm and fucked her with his fingers. He continued to murmur praise and encouragement. Very quickly, she was cumming again and again. When it became too much, she tried to pull away. Shaking head back and forth.

"No Caden. No more."

With a devilish smile, he said.

"Yes, Honor. You can. One more for me. Then you can have my cock."

She still was shaking her head when he continued.

"You do want my cock. Don't you, my girl?"

Unable to deny him, she nodded her head.

"That's my girl."

She watched as he lowered his head. Wrapping his lips around her nub, he sucked hard while increasing the rhythm of his fingers. When he bit down, she screamed, flying into oblivion.

Once again, she was flying. Landing on her belly, Caden made quick work of lifting her knees before running his now engorged cock through her wet lower lips. The groan of pleasure that left her was quieter than her wetness.

Embarrassed, she borrowed her face into the covers, hearing his laughter.

"It's good to know I can get my girl good and wet for me."

Gripping her hips firmly with his hands, he lined himself up to her entrance, saying.

"Brace yourself. You may cum whenever you want."

With that, he slammed into her. Fucking her hard. When he hit her cervix, she came screaming his name. One orgasm led quickly into another and another. She lost count of how many when Caden lowered, wrapping himself around her. Placing a finger hard on her nub in gentle circles. Using his other hand, he wrapped his fingers around her neck and squeezed.

He issued a simple command to "Come" as he pinched her clit and bit down on her neck. Her body responded before her brain processed the command and she shattered into a million pieces. She could feel his cum exploding inside her, before leaking out and running down her leg.

CHAPTER 31

*H*e couldn't believe the plan they were about to execute was brilliant, simple, and something he should have thought of. When their newfound member had mentioned it casually while in conversation. Everyone raved at its wisdom.

This man who refused to give his name was content to sit back and watch all the action.

Continually offering hints and making suggestions on how to do or approach something. Never once acknowledged that this group of followers were not his. Nor that he hadn't put in all the legwork of recruiting these idiots either.

It royally pissed him off. That, yet again, someone was taking credit for all his hard work. Damn it! Now they were all hanging onto every word, this nameless man said. He was beginning to regret offering him a position within the group.

Still, he was a magick and one of them. He knew all kinds of powers, dark and light. Anything they needed access to, he provided. Like a walking library. At first, when he arrived, he had hoped simply to pry the man of his intelligence.

He should have known better. A man with so much knowledge wouldn't offer it freely for long. Sometime soon he would want his due diligence. It was only a natural thing to do. However, he had not expected this.

Nevertheless, he would allow the double cross to go. Eventually, he would get what he always desired. His rightful position of Overseer. The men and women from his time would be under his rule. Ready and willing to do all he commanded of them.

Like taking over the compound and all the surrounding towns and villages. All magicks and nonmagicks alike would cater to his every need. It was only a matter of time.

The smile that spread across his face reached his eyes this time. It would all be happening soon. Thanks to the plan, they were all about to execute. He eagerly anticipated seeing the expression on Caden's smug face when he realized who had done it.

Looking around, he took in the small one-room cell they had created. It was a room built of stone deep within the ground. After casting a magick spell on each stone, they placed them together to create one massive spell. One that would not allow its resident to use their gifts. All the while siphoning the prisoner's power.

He couldn't wait till he had their prisoner here. The list of questions he had was growing at a steady rate. Any advantage he could gain and use over the Faxons was a blessing. Not to mention the joy he would have of finally taking his anger out on their upcoming prisoner. It would be long overdue justice being served for crimes.

Not having access to any powers within the room, he was grateful for his godlike strength. It would give him the upper edge when questioning and dueling out punishment.

All that remained was to prepare for accepting their new guest. As Cory was going to be providing their prisoner with transportation, they needed a room he could blink to. One that was close enough to the underground cell and allowed for the use of magicks. Where they could receive the new guest before hurrying them to their temporary new home.

He had no intention of allowing this person to live. After he had gotten all he wanted from them, he would gladly turn them over to their nameless member. The skeletal man said he had use of a magickal being. Once he finished, there would be no need for him to dispose of anything.

It had creeped him out just thinking about what he might be doing. However, in the end, he simply didn't care. Less for him to do. Nothing for him to worry about.

Trekking his way through the back portions of the farm they had commandeered, he made it to the landing pad. It was what they had dubbed the location with which Cory would use for blinking. This man's gift was coming in handy, that's for sure.

He had been making regular trips in and out of their old compound. Taking anything of value. Plus all the things they needed here. Using magick, they had created a compound to rival the other one. The land here was far larger. Plus, he now knew all the secret places they had created. It made sense to stay here. Hence, Cory's repeated trips for pilfering.

They had accumulated quite the stash now. Impressing many of the locals with new technologies and more. He wasn't worried about news spreading and going against the True Guard code. He was the true leader now and what he said goes. If any of these beings survived till the end of his conquest, they would be his servants anyway.

The sun was just rising over the horizon when he reached the entrance. Opening the door, he stepped over the threshold. This room, too, was just as cold and dark as the other. Its door on the opposite side leads down and into the single prison cell.

From what he could see, it was time. They were ready to welcome their guest.

CHAPTER 32

*H*e watched Honor as she snored softly beside him. Last night he wore her out, taking her every way he could. Sex with her was too good. It was never enough. Smiling, he ran the back of his finger down her cheek.

Despite being asleep, she couldn't help but feel drawn to him. She turned into his touch, purring in pleasure.

Bending, he gently pressed his lips to her forehead. Lingering there for a moment. He couldn't seem to get enough kisses, either.

Rising from the bed, he went into their wet room to get ready for today. Turning on the spray for the shower, he waited while the temperature warmed. This week of telekinetic connecting to his sister so he could attend the meetings was exhausting.

To maintain the connection, it required lots of concentration. Not to mention power. He needed to increase his food intake and start meditating. Just so he could maintain any sense of normal. His true Mate was also a godsend. She knew exactly what he needed and when.

Stepping into the shower; he tilted his face toward the water spray. Enjoying the warm water trickling down his face. Allowing himself to zone out, he washed on autopilot. Enjoying the refreshing steam building around him.

He wanted to do something nice for Honor. He planned to ask his sister what she would recommend. As much as another sexcapade would be appreciated, he wanted to do something for her that no one had ever done. Having grown up an orphan, she wasn't lucky enough to have a sibling like he was.

There were a few things he was thinking about doing for her as a surprise. He was second-guessing himself. Plus, with their mating bond, it was hard to surprise her. He could hopefully keep it a surprise by gaining Harlow's help and advice.

After stepping out of the shower, he reached for a towel and dried off, only to feel a wave of terror wash over him. Before he could move, he heard Honor scream in fright.

"HONOR,"

He shouted while racing to get to her. Someone was in their pod that didn't belong. As he ran, he could hear a scuffle and dishes crashing. They were in the kitchenette. Why wasn't his Mate using her gifts and disappearing from their pod and going to Cormac's cabin?

Could it be that she knew the who was attacking her?

He was just rounding the corner when he heard her shout his name.

"CADEN,"

When suddenly she was gone. He knew it before he was standing in the middle of the abandoned chaos. A loud bang of the front door exploding in saw Garth rushing in and demanding.

"What happened?"

Holding up a finger. Pausing briefly, he surveyed all the wreckage. Reaching out through their connection, he could feel her fear. Then, in a flash, there was nothing. She was gone. Which told him she was not the one to have taken them wherever it was they were now.

Looking at his friend while he spoke.

"We had a visitor who took Honor. I can no longer sense her."

He watched as concern and anger crossed over the other man's face.

"Your sister is still with Cormac, right? Link with her. Tell her what has happened. Perhaps they can help."

Closing his eyes, he tried to calm down as he connected with his twin. His Mate was in trouble.

"Harlow,"

Relief filled him when she answered immediately.

"What's happened, Caden?"

"Are you with everyone for the meetings?"

'Yes, we are. What do you need?"

Relaxing slightly, he continued the conversation while watching Garth taking in the destruction. Relaying everything that happened, saw Garth sniff the air and a few of the splayed items across the floor. Was he scent tracking? He snapped his head up, growling in anger. Through clenched teeth, he said,

"Cory."

Shocked, he too joined in with a growl.

"What is it? What happened, Caden?"

"Cory is the one responsible for kidnapping, Honor. Garth just scented him."

He heard his sister's shocked gasp. Before saying any more, Harlow urged him to continue his efforts to try to reach out to her. Cormac insisted, reassuring it was going to be possible. Harlow also informed him Aramis was readying a small battalion to travel along with them.

"We're coming, brother mine. Kieran is gearing up along with Aramis."

Just as he was about to ask.

"The meetings will wait, Caden. Your Mate is more important."

After a pause, she continued.

"Remember, Caden, she is powerful in her own right. With her training, she can handle herself. Have faith in her."

Her words helped to calm him. After his shock had worn off. He knew his sister was right. He, therefore, channeled his energy into his anger instead. Looking at Garth, he said.

"They are coming with Aramis and a small battalion."

The enormous man in front of him eased up a bit and then called over another teammate by snapping his fingers. Shouting orders and demands. After an instant, a multitude of members rushed into the pod, using their unique gifts.

Shaking his head to regain his focus. He took a deep breath to calm his waring insides. In case Honor messaged him, he wanted to know the moment it happened. He could only surmise she was unconscious.

Hence the no contact. That he couldn't sense her whereabouts there must be magick involved.

Looking at Garth.

"Have everyone readied and waiting in the main building."

Without pausing for a reply, he entered the bedroom and proceeded to grab and pull articles of clothing from various drawers. Inhaling deeply, he made another effort to reach out to Honor. After discovering nothingness, he ground his teeth while getting dressed. After finishing, he stormed from their pod while cursing Jasper and his crazy puppets.

Enough was enough. He was going to end this once and for all. He used his stupid cronies to do his bidding and take his Mate. She has done nothing to deserve the treatment she received at Jasper's hands.

Honor wasn't the only one to gain the ability to travel in a blink. Cory has the same gift as well. However, he doubted he possessed the same Oracle abilities his Mate and Cormac had. It would explain how Jasper and he had escaped, plus all the gear and supplies that had gone missing.

Their dining hall was about to become the war room. One in which he would soon share everything. All the treacherous deeds of former team members. As well as all the new friends and allies they formed. They were no longer alone in the world and would soon host their new friends and family.

Preparations needed to be made. Suddenly, he heard the faint whisper,

"*Caden.*"

. . .

HOLY CRAP, she hurt. What the hell had happened to her? Why did she feel as if she had been in battle? Taking a moment, she tried to recall recent events. The last she remembered was waking up to an empty bed and hearing the shower running.

Realizing Caden was in the shower, she had debated following him. Instead, she made them breakfast and coffee. After their sexcapades the night before, a good stiff brew would help. It wouldn't cure the aches and pains, but it could help with the concentration.

She liked the idea of walking around smelling like him. Wearing all his love bites with pride. Her Mates inner cave man would love it. The percolator beeping pulled her from her thoughts.

As she was finishing pouring two steaming cups, someone grabbed her from behind. Freezing in fear for only a moment had cost her. As to had the shattering mugs filled with scalding liquid. Giving her captor the upper hand. Try as she might, she remembered fighting hard. Giving it her all with her True Guard training and her newfound Oracle skills. Her captor ultimately gained the upper hand.

They both had disappeared in a blink. When she felt a sharp prick in the neck followed by a burning sensation before blackness overcame her.

She briefly remembered calling out to Caden. After that, there was nothing. She felt scared. What was happening?

Blinking, she tried in vain to look around her. All she could see was inky blackness. With fear rising, she reached out with her hand, waving it in front of her eyes. Again, nothing. Taking a moment, she tried to breathe deeply and slowly to calm her rising panic. It was important to stay calm and focused.

Using her newfound gifts to sense her surroundings. Wherever she was, was below ground in a room constructed of stone and magick. Dark magick too. How she could tell the difference, she wasn't sure. But it felt icky and wrong to her. Thankfully, with some concentration, she could push past it. Even if someone meant it to restrict her.

It had been a wise decision to keep who and what she was a secret. This prison wouldn't hold her for long. It simply would slow her down. Knowing she would still need help, she needed to send as much info as she could to her Mate.

Closing her eyes and taking stock of everything magick and nonmagick alike. She was lying on a stone-cold floor. In a small room big enough for two, maybe three people, max. The chamber was deep beneath the ground with a tunnel leaving it. Leading to another, even smaller room which exited to the outside world.

Three to five persons executed the magick. She wasn't positive, though. It was also dark and tabu spells. Quite possibly, old and feared magicks. Its knowledge had come from one being and one alone. Who that was, she didn't know. It was not someone she had met before.

However, Jasper and Cory had touched this place all over. It had been Cory who had blinked them here for Jasper to drug her. With what, she wasn't sure. It was a drug from their time, but someone had also touched it with magick. Leaving a funny taste on her tongue.

Compiling all this information into a massive visual bundle, she blasted it toward Caden. She was going to need his help to get out of here wherever here was. Hopefully, her Mate would hear her. This was a magick-protected prison.

Before she could try again to send her message, the door slammed open. The torchlight in the person's hand blinded her. Gasping in pain, she raised her hand to cover her eyes. While scurrying backward and away from them.

Her movements were so fast that she slammed her the back of her head onto the stone wall. Causing her to cry out in pain once more. Holding her head in her hands, she allowed silent tears to fall as she took deep breaths. It was imperative she remain focused at all times.

That was her last thought before an evil laugh broke through the air, and a vicious beating ensued.

CHAPTER 33

*U*pon entering, he had been tossing between anger and helplessness. Yet, as he looked at the faces of those gathered, he felt overwhelmed by a tidal wave of emotion. Standing in front of everyone in the main building, he was pleading for their help.

Watching, he could see they were on the edge of their seats, listening to him. Some were gripping their seats so tight in frustration their knuckles were now white. Others standing with such force their chairs toppled backward as they paced.

His mate's life was at stake. He would do anything to help her. Including pleading for help.

"I need your guy's help."

Ashamed, he tilted his head as he rubbed his hand over his face.

Garth's timber voice echoed through the room.

"Caden, we'll do anything to bring your Mate and our teammate home. Won't we?"

As a unanimous "Hell yes" reverberated through the room, he snapped his head up. Looking into the eyes of all gathered in front of him. Each person nodded their head in total agreement. Everyone gathered sympathized with him.

Slumping his shoulders. He could only whisper his thanks.

"Thank you."

His new friend's massive hand rested on his shoulder, offering a squeeze of support. Looking at him, he offered a nod of thanks in reply.

Watching in an emotional daze as Garth took over. Explaining what had happened this morning. How Cory could blink travel from one place to another, how he had come and taken Honor. Likely was the one to steal all their other missing items too.

Just the mention of the other man's name caused outrage and anger. How one of them could treat a fellow member with such disregard and a woman, too? Many shouted that they were to be protected and cherished.

Scanning the room, he saw many of them turning purple with rage. As they murmured, you never took a Mate from their partner. That just was not done. It amazed him how much this team had naturally picked up his mating connection with Honor. They had never announced their bonding. That they all knew, however, amazed him. He was still adjusting to this world of magick. It would make sense that they could feel his bonding with her.

He had done the same when he encountered Harlow and Kieran. Immediately knowing they were a bonded pair. The magick entwined and vibrated through them as one unit. You could see, smell, and taste it. Yet, they were each an individual too.

His heart warmed as he took in everyone. Remembering that once they entered this time, they all altered their perception of Honor. Like they finally opened their eyes. While others expressed their acceptance openly despite Jasper's distaste. Others remained quietly supportive of her.

Why the man had it in for her was anyone's guess. Many had forwarded their guesses, and that was all they had. Only speculations of why he had gone to such lengths.

Unlike his hatred of the Faxons as a whole. That dislike, he had always broadcast loud to anyone and everyone. Whether or not they wanted to hear. It was common knowledge of his jealousy. So his behavior now was both in and out of character for him.

Honor was the person always in the background, performing the tasks with skills that outweighed everyone else. So underutilized. So much like his sister Harlow. The similarities between the two of them were eerily similar. Most of the members of her True Guard team at least saw the real woman. They were now willing to go to bat for her.

All because of her. Not because of him and who he was. The leader of this small magickal compound. Or that they were a Mated pair. It was who she was. The kind and loving, supportive woman who held this team together in the background.

Pulling himself from his internal remembering, he shook his head. Allowing the energy of those around him to flow through and around him. Inhaling deep, he closed his eyes. With his new gifts, well, they weren't new per se, but still. His natural born talents he was learning to embrace.

He would use and store this energy for later. He would need it. Of that, he was positive.

Now that everyone had voiced their outrage, they were demanding what the plan was. How to get their leader's true Mate back. While simultaneously giving karma to Jasper and Cory.

Thankful for their combined faith and camaraderie, he raised his hand. Hushing the crowd.

"Thank you."

He choked on his words. His emotions were running high.

"I am touched and honored by your loyalty and support."

He took a moment to look each of them in the eye.

"Mark my words. We will find and bring my Mate home. Together as a united family, we will bring justice to all."

A hush swept through the room like a soft summer breeze. All eyes fixated on him. Their bodies relaxed and attuned to his movements. Was this another of his gifts? He wondered.

Shaking off the thought. It was now time to share all that they knew. Together, he and Garth filled them in on Harlow and her true Mate Kieran. Also explaining the connection to the locals and the overall basis of their ruling system. How this past week the leaders had gathered together to discuss current events and recommendations for changes.

Their appearance in this time had changed events. Causing

happenings that now required significant changes. Decisions that included everyone. It had been why the three of them had been so busy and yet absent at the same time.

Addressing them, he said.

"We have not yet finished the meetings. Therefore, I don't have all the information to give to you."

After several nods and mummers,

"Not a problem. You'd tell us what we need to know when we need to know it."

The room seemed to hum as one the more he and Garth spoke. Explaining that one ruler would come to aid them, along with his family. Minus Rowan, who was still in need of recovery. A small battalion would accompany them.

Their unanimous outrage on Rowan's behalf didn't surprise him. His surprise came when they also insisted on being allowed to exact revenge on those responsible. Also further expressing they were thankful his nephew was getting the care he needed to recover.

Overall, he was happy with how this impromptu gathering had gone. They accomplished so much. Not only had he filled them all in on the past events, but he learned so much more about theirs and their respective talents.

They now had a plan semi-put together based on what they knew and their many gifts applied. Leaving room for alterations when the aid finally arrived. He had used his link to talk to Harlow to help in forming a rough outline of a plan.

With all the support, his confidence was growing, and he truly felt blessed. That was until his Mate sent him a message. One that had him falling to his knees and gasping for air.

. . .

HOLY SHIT! She hurt everywhere. From her tippy toes to the top of her head. What the hell was wrong with that man?

The first time he came to see her in her little prison cell, shocked her. The beating she had received comprised kick after kick. He only bent down to grab her by the hair, holding her as he kicked her some more.

Not once had he said a word. Or even made a sound. Only his deep, even breathing filled the tiny stone room. After finishing with her, he turned abruptly and slammed the door on his way out.

His second visit started with the door hinges creaking as it slowly opened and his question.

"Now, how is the princess doing? Better, I hope."

Then he pulled her up again by her hair. She cried out in pain as he ripped some of it out. Shoving her against the cold, hard wall, he swung his arm back, slapping hard across the cheek. The pain filling her head made her dizzy. Licking her lip and tasting blood., before turning to look at her captor. Asking.

"Why? Why are you doing this, Jasper?"

He had only stared at her with vacant eyes before an eerie smile crossed his face.

She could help but ask her next question.

"What have I ever done to you?"

She couldn't fathom why she was receiving such treatment from him. Each time he stuck her, he seemed to grow stronger. As much as this hurt, it scared her he was getting something from it. He seemed to know when she was about to pass out or give up. He would abruptly stop and leave.

She would collapse into a heap on the floor and sleep a healing sleep. As best she could, anyway. It took a lot out of her to heal in this prison cell. It was taking its toll.

She was losing count of the multitude of visits. He hadn't spoken a word outside of that second visit. However, each time, he would use a unique method of beating her. Everything from his feet, hands, fists, and even his fingernails.

At some point, she wasn't sure when she had realized she could siphon some of his energy to help heal herself. It seemed only fair. He was taking from her, so she gathered what she could from him. It meant that their meeting was now shorter in length. Sadly, it also meant there were more of them.

Still, she wanted to stay alive. She wanted more time with her Mate. A life filled with love and, hopefully, children one day. He gave her a reason to be sneaky. Carefully using her gifts in a room created to stop just that.

Despite the reduction in her powers, Jasper had not yet realized that she could still access and use them. If he had, she was positive she would be dead already.

Why he had such a hatred for her that seemed to grow with each visit she could not fathom. She had asked repeatedly, never getting an answer. As frustrated as she was, she had long ago stopped asking.

She was also unsure of how long she had been here. With the repeated Jasper visits, followed by her napping sessions, she had lost track of time. She focused her remaining energy on healing herself and gaining as much strength as possible.

Not wanting to worry Caden, she refused to contact him again. Praying her last message was enough to get the ball rolling. That he could gather enough forces to come and get her. Knowing Japer as she did, he wouldn't like to get his hands dirty. Allowing others to do his dirty work for him.

However, his treatment of her lately was proving otherwise. Now he seemed all too happy to get his hands dirty. Each time he had entered her tiny prison; he was happier than the last visit.

It was turning her stomach just thinking about it. What happened to him to make him this way? Was it coming here and losing Sally the way he had down something to his brain?

Usually, he was waking her up as he entered the cell. This time, however, she was waking on her own. Had much time passed? Or was she healing herself better and faster than before? Maybe that was it. She hoped.

Perhaps something had happened topside? Could her Mate have come to her rescue already? She doubted it. That shared connection they had was weak, if at all present. He wasn't close by. So something else must have happened then.

Well, if that was the case, then maybe she should allow her body more rest and healing. She was definitely going to need it. Of that, she was positive.

CHAPTER 34

*T*hings were finally flowing in his favor once again. He had an endless supply of willing victims to his sustaining spell. If only it didn't repulse him so much. Drinking the life of another, yuck. As foul as it was, its taste was growing on him. The more intense the magick in any creature, the sweeter it tasted.

The cumbersome spell it required each and every time was getting old. He wished there was a way to circumvent it. Nevertheless, it was serving its purpose and then some.

Looking in the mirror this morning, he had noticed he was starting to look like his old self. That dashing young man who could get anything he wanted whenever he wanted it. Things were looking up.

Despite the negatives, he was willing to overlook them because of this side benefit. He even contemplated not seeking out a more gifted magick to make alterations to the spell process. However, in the end, he wanted the process to be more streamlined and, shall we say, quicker.

At the moment, his focus needed to be on his host. He was becoming obsessed with their latest prisoner. Coming and going at odd times. Often wearing an eerie smile. For him to say he thought the man was eerie was saying something. That was usually his crown to bear.

So this was how he found himself following the man into one of the newly created prison cells. However, this one had the blessing of magick. More magick than he had ever seen before. It made him wonder what kind of creature the stone walls held within.

This was the reason for all the repeated questioning about his magickal knowledge. Using all the spells and positions during construction. He hadn't assumed they would amass it all into one single cell. Now he was even more intrigued.

Entering the cold and damp space, it took a moment for his eyes to adjust to the lack of light. As they descended through the tunnel, he could sense the energy shift. Staring at the back of his host's head, he wondered if he too could feel it, or was he oblivious? The man had been down here so many times before.

The power of the magick was far greater than he had expected. Who were these people? How had he not sensed all this power before, above ground? Or did this magick belong to the guest within? If so, it was his lucky day.

Smiling to himself, he followed quietly. Thanking the stars, he had convinced his host to let him come too. They had promised him this prisoner at the end of their usefulness. It was only fair he was present for integration.

So he was taken aback when they entered the tiny stone room and Japer abruptly reared back, slapping the woman awake. She whined, curling into a protective ball.

The tiny thing didn't stand a chance. Her abuser grabbed her by the hair, lifting her while demanding.

"Stand up dam it."

The poor woman, suffering from a clear concussion, struggled to focus her eyes on the man in front of her. Still, she processed more magick than he had sensed in a being in a long time. Well, that wasn't entirely true. Only a short time ago, he had another powerful being within his grasp. Alas, she had escaped. On her own, no less.

It took a lot to impress him. That woman certainly had. One day, he would find her again and take from her what he wanted. For now, though, the woman in front of him would do nicely.

Crossing his arms, he leaned his shoulder against the wall. Content to watch and listen.

A spitting Jasper was talking at the poor woman.

"Not so smug, are you now?"

He was shaking her, rattling her brain even more. He was sure of it. What he couldn't understand was the way the woman needed to be treated like this. He was sure it wasn't necessary. Well, other than Japer's pleasure. The man was getting off on every slap, punch, and kick he inflicted.

Still curious, he asked,

"What has she done to deserve such a treatment?"

To his surprise, the woman before him looked right at him. The strength he saw there stole his breath. Jasper's growl pulled him from an almost revelation.

"This bitch has taken everything from me. Always has."

The annoying man then began to pound some flesh. Wanting to give the woman a break. If she died, she wouldn't be of any use to him. He needed her alive to drain her life force power into himself. So he kept Jasper talking.

Appearing nonchalant, he inspected his fingernails as he asked.

"What has she always taken from you? I mean, she's only a woman. What could she possibly take from you?"

His host whipped his head around before turning to face him. When he did so, the poor woman dropped to the ground with a thud. Placing his hands on his hips, he angrily sputtered.

"Everything."

He couldn't help but laugh, further angering the man. Still, with a shrug of a shoulder, he asked.

"She take your virginity?"

This time, he held his laughter back. The man was growing increasingly red about the face.

"No, she did not take my virginity. She did, however, take my family from me."

A tiny, shocked gasp echoed around the cell. Clearly, this was a surprise to their guest. Ignoring her, he continued to focus on Jasper as he vomited his story.

The not-so-perfect woman, who was a member of his team.

Thinking to himself, whatever team that was, he didn't care. She had, for her entire life, been taking from him.

First, she had stolen his mother in childbirth. She had been told not to have any more children, but she had so wanted to have a little girl. So their father had granted his mother's wish. They had kept trying and finally, they were pregnant with her.

The pregnancy was rife with challenges for both mother and baby. When his mother made his father swear he was to protect their baby at all costs. He was furious when their father agreed so readily. Shouldn't a man protect a wife? Who cares about an unborn baby?

So after his mother died birthing her sick daughter, their father did everything to care for the child. Even forgoing caring for himself. He quite took his oath to his wife, literally. Making sure their daughter survived till the day he died.

His death was one year to the day of his beloved wife. Leaving behind all their children. Forcing all of them into permanent care of the boarding house. Why they had to live there and not in the grand house was her fault as well. The doctors recommended that she have her siblings around her because she needed too much care. That perhaps it might ease the job of the elders, having her family around her.

Instead, the Faxons lived within the grand house with the Overseer. Whoever the hell hat was. This man was a floodgate of information. Knowledge, it seemed, the woman on the floor did not know.

She stared wide-eyed at her assailant. Shock marring her facial features.

She whispered.

"You lie."

Shaking her head as if to dispel the knowledge.

However, he knew the man was speaking truths. He could tell. Like so many of their kind. He possessed some skills. Just not any of the active gifts most of their kind received. Hence, his travels down the road that lead him here to this place.

He snapped out of his remembering when Jasper shouted.

"It's no lie. You are my sister, Honor. The one that killed. Death follows you everywhere."

She was shaking her head in clear disbelief while he continued.

"It's true. Look at what happened to our brother. He's gone now too."

When she looked up at him, confused. Jasper pulled back and kicked her in the stomach.

"Clay died because of you, too."

Again, she was shaking her head. This time, though, when she spoke, it was cold.

"Clay is gone because he raped and beat Harlow, not because of me. There is no proof he is dead. Though he deserves it. That bastard."

Her statement renewed Jasper's anger. He once again hauled his hand back and slapped her hard. Her head whipped around, causing her to tumble backward from her sitting position.

Their interaction was interesting and informative. Found siblings, that hated each other. One is a jealous monster. The other was a powerful creature with more magick than he guessed she possessed. He suspected she was hiding most of it.

While also siphoning what she could from Jasper with slight and subtle touches here and there. The woman was smart and talented. It was wise for him to keep his mouth shut. For he wanted all her power for himself. If she could finish off his host herself, he would be ahead of the game.

Perhaps if things progressed as they were right now, all that would come to fruition. He could walk out of here a new man.

CHAPTER 35

*H*onor's message was full of pain and fear. At the same time, she had given them all the information she could. There was so much of it, he was having trouble sorting through it all. He experienced it as a mass jumble in his mind.

When he collapsed, Garth had been right there to break his fall. Meanwhile, another person from the group hurried towards him. Gabbing his hands. At the contact, he felt a wave of power exchange between them. Then suddenly his vision was playing between the two of them. As if it were on a screen.

So shocked by the experience, he pulled his hands free of the man's grip. He felt that someone was violating the bond between him and Honor. Their visions were private. Even though he knew that was not the man's intention. The goal was to help.

It worked too. This person could, and with the help of others, gain the location of his Mate's prison. But also give details on the unknown magick used.

Her Vision as scattered as it was, she managed to convey so much detail and information. Grateful for her ability to think on the fly in the face of danger. This knowledge would go a long way into assisting her.

When he looked at the man, ready to apologize, he insisted it was unnecessary. He understood Caden's reaction was based on a need to protect that which was special between True Mates. It was he who should apologize for violating it.

Acting on instinct, knowing that his talents could help. This mans gifts were like a Wi-Fi signal and a router combined. It was the best way to explain it. He could also confirm Honor was right about dark magicks being used in and around her prison cell. There were excellent reasons for forbidding them.

Not only did they require a sacrifice, but they also surrounded her to imprison her magick while simultaneously absorbing her life force. It was dire that they acted fast if they wanted to rescue her alive.

Hopefully, Aramis would have more knowledge of how to deal with this rare type of magick. If not him, then perhaps Cormac would know. He was coming with their entourage. The man had more knowledge than he let on. His fear was how could they rescue her without themselves falling victim to the magick of her prison cell.

In her vision, she sent, however; she was using her gifts. Was her magick stronger than that of the darker magicks? If so, perhaps his Mate would also possess the ancient knowledge. She was an Oracle just like the old man. Maybe it had something to do with the powerful gifts they processed.

Regardless of all the efforts put in and the information obtained, his panic was rising. The separation from his Mate was causing a physical ache. An ache that grew at a steady rate. Rubbing his chest, to ease the pain repeatedly, only garnered more staring go concern rather than relief. That she was in grave danger and with a man who hated her weighed heavily on him.

He kept running through past events. Wondering if he had done something or anything different could he have avoided this? He wanted, no, he needed, his Mate back.

A haze of red tinted his vision. He needed Honor by his side. Where she belonged. Hopefully, his sister and their friends were quick to travel. So they could all take action soon.

THE THOUGHT of food turned his whirling stomach. Still, he ate, knowing he would need the energy. If they were to have the best chances at rescuing his Mate, being well-fed and in a proper frame of mind was an asset. One group even suggested they all take part in a meditation, followed by a training session.

Maintaining a habitual routine helped with his frame of mind. He was better able to focus. Giving him the ability to gain control over his emotions helped. Now he was able to think clearly and rationally. Instead constantly being emotionally driven.

As much as he wanted to fuel his anger, it wasn't the best idea. He could do that after Honor was safely back in his arms. For now, he needed to maintain his leadership. Delegating tasks, while preparing of guests and battle. Still, it wouldn't hurt to reach out a little bit, would it?

Gazing around the room, he stopped when he found those wanted to talk to. Determined, he crossed the room to them. Sweat drenched their bodies, and they were panting for breath, just like him. They looked at him, surprised when he stopped in front of them. He smiled before asking,

"Will the two of you give me a hand in another mediation session?"

Still wearing their surprised looks, both men were quick to reply.

"Of course."

Nudging his head behind them, they all turned and made their way to an empty corner. Once there, they all sat facing each other.

"I would also appreciate your help as I attempt to support Honor."

Confusion still marred their faces, as both men agreed to help him.

Nodding his head, he explained.

"I know I can assist her with magick through our Mating bond. Knowing what we know about the magick being used against her it will help."

Again, he watched as the men nodded in agreement. How he knew this would work he couldn't explain, he just knew it would work. It was revealing his vulnerability next that was hard for him.

Honor deserved the best. He was determined to give that to her. Even if it meant rescuing her from a psychopath. One he should have protected her from. Rationally, he knew no one had known how crazy he had become in this time. Still, his feelings were just that: his feelings. The need to protect one's Mate from everything was strong.

He now understood that those feelings were growing stronger with every moment. It was a part of the True Mating process. The kidnapping of Honor only intensified them. Thankful that his meditation had helped.

The bond between them he was seeing more clearly with each moment. Instead of a slow natural building of their connection. This situation caused it to expand and intensify. No wonder his emotions were all over the place and so intense. What should take eons to develop was happening in hours, minutes, and seconds. Now, with that understanding, he could reach out to his Mate.

He could maintain his emotional focus and give Honor a little of what she needed with the help of others.

Looking both men in the eyes, he said.

"I need your help to calm my emotions and to stay focused on the task at hand. I don't want to get distracted. Will you help me so I can help her?"

Suddenly, fear filled him. He was their leader and shouldn't appear weak or in need. This rollercoaster of emotions was really getting exhausting. He appreciated how much Honor did for him in her ability to calm. That fear quickly disappeared when both men reached out, each grabbing a hand.

"We will gladly help you, sir. We will also help Honor."

Determination gripped him as they all closed their eyes and breathed deeply. Creating a rhythm of breathing in through the nose and out through the mouth. Soon he felt their combined magick swirling around them.

Not wanting to worry Honor, he kept to the background of her mind. Like a gentle hug, offering her support for anything she was enduring. He knew he shouldn't make a full connection. He likely would be angry with what was happening. That would only cause her to worry about him.

So instead, he offered her his magick. Giving freely, all she would need. He planned on repeating the process as many times as needed till the arrival of their aid.

THIS WAS BAD. Very, very bad. Looking over at her Mate she grimaced. He, too, wore the same grim expression. Hearing her twin's plea for help had brought so many feelings to the surface. Plus memories from when they were in a similar situation.

Needing comfort, she turned, whispering.

"Kieran."

Sighing in contentment when he instantly embraced her in his loving arms. He bent, kissing the top of her head.

"I know, little one. I remember too."

He always knew exactly what was on her mind. Even though the binding connection didn't work that way. He is so in tune with her.

Pulling back, she searched his face.

"You think we'll get there in time?"

He smiled, rubbing his thumb along her cheek. Nodding his head, he said.

"Yes, little one, we will."

With that, he turned her around, slapping her ass, saying,

"Hop to it."

Laughing as he walked away. Shaking her head. Even though she had tried to reassure her brother, worry still swamped her. Honor was a True Guard member, a good one, too. Still, there were some things that, no matter how prepared you were, would still send for a loop. Plus, Jasper and Cory were crazy. Instead of dwelling, she finished gathering their belongings and stuffing them into bags.

Now, with the official meetings cut short yet again. They had still yet to discuss the meaning of her son's statement of "he's coming."

She was positive both she and Caden knew who he was referring to. The Overseer. Who else could Rowan have meant? How that man had any knowledge of the portal or how to use it, she didn't know. Had he found the clues she had left behind?

Those were some of the multitude of questions she had planned to ask. These meetings had stretched on for days. Various topics being discussed. As well as various decisions being made. Changes needed to be made and applied.

The list seemed endless. New questions always arose when discussions started. Wanting to dot every I and cross every T, they were in no rush to hurry Rowan. Content to allow him all the breaks he needed. Her son was still dealing with his transition. Everyone had agreed to give him grace and they could work at his pace.

Smiling to herself, she remembered when Aramis had pulled her aside after one such meeting. He wanted to reassure her he would personally see to Rowan. That he would help during his transition. Admitting he rather liked her son and wanted to nurture their growing friendship. He would also aid the man in finding his center in his newfound alpha abilities.

Her respect for the ruler grew. Not only did he care for her son, but he cared enough to build a relationship with her. Keeping her in the loop while also reassuring her. She was glad her son had made a new and close friend, and he didn't even know it yet.

She had to laugh. Her son, like his uncle, drew people to them.

They were the likable and genuine people everyone gravitated toward. So, leaving him behind, while the rest of them went to help Honor. She was confident he was safe here. The time might allow him the rest he needed.

Now, though, she needed to focus on helping to save her sister-in-law from a crazy man. Jasper really was a nut job. His picture should be in the dictionary beside the definition. The guy had always given her the creeps. What Sally had ever seen in the guy left her baffled.

Regardless, Jasper was a True Guard member and leader of a team. Therefore, he was above board, and she was the crazy one. People were stupid. Thinking about it made her angry. Their former compound housed some real wankers.

Feeling eyes on her, she looked up to see Kieran was watching her.

"It will be ok Harlow."

She accepted his outstretched hand. Smiling at him as he said.

"Come along. Cormac has requested we meet in a private court-yard. Cillian is already waiting with Aramis and his right hand."

With that, he gave her a slight tug forward before placing her hand in the crook of his elbow. He led the way to the agreed meeting place.

Before she could ask about the all their bags she had packed for them; he said.

"Don't worry, little one, our belongings will arrive at our destination."

Laughing at her confusion about how that would be, he playfully tapped the tip of her nose with his finger.

"Relax. Ok? There is more to this world you have yet to learn. Trust me."

Looking at him, she couldn't help but love him more. She trusted him implicitly.

"Alright, Kieran."

The beauty of the courtyard surprised her as she arrived. Stopping, she looked around as she gasped. The sunshine was dancing around and sparkling at everything it touched. Many of the plants and flowers she had never seen before.

She was discovering there was only so much you could learn from books. It was far better to actually see first hand and discover for yourself.

A deep voice broke her from the garden's spell.

"Thank you. I think it's beautiful as well."

Whipping her head towards the owner of the voice. Aramis smiled at her.

"This place is my most treasured sanctuary."

Smiling, she replied,

"It's stunning."

Cormac interrupted their interaction.

"Now that we all have arrived. Please take the hand of the person on each side of you."

He nodded his approval when everyone completed his directive.

"Good. Now hang on, no matter what happens. I want you to close your eyes and listen to my voice."

He began to chant. His rhythm ebbed and flowed through them. Taking them with the wind, lifting them. A pop within their ears had them all gasping for breath.

"Not bad. Not bad at all. You all did very well."

Opening her eyes, she saw they were no longer in the stunning courtyard; they were in a cabin. A smaller version of the one she had woken up in recently.

Cormac was gesturing for everyone to follow him.

"Come, let's go. Caden is expecting us."

They had just blinked traveled. Looking at Kieran, she whispered.

"Wow."

Her tongue-tied Mate could only nod his head in reply. Though he was looking a little green. She could help the laugh that bubbled up.

CHAPTER 36

A sharp voice rang through the air. Pulling him from his meditation.

"Caden."

Thankfully, he had offered Honor enough magick to sustain herself for a little while. After performing the task several times before with help, he could now do so on his own. Allowing his fellow compound members to help the others.

Blinking, he turned in the direction he heard the voice. Garth was standing there bouncing on his feet. The man was excited. It was an odd thing to see; he thought before asking.

"What is it, man?"

His bouncing stopped as he became serious.

"Your sister is here with everyone."

Surprise filled him. He had not felt her coming. Still, this was good. Standing, he brushed the nonexistent dirt from his pants. Asking.

"Where?"

"They'll be coming in the North entrance."

Nodding his head, he followed Garth from the hall. It had been the best place for him to connect with his Mate. Offering his magick to

her. It was the one building they had constructed of all natural mate-
rials. That, along with its open interior design, he could connect with
all the elements. Sustaining himself all the while, assisting his Mate.

As much as he wanted to go storming in, and saving his woman
from her captor. It was wise to wait for the support of the cavalry.
Especially when said group comprised locals and magicks. They were
an unknown, forcing them to rely on Honor and her training for the
time being.

He could hear the shouts of excitement when they left the great
hall. Their joy was contagious. He smiled, looking around at their
home. What they had built together was amazing. A blend of all the
tech they had access to, and some beautifully crafted wooden structures like that of the kitchen hall.

The preparations being made for their guests since hearing of
their immanent arrival amazed him. Beautiful gardens surround
many sleeping accommodations and entertaining spaces. With the
help of Magick, many of the structures reached a height higher than
he ever expected it to be possible.

It was stunning and magickal in its own right. They were truly on
their way to creating a beautiful sanctuary for magickal life. He could
only image what was to come when locals lived here as well. Home, he
thought.

People greeted them with handshakes, fist bumps, and congratula-
tions as they walked through the compound toward the North gate. It
was a relief to live in a place where people were happy, confident, and
giving to each other.

He was a few steps away from the gate when he heard.

"Caden, we are here."

He couldn't help but laugh. His twins, hesitance, was a typical side
of her personality from back home. However, in this time, she was
finally showcasing her true self. The side she had only allowed him
and her son to see. Cora to of course.

It was a blessing to see. Her Mate Kieran brought out the best
of her.

"We know, sister dear. The gate will open soon."

Looking over at the man in charge of the door today, he nodded.

Showing he could open the door. He wondered how they would all react to the changes in his sister. She outranked them all now. When Kieran and Harlow bonded, the priestess, who presided over the ceremony, blessed them with a gift.

He knew they wanted to keep their new status a secret. Which made him laugh. When Magick was involved, all intentions went out the window. The couple in question carried an aura around them. Anyone who came near them immediately knew and recognized who they were. If that wasn't enough, there were the tattoo markings displayed on their left arms. A telling of their story and their vocation.

Once the doors opened, a hush washed over everyone, as if on cue. The couple in question were leading the group walking into the compound. As usual, his twin was oblivious to her effect on people as she rushed toward him, her arms wide.

Shouting his name, she flung herself into his waiting arms.

"Caden."

Laughing, he twirled her around before setting her on her feet.

Pulling back, he studied her face.

"It's good to see you, sister, dear."

Pulling her in for a hug. He wanted the familiar comfort.

When he released her, her blush slowly crept up her face. Displays of affection were hard for her. Her instinct was always to hide and be invisible. She took a few steps backward, backing into Kieran's chest. He watched as his brother-in-law wrapped his arms around his Mate. Bending, he whispered into her ear, causing her cheeks to turn redder.

Deciding to give her a break, he said.

"Come with me. We can go to the kitchen hall and eat while we talk about a plan."

It was like they were walking in a parade. As they trekked through the compound, everyone gathered to watch them. Complete with oo's and ah's. Everyone bowed their heads when the couple passed by.

He was right they had no hope of keeping their secret. What did that mean for Honor and Cormac? How long would it be before someone found out they were Oracles, he wondered?

THE MEAL they shared was amazing. Whoever had cooked outdid themselves. So much so that Aramis threatened to steal them into his kingdom of this personal chef.

With bellies full, everyone took this time to talk and get to know one another. Discussing gifts, talents, training tactics and the like. Some even went so far as to spar in the far corner of the room. While others were content to continue chatting, and learn from each other.

Aramis's people were intense, but cool. He ran his battle guard, similar to how he had run his True Guard team. He could see why his nephew and the shifter leader got along so well.

They were still joking around and laughing when a sonic boom reverberated throughout the kitchen hall. Shaking everyone and knocking a few to the floor.

Some were asking.

"What the hell was that?"

While others asked,

"Was that a person who did that?"

Shaking his head, he knew right away what that was. Someone had just come through the portal. Likely a lot of someone's too. Through gritted teeth, he said.

"No. It is the archway. Someone had come through."

Looking at his sister, then at Garth, he said.

"He's here."

The timing sucked, to say the least. They had been preparing for an attack on a local farm, with magicks and nonmagick. To bring Honor home. Not defending their new compound.

Like a well-oiled machine, all of his members within the compound swung into action. Increasing surveillance, assembling a scout team, and even Kieran was discussing with Cormac. Following a few nods and shakes of his head, the old man vanished in a blink.

He was thankful for the shifter ruler's battalion had arrived not that long after Aramis himself. So they would have back up, should they need it. It was just they had no experience with their tech or techniques. It was a blessing then that after the meal, some had broken away to spar. Receiving a tiny education into their world.

Now his brother-in-law was talking to his man Cillian. He sought his sister Harlow. She would be privy to the reason for Cormac's departure. He had a feeling there was something more going on.

His twin confirmed his suspicions.

"He's gone to retrieve Corrina."

They knew her as Cora in their time. But someone had murdered that woman. There was speculation that Jasper had done the deed himself. Even amongst his very own True Guard team, speculation ran rampant. There was no proof he had, sadly. It was not for the lack of trying, either.

He had learned many had conducted inquiries secretly, in vain, to find out information. Hoping to give to him or Harlow solace. Taking said findings to The Overseer as well, so justice could be served. Sadly, that hadn't happened.

Most everyone had shared such their personal revelations with him at varying points since arriving. Expressing their true feelings about their former leader, too. At first, it had been unnerving, while also thrilling.

Now he was hoping they could act as a unified family of magick. They were beings who possessed a multitude of powers and talents. Who, through the many meetings this week, had sworn to protect magick and all magickal beings.

With their technical compound combined with magick, it made a unique place. A sanctuary for all magickal persons and the archway. Their mission was now sound. Their goal is obvious.

There were multiple construction projects in the works. All to better prepare themselves for the many tasks ahead. A state-of-the-art temperature-controlled library to house all magickal documents and tomes. More living quarters with a verity of features. With the multi-tude of varying magickal creatures, they needed to accommodate the uniqueness of everyone.

Not to mention a new grand hall since this kitchen hall had now become their war room. It would not accommodate the growth of the compound. Which was just as well. It was plain and basic. But as a war room, it was perfect.

What further surprised him was the response of the community at large. Many of the kingdoms were already duplicating their works to add them to the many existing works. Kieran and Cormac had supplied most of them already. His sister was champing at the bit to read them. Their kind went back for eons. Even the elders among them had forgotten most of what the tomes contained.

The archway that housed the portal was also in need of protection. Not to mention some serious guarding. They were perfect for handling the responsibility of the task. By traveling through it, they gained some knowledge of how it worked. It was basically right at their doorstep. Add in all the True Guard training and experiences, along with their gifts, they were the perfect guardians.

So if it was who they all thought it was, that came through the portal. Then they would have some time. The journey took a lot out of a person, most times rendering the person unconscious. However, if The Overseer had learned about the archway, he might have discovered a workaround for that arrival issue.

The man had in the past always was one step ahead of the rest. He wonders was he too one of them? Could that be why he was ahead of the game?.

Time would tell, he guessed. Soon too. There was no need for them to leave the war room. He knew their new arrivals would come to them. Curtsy of the collection team they had created. In the event that something like this was to happen.

So they waited. He, along with Harlow, Kieran, Cillian, and Aramis, sat up on a platform at the end of the hall. Shortly after a few more popping sounds, Cormac appeared with Cora and another man. Quickly, they joined them where they sat. They didn't have to wait long. Others filed into the war room.

Waves of semi-conscious True Guard members were brought in. All of whom were members of his very own True Guard team. That surprised him. How had they become the personal guard of The Overseer? He knew the change in their rank based on the badge they all now wore. What happened to the other team of men and women who were serving this position?

With more questions than answers rising, he filed them away for later. They sat there waiting and watching. When the man in question was among the last group to enter the war room. He, like the rest, was semi-conscious.

It didn't take long before the new arrivals were all coming around. They seemed to fare far better than they had when they had traveled through the archway. Looking around, he watched those seated beside him studying their guests. He felt a little strange now. Being he was the one in complete charge.

Regardless of his twin and her Mate's official status. Aramis a ruler in his own right, as well as the unnamed man he to a leader himself. They respected this as his territory, supporting his decision. It was what they had all agreed upon while in the meetings this week.

Their wait was brief before they could begin with questioning. Many of his people proficient in healing were attending their guests. They applied their magickal knowledge combined with the tech they had access to. Plus, if these men were like the rest of them, they also had the ability to self-heal.

He knew when The Overseer was back with them. He wasted no time in addressing them. Nodding his head. He said.

"Hello Caden, Harlow."

He acknowledged their places of power. Interesting. He thought. There was more to this man than he thought. He had always been aloof and absent before. Now he suspected that was because of his ageless appearance as opposed to a personality type.

He didn't look much older than himself. When he knew that was impossible. He had been the Overseer when he was born. Come to think of it, how long has this man been the Overseer?

The more he stared, the more he realized he was like them. Eerily so. His face had freckles dotted around, framing bright green eyes.

Their eyes. It was like looking in a mirror, except for his graying ebony hair. How had he not seen the similarities before?

Looking sharply at Harlow, he wondered if she was seeing what he was seeing. Did she realize the possibility?

"I see what you see, brother mine. Let him speak. See what he will reveal."

Nodding his head. Giving her his usual smirk. He said.

"Then we'll know what to ask. Smart. Very smart, my queen."

He roared out in internal laughter for only them when she scrunched her nose at his new nickname for her.

"Enough Caden. Let's get this over with. Perhaps the extra people could help us."

Liking her thinking, he turned back. Waiting for answers that clearly everyone sees wanted as well. This needed to hurry along. Honor needed their help.

From the corner of his eye, he noticed they were now observing the same thing he was observing. Was this another reason for his limited appearances?

When the Overseer cleared his throat and said.

"Hello, Corrina."

He nodded his head toward her.

"I hope you are well?"

All heads whipped to her, their eyes staring. Waiting in earnest. She did not disappoint them. First, she looked back in shock, followed by skepticism. Cautiously, she replied.

"I am well."

Regardless of her perfect vision, she squinted at him. Studying him.

He squared his shoulders while saying.

"The Ravens shall light your way."

Corrina sucked in a shocked breath before leaping off the elevation to stand before the man. Staring him down with hands on her hips, she firmly demanded.

"Who are you?"

Maintaining eye contact, he said.

"A dear friend of yours for many centuries."

He continued to speak while he shifted his glance to Cormac.

"I am not of this time. Clearly, as I am here now. A soul can only exist in one time. Otherwise, I could not survive the trip. Nor could I have entered had I not been a magick."

Tilting his head when he stated.

"Isn't that right, Cormac?"

Many shocked gasps sounded around the room. What else did this man know? Biting his tongue, he allowed him to continue.

An eerie smile spread across his face. He knew the effect he was having. Pausing, he continued when the old man stayed quiet.

"Yes, I know more than you suspected."

Looking at the twins. He directed the rest of his words to them.

"I did what I did to protect the two of you and, later, your son Harlow."

Indicating Harlow's son Rowan.

"It's what you do when you protect your family. Anything and everything."

Before he could continue, a forceful door slam caused it to hit the wall as someone forced it open. Everyone turned to see Rowan storming into the room larger than life and fuming. As he stocked through the room, all eyes were glued to him.

As he came to stand in front of them, just below the platform. He faced The Overseer.

Growling through clenched teeth.

"Hello, uncle."

The Overseer nodded his head, closing his eyes.

"Hello, Rowan."

Raising his head, he sniffed the air. Before asking.

"Are you well? There is a change in you."

Tilting his head, he studied his great nephew.

More growling through Rowan's clenched teeth. Had Aramis carefully stand, coming to stand behind him, and placing a hand on his shoulder. Instantly, he calmed. When he lowered his hand, his nephew replied.

"I have changed and am adjusting, ... slowly."

He turned, nodding thanks to Aramis before turning back to face his uncle. Well, their uncle.

The Overseer nodded his head, saying.

"That's good."

Giving his focus again to the twins, he told them.

"Your mother was my twin sister. As you know, she died giving birth to you both. To save your lives, I had to hide the two of you. Not willing to leave you's I hid you both in plain sight."

Before their uncle could continue, all hell broke loose. With several things happened at once, causing confusion and hysteria.

CHAPTER 37

*H*e hadn't felt this energized in days. This self-imposed therapy of a daily ritual was doing wonders for him. Well, it could also be that his little sister held quite the magickal punch. He couldn't help but laugh at his joke.

The darling Honor had become his personal punching bag. Every time he made contact with her, he could feel the energy flow. Maybe he should keep her instead of giving her over to their powerful guest. It didn't matter what he had promised him. She was his by blood.

Yeah, he liked the sound of that. Screw the other guy. She was his. A personal battery for himself. How she managed it, he didn't know and didn't care. Only that she should continue to do so. Otherwise, she was dead.

He was going to kill her, anyway. So it was no skin off his back. Now he got to have a little bit of fun. The fact it was with his little sister was a fringe benefit.

Now he had to figure out how to get rid of his knowledgeable guest. He regretted inviting him here. The longer he was around him, the more he disliked the man. As creepy as he was, it was not why he wanted him gone. The man was trying to usurp his authority.

This was his time to shine. His time to rule. All his hard work would not be in vain. Again. He would take care of the scrawny man himself if he had to. Although he suspected Cory would again come in handy.

He disliked their new friend just as much as he did. The reason he did so, he refused to reveal. Nevertheless, he would use that hatred for his purpose. Like he always had. It was what he was good at. Reading people and making do as he wanted.

It was the purpose of lesser people. He himself is one of the better ones. Why else could he achieve so much? It just further cemented his belief.

He had convinced Cory to go and take Honor. Bringing her here where she belonged. She had even been given to him when she joined the True Guard. Justice needed to be served for past wrongs, and now was the time.

They would not tolerate her abandoning them for someone like Faxon. She needed to be dealt with. Cory had readily agreed. Blinking when told and bringing her to him. It had easy to drug her and place her in her new room.

His first mistake had been allowing their guest with no name to go into the prison with him. What he witnessed then had changed the man somehow. The man was now smiling and spunky, almost. It made even creepier, if that were possible.

He was pretty sure the change was not in his favor, either. Which sucked. He had been hoping the man would be an asset to him. Instead, he was turning out to be a leech. One he would quickly remove and squish.

He had to time it just right, with all the right players. Perhaps Caden could be of some use after all? Rubbing his chin, he started to plan. Ginning, he knew he was on to something here. This would work. Work very well indeed.

Rising, he dressed quickly. All he had to do was say the right words into the right ears and things would progress. With a helpful nudge, of course. He allowed the grin on his face to spread.

THE ENERGY SURROUNDING her was shifting at a rapid rate. Something was happening topside. Something big. Sitting as gently as she could, she sighed in relief when she leaned back against the wall. As hard and cold as the stone wall was, she was thankful for the support while sitting. It was nice to change positions now and then. There weren't many options in this tiny room, however.

Closing her eyes, she recalled all she had learned after her last visit with her brother. Her brother. That was still hard for her to wrap her mind around. She could never find out any information about her family. Therefore, she assumed, like her, they were unimportant.

Not only was Jasper her brother, but so too was Rowan's father. It disgusted her with what Clay had done to Harlow. Were all the men in her family crazy? Well, not according to Jasper. Their father had been a standup guy. In her perspective, he was. From what she had learned in all of Jasper's ramblings, in between his beatings.

What was the point of worrying over it now, though? She had bigger problems. Like getting out of here. She was barely awake long enough to formulate a plan. Otherwise, she dedicated herself to staying alive during her brothers' frequent visits.

It took all she had to maintain her healing and strength to deal with him. Plus, during his last visit, he brought a friend with him. A creepy scrawny-looking man. That was just as sleazy as her brother was. What bothered her more than the intentions that man had. Was Jasper's parting admission.

Oh, she could very easily deal with the other man. In time. It was the admission her brother made. He had killed Cora. It was like a slap to the face when he said it. She had always suspected as much, but couldn't find any proof. He had taken her life because he could. It was just a fringe benefit that it bothered the Faxons so much.

Chills ran down her spine. Her brother was cold and heartless. To murder someone just because you could. Yuck, it made her sick. Part of becoming a True Guard member was about protecting life. Closing her eyes, she tried not to vomit.

That was not something she could afford to do right now. She couldn't remember the last time she had eaten. Somehow, though, she could access enough magick to sustain and heal herself. If she had to guess, Caden was the reason behind that. There whisper touches of him every so often. Making her feel loved and reassured. While enough to sustain her and keeping her alive. It wouldn't do forever, though.

The touches and slight grazes she had made when Jasper was here weren't enough. He did not possess enough magick for her. As time wore on, she suspected he was doing the same to her. Feeling the energy flow from her to him. Though she doubted, he realized what he was doing. It would explain why his strength never wavered.

Still, she pondered. Why else was she so tired all the time? Her gifts were far more powerful than his. Even more power than the ancient one that had come with him. It was likely because of the type of spells cast around her cell and the fact she hadn't consumed food in a while. It was becoming more difficult to focus, let alone to think.

Shaking off the memories and trying to figure out the exact magicks, it was redundant. It was better to channel what mental focus she could on getting out of here. With all the ruckus going on above, she was betting now was the time for her to escape.

So far, she had only learned that the door could only open from the other side. Jasper always left the door open during his visits. She doubted it had anything to do with claustrophobia and everything to do with magick. Would explain why every time she had tried, it wouldn't budge. The simple wooden handle had given her false hope.

It was going to take someone coming down here and opening the door for her to make her move. Her instincts were saying it would be the mystery man that came.

Any reason to fight or create conflict and Jasper was there. So he would be otherwise occupied. No doubt he was the reason for all the chaos happening above her. Could that be how gets his immense strength? Inciting mischief and ruckus in others? Shaking her head again. Those were questions best left for later.

Her plan would have to be a simple one for now. Taking the situations as they came. Then going for whichever option leads her closer to freedom. Like a 'choose your own adventure.' Laughing, she liked that idea.

Once she was topside, she knew she would regain the ability to access all of her magicks again. Now she would wait for the ancient one. She would follow his directive to a point. Ultimately, she would make sure that he received what he had always been seeking.

It was her turn to smile an eerie grin. During her imprisonment, she learned how her powers worked. Her brother's scrawny friend had been a perfect test subject. She would grant his wish while also doling out his rightful punishment.

As if on cue, the very man she suspected walked through her prison cell door. He was haggard and winded. His eyes whirling around in fear. When he saw her in the far corner, he rushed to her. Grabbing her by the upper arm, he brought her to her feet.

Despite being frail, he had a surprising amount of strength. With a crackly voice, he demanded.

"You're coming with me."

Trying hard not to laugh, she sobered her facial features before replying.

"Ok."

His resulting squint at her had her second-guessing her response. Had she been too perky and quick to reply? Or was there something else?

In the end, it didn't matter. This was her chance, and she was going to take it. Even though she still felt like shit and wanted to sleep for a week. She wanted her freedom and Caden even more.

CHAPTER 38

*M*en and women he had never seen before now appeared from thin air all about the kitchen hall. To the untrained eye, they all looked as though they were blinking into the place. Being he had traveled in such a way before, he knew this was not the case for these individuals.

They were all perfectly positioned between every True Gaud member. Like they had all walked in here under an invisible shield. Picked out their victim and stood before them. Was that how they entered? Under a cloak of magick.

He had a moment to look at the weaponry they carried before they started attacking. It looked like what they had seen in history teaching as children. Shouts and cries echoed across the great space. What he found interesting was they were only attacking what he guessed they assumed to be locals and not their newly arrived guests. Many of whom were still coming back to themselves after their portal travel. Since they were all dressed the same, and that was the only difference, he went with that theory. Or did someone assign them direct targets? If so, then who by? Jasper?

What irked him even more was he still had yet to recuse his Mate. Let alone plan an attempt. Life seemed to throw every obstacle in his way. While each one seemed to result in side benefits for him. Finally, answers were coming for age-old questions. The timing, however, sucked.

A mass of screaming warriors charged the platform where he, his sister, his brother-in- law, and the others were all now standing. Raising their weapons, they shouted obscenities at them. Confused, he looked at Harlow and Kieren, who looked just as confused.

With a twinkle in his eye, his sister's Mate said.

"Let's not hurt them. Much."

Before, he jumped off the platform, entering the battle. Using his magick to block blow after blow from a blade before sending his opponent sailing through the air. They landed on another of the attackers, knocking them both out. Rendering them unconscious.

Energized and seemingly enjoying himself, he watched as his brother-in-law skipped to the next duel. Shocked by his odd behavior, he turned to gape at his sister. Only to find her bent to her knees, laughing and shaking her head.

Well, if she was content simply to watch. He would join in all the fun. Knowing she would have their backs covered. Jumping down, he allowed his electrical charge and current to spread across his skin. Not only could he hear the crackling sound, but he could also see the popping light effects, which made him smile.

Reaching out, he grabbed the first attacker he saw. Watching as their eyes grew at the shock of pain before they rolled into the back of their head. Keeping his voltage low. It wasn't enough to kill, only to knock them out for a few hours. Like a dance, he moved across the floor. Twisting, ducking, and spinning to miss a thrust of a sword or a swipe of an ax. He understood now the reason for Kieran's skip in his step. This was fun.

Their attackers were intent on killing them. Despite being outmatched. Not having interacted with many locals before, this seemed like odd behavior to him.

When a slice of a blade swiped across his back, he hissed through his teeth at the sting. Arching his shoulders at the pain. Damn, that was painful. It was taking more of energy and power to heal himself.

Someone cursed these blades with magick. It was not those wielding the weapons either. If they had gifts to curse, they would use them to fight and not on armaments.

Something more sinister was in the works here. Time they finish this before more damage could be done. They need to find answers and find the real culprits. Quickly, too, he needed to get Honor back. His only reassurance was she was an Oracle possessing immense power and powers. For a time, she could handle herself.

Cormac had reassured him just the same. While also saying this was a trail she needed to go through. Along the way, she would find the answers she had sought. That man was sometimes far too cryptic for his liking.

Scanning the room, he noticed Kieran, Rowan, and Aramis were herding the attackers into the far corner. He wasn't a fan of violence for the sake of violence. From looking around, the others weren't either. Which was nice. Perhaps they could get some answers.

It took almost no time to subdue the remaining fighters. With a quick swish of his wrist,

Cormac had tied them all at the hands and feet in one long chain. Which, when complete, saw them all topple like dominos to the ground. It was a funny sight to not bend over laughing. Everyone joined in before he blurted the first giggle. That was when the air began to crackle and sing before the main doors flew open with enough force to bang against the wall.

Jasper strolled in, like he owned the place. Strutting tall and proud, completely ignorant of those around him. When he made it to the center of the room, he froze. Finally, taking in his surroundings. Shock spread across his face. Quickly followed by anger.

His head whipped around the room till he located Caden. Pointing his finger, he shook it at him as he sputtered.

"You. You're supposed to be dead."

Confused, he scanned the room again. Finally, seeing all the men and women he had sent in to do battle were either tied up or unconscious.

With more sputtering, he asked.

"How?"

The man was really confused. He thought his plan was successful. Never once considering it would fail. It was almost comical. But he had once again brainwashed and recruited others to do his dirty work for him.

All so he could have power? He was no leader. Only a bully and a cheat with a nasty temper.

Slowly, he advanced toward the man. Staring him down. He wanted his Mate. He demanded.

"Where is Honor?"

He couldn't care less about the events of today. This sleazy man had his fingers in his Mates's kidnapping. He wanted answers.

Jasper's face shifted from anger to smug pride. When he said,

"You'll never have her back. I have only taken what is rightfully mine."

The Overseer's intervention stopped him from rushing and grabbing the man. He swung his arm out, barricading his path.

"What is rightfully yours? Hah."

He seemed to grow even taller as he spoke.

"Women are not things, Jasper. Just because you killed Cora does not give you the right to harm your sister."

Caden felt as if someone had punched him in the gut. He had always suspected it was Jasper who had killed his friend, but lacked any concrete proof. But the man was his Mate's brother. Suddenly, all the pieces added up and made sense.

Sucking in a few shocked breaths, he heard the echoes of others doing the same around the room. Watching as Jasper started to transfer his weight from foot to foot. He had the deer caught in the headlights look.

He used to make fun of his sister for always trying to resurrect the old colloquialisms. Now he was finding them more fun to use. It was a fun way of expressing yourself. In this case, it was also a welcomed distraction.

The former True Guard leader had nothing to say for once. The man always had an excuse for everything. It usually was in his favor, too.

"Just as I thought, always the bully, aren't you, Jasper? Just like your brother Clay."

Upon hearing the mention of his sister's rapist, she gasped while he growled. Also had Kieran and Rowan joining in, it seemed.

Jasper's eyes seemed to sparkle. The tiny man stood straighter and squared his shoulders. He liked what his brother had done. He was proud.

What a monster! Once more, he tried to charge the man, but his uncle prevented him, again.

He watched as the man he only ever knew as their leader defended his family. Like he had been doing his entire life.

"Your actions have consequences, Jasper. Just like your brothers did."

This only seemed to infuriate him to where steam could be seen coming from his ears as he said. Shoving his finger in Harlow's direction.

"She asked for it."

He could hear his sisters whimper in pain.

Their uncle shook his head, saying.

"No, Jasper, she didn't. No one asks for that. Not even Caden when you had Sally do the same to him."

Shock filled him at his uncle's insight. How had he known? He had only recently relieved that insight to himself through Honor's help. His Uncle was really a wise man, a wise man indeed. Standing here defending his family while also governing, as was his duty.

Jasper, on the other hand, looked as though he was about to burst into a rage. He kept opening and closing his mouth.

"Your sister is not the reason for the destruction of your family, Jasper. Your parents died of cancer. They were heroes. Surviving long enough to make sure Honor had a chance. Had they gotten their treatment, she would have died. Even then, she needed medical help."

This time, he looked up at Corrina and smiled.

"I took it upon myself to help your family, Jasper. I searched high and low crossing the globe looking for my very old and dear friend, Cora."

Corrina had her head tilted, studying The Overseer. She was learning about her future self. How must it be to be in her shoes? To learn about your future death from future friends.

"For she possessed the ancient knowledge to heal. The kind of internal knowing we had long since forgotten."

Looking back at Jasper, he continued.

"It's my fault, Jasper. I could not find Cora in time to save your parents. For not giving you all the information, and I'm sorry. You should have known the truth before now. I thought I was sparing you more pain and suffering."

In a whisper, to himself he said.

"Perhaps if I had, we wouldn't be here now."

This is where Cormac chimed in, saying.

"Hogwash. That man's transgressions are not your own. He made the decisions just like his brother did. All you could do was deal with the aftermath of their destruction."

When he finished, he grunted his disgust toward Jasper, waving his arm like he was swatting a fly.

During the entire conversation, a select circle of True Guard members was closing in on Jasper. Any knowledge they were hoping to gain, The Overseer already knew. They just needed the exact whereabouts of Honor. They could restrain the bastard for that interrogation.

Just as the thought crossed his mind, the men pounced. Tackling him to the ground and hog-tying him in a matter of seconds. His men were good. Of course they were. He had trained them, after all. That had him smiling ear to ear.

That was when more crackle and popping sounds echoed around the room. When suddenly Honor was standing before him. Her smile was stunning. She whispered his name just before she collapsed. Thank god for his super reflexes. He caught her just in Time.

THE MAN WAS STRONG, yes, but slow. It took them ages to reach the topside. Once there, he had to stop to catch his breath. While he leaned against the door, hands to his chest, she fell to her knees on the ground. Sinking her fingers in between the blades of grass and closing her eyes. She asked for the rejuvenating essence of the earth. Wishing for just enough to perform her next task.

Feeling a warmth fill her with its loving hug. She thanked all the powers. Knowing she could now freely talk to Caden through their mating bond. She maintained that barrier just in case this didn't work.

Needing to act fast but not raise any suspicions, she used what little acting skills she had. Moving slowly and with an awkward gait, she tried to simulate injuries while moving closer to the ancient man. Copying his pose, she reached out with one arm and when she made contact; she blinked.

Hurtling them through space. Keeping her mind focused on Caden, instead of a specific destination. She needed to make it to him. After that, she could relax and sleep. Hopefully secure in his arms.

With all the recent revelations she had learned, her mind hurt. The deaths of her parents and their story. Brothers, she didn't know she had. The monsters that they were. Then there was her nephew, Rowan, and not just by a marriage. But by blood. He was a blood relative of hers. One she liked, too. He was a good man.

Was that why and how she had created the unbreakable bond with Caden and Garth? With a mental slap, she needed to stay focused. She wasn't out of the woods yet.

As the energy charge ramped up, she knew they were getting close. She tightened her grip on the ancient one. He was barely conscious but trying to fight her. He knew she had hoodwinked him. The thought made her smile.

In another blink, they were both standing in front of her Mate. With her ears buzzing and her vision blurring, she looked up at her man. When he smiled back, she let the blackness swallow her.

CHAPTER 39

*C*radling Honor to his chest, he watched as yet again, all hell broke loose. The scrawny, ancient-looking man his Mate had brought with her was now in vain trying to escape his uncle.

He looked like a clown doing a bit, the way he was tripping over nothing and swaying this way and that. The laugh he allowed to escape startled the precious bundle in arms. A bundle he wanted very much to run back to his pod with and care for her.

Looking back at the chase, ensuing, he couldn't help but think there was something familiar about this man. He didn't recognize the man per se, but there was something about him.

There was also something wrong with him. Was it because of something Honor had done to him? Or was he just like that? He wanted to laugh again at the sight of it until he heard Harlow gasp, "You." Turning to look her way, he saw Cormac clutching a hand to his chest, saying, "Gawyn." All the while, The Overseer was chasing him around and shouting.

"Craven, you'll not get away this time."

Who the hell was this man? His head hurt from whipping it in every direction to discern the connections, if any.

Finally, Aramis's shout distracted the man enough to trip and fall. Ending the chaos.

"Enough."

True Guard members were ready and waiting to hogtie him, too. It would seem they had been just as taken in by the crazy display as he had been. When he was secure, they flipped him over and seated him near the platform. With enough slack in the binding to fasten him to the chair now. The sickly looking man sneered at his uncle.

"Cade."

There was so much venom in his voice that everyone could feel it. While finally revealing The Overseer's name. It never occurred to anyone to find out what it was.

His uncle said through clenched teeth.

"Craven. You'll no longer harm my family."

In a move so smooth, the old man stepped down to stand beside Cade. Tilting his head, he said.

"Gawyn, I thought you dead."

Filled with emotion and concern, he continued.

"What have you done?"

As he spoke, the man with two names merely shrugged. Taking a double take of Cormac before his face looked as though he had come to a realization. Then just as quickly reverted back to anger.

With anger thick in his voice, their uncle said.

"This man." Pointing a finger. "Seduced and abandoned, my sister. His torture of her was so severe when she found out she was pregnant, she went into hiding."

Watching in shocked silence, as more revelations were being told. Cade continued. Speaking as if he were relieving the events.

"She told no one of the pregnancy out of more fear. Not even me, her own twin." He heard Harlow gasp in shock. Their mother was a twin, just like them. Turning to look at his sister, he felt their unique bond. He could only imagine how his uncle felt.

"I didn't find her till it was too late. She had been in labor for days. I was able to get her to the hospital, where they performed a C-section. All the while, she insisted they save her children. Harlow was the first baby removed, screaming and yelling bloody murder." He smiled at the memory. Before he frowned and continued. "The doctors had wanted to save my sister, as the other baby was stuck in the birthing canal. Had been for days. And likely already gone. She refused and prioritized saving him first, resulting in her death. When Caden was free, all efforts were used to revive him and bring him back to life. There was no way of knowing how long he had been gone."

He had been dead, born dead. Shocked at his core, he stumbled back a step.

It was then his uncle looked at him as tears filled his eyes.

"It was your mother's dying wish for you to share my name."

His uncle smiled then. A handsome smile, one filled with love. When he turned back to look at the scrawny man, he grew in stature. The softness and relaxed posture gone.

"I also swore to her I would protect her children from their father. Whatever it takes."

Cade moved so fast. Hauling his arm back, punching their father in the face, breaking his nose with a discernible crunch that echoed. Shaking his fist, he turned, storming from the war room.

Silently, everyone watched him leave. It was Cormac who broke the silence.

"Well, that explains a lot."

SHE COULD HEAR a man whining about his nose being broken through gargles of what she assumed was blood flowing. Blinking, she tried to find the source of who woke her up. She had been having the most wonderful dream about Caden. He embraced her tightly with his arms wrapped around her.

When she saw who it was, she couldn't help but roll her eyes, whispering.

"Oh, it's you."

Then she realized her dream wasn't a dream at all. She was being held tightly within her Mate's loving arms. Smiling, she looked up to see he was studying her. Reaching up, she cupped his cheek in her hand.

"I'm alright now."

Rubbing her thumb over his cheek in a loving gesture. She moved, telling him he could place her on her feet now. He granted her wish, but not before he bent his head and locked their lips together. Causing her to moan in desire. Man, he could kiss.

When her feet touched the ground, and he tried to pull away, she stopped him. Wrapping her arms around his neck, she deepened the kiss. Sighing in pleasure, when he accepted the challenge and took charge of the kiss. Thrusting his tongue into her mouth, dulling with hers.

Too quickly, he stopped, pulling back and resting his forehead against hers. She couldn't help the moans of displeasure. He responded by rubbing her cheeks with his thumbs as he cradled her head in his massive hands. Kissing the tip of her nose, he whispered.

"Later, my girl."

He pulled back farther, searching her eyes, before he asked.

"Are you really ok?"

Without being able to voice it, she nodded. She couldn't lie to him. He was her True Mate. The repeated beatings from her brother left her hurting from head to toe. Not to mention the metal toll he left. A toll she suspected she would deal with for a long time.

For now, though, she needed to put it all aside. There was more going on here. She could deal with herself later. She would have help. Smiling, she expressed all her love toward Caden in her eyes. Pleading him to understand. At least for now.

Still, he studied her, before squinting at her and nodding his acceptance. The unvoiced conversation was later, he would see for himself. They both turned. He placed her back to his front, wrapping his arms around her middle as best he could. He was several inches taller than her. It meant he had to bend slightly, resting his chin atop her head. The move made her giggle.

He whispered.

"Shhhh."

Snapping her out of their private moment. It was then she realized they were standing in the kitchen hall surrounded by people. Who all saw their display of affection. Her blushing cheeks grew steadily hot. She wanted to turn and burrow into Caden's protective embrace. However, his grip, suddenly firm on her hips, held her in place.

Unable to move, she stood there as Caden demanded.

"So which is it Gawyn or Craven?"

She noted he was addressing the scrawny man she had brought with her. All the man offered for a reply was a grunt and a shoulder shrug. Interestingly, he didn't seem as confident as he had before. That could be because someone had bound him to a chair. Though she doubted it. She had missed some vital interactions while she was out cold.

So remained silent and listened to Caden's questioning.

"What? No answer for your son?"

Unable to hold back her gasp, she covered her mouth to lessen its sound. This was the father of the twins. But how? She turned, looking up at Caden, silently asking her question.

His answer was to shrug his shoulders. So he didn't know either.

Turning back, she studied the man in while her Mate peppered him with questions. All of which were met with the silent treatment.

It pissed her off. This man was a snake of the first order, and he wouldn't give his children anything.

They deserved to know. She could do something about that. Taking a deep breath, she zeroed in on her target. Staring him down till he made eye contact with her. Perfect, she thought, as an eerie smile crept across her face. She could feel him tremble in fear.

As he should, she thought. In the distance, she heard Caden shout.

"No. Honor, what are you doing?"

Cormac's reassurance chased it.

"She'll be ok, my boy. I'll make sure of it."

It was then she felt the touch of his magick at the edge of her mind. Then together they dove into the mind of a monster.

CHAPTER 40

hat the hell was happening? His Mate was a pillar of ice in his arms. She kept her stare fixed on his father's gaze. Both were unmoving. Cormac stood just to his side, his hand resting on Honor's shoulder as he too, stood still, like a statue. The only difference was that his eyes were closed and moving rapidly.

Turning, he sought everyone still standing on the platform. He demanded.

"What the hell are they doing?"

Harlow was the first to move, coming to stand at his side. She said in her concerned, motherly voice.

"I don't know Caden."

Reaching out, she grasped his arm, gasping when she made contact. Eyes wide in surprise, she looked at Caden, stating.

"Their Oracles."

Her mouth formed an O as she turned to seek her Mate. He should have known his twin would figure it out sooner rather than later. The response she got surprised him more. A chorus of,

"We know."

Rang out behind him. So they all knew but had kept it a secret. His respect for them all grew a bit more. However, now everyone in the great hall knew their secret. Before, he could worry even more. Kieran spoke.

"No need to fear, brother. Their secret is safe with everyone in this room."

He was about to question about Jasper and his father when it was Aramis who spoke.

"No need to worry about the scum."

The man possessed an eerily cheerful smile with hungry eyes. He wasn't so sure he wanted to know what he was planning. The man seemed to read his mind there, too. He slowly shook his head.

But what about all the others in the room? They were from this world, and knowing Oracles existed could be problematic. Even though they were all still unconscious, he was still worried. This was his Mate.

Harlow pulled his attention back to the moment.

"Caden, if we can all connect to form a magickal chain. We will be able to support our Oracles in the task they are performing. I suspect any magickal assist would be beneficial."

He watched in awe as every single person in the room swiftly moved. Creating a chain by gripping hands. When Kieran joined hands with his Mate, an electrical charge like he never felt before flowed through him. Their combined magick was intense, powerful, and so bloody good. He was euphoric.

He still had no clue what the Oracles were doing to his father. No one else did either. However, he suspected his sister knew. Just a feeling he had. Why else would she have suggested this action? Watching her as she maintained eye contact with her mate. It looked like they were having an internal conversation. That gave him an idea.

Closing his eyes, he focused on Honor. Reaching for her through their mating bond. When he hit a wall, frustration washed over him. Until he heard her say,

"Be careful, Caden. I'm not sure you're ready for this."

What was she doing?

Wanting to know, he pushed ahead. Mentally stumbling when they realized where they were. Inside his father's head. The head of a monster.

HE WAS FIGHTING the urge to vomit. Inside his father's head, he was privy to everything. His endless torture of their mother. How he had hoped to steal her life essence to further his magickal abilities. His father was born into a magickal family with no magickal abilities himself. He had learned through the use of dark magicks how to garner his own powers by theft.

The trail of death and deceit he left was long. From what he could tell, he was unfazed by his actions. Instead, viewing it as though every victim owed it to him. Even so, he needed magickal persons with powers to perform most tasks. Therefore, he was keeping his hands clean. "So to speak." Disgusting. Utterly disgusting.

The man had so much blood on his hands he could smell it. As well as taste it. Had he always been like this? Or had the repeated use of dark magicks made him this way?

Based on Cormac's reaction, he was guessing the latter. Did this cause dark magicks to be forbidden?

Thankfully, his mother had outsmarted him and disappeared. Otherwise, who knew what could have happened? They might not be here at all. Any of them.

Another revelation was this man knew how to use the archway portal. It was how he had been seeking and finding the multitude of victims. In his dad's time, there had many more of them. All of them serving different purposes.

During the epic battle of the gods, all were destroyed except for one remaining archway. They thought that by destroying them, they could protect all life. Only it would seem they were too late.

Weaving through more thought and memories, he had the answer. His mother had tricked him into coming to this point in time. Craven had wanted the Ravens spell book and had come to her time looking for it. He figured it would have gained many spells by then and be immensely powerful.

So he sought his mother in order to seduce her so he could take the book. Since she was its guardian. His plans, however, evolved along the way when he discovered her uncanny resemblance to the prophecy.

For the one to see the futures past,
Is thrice blessed to conquer lightfast,
Fire be true,
With leadership firm.
Changing destiny right.

He knew of the vision it had invoked and heard it described many times.

Figuring destiny owed him for his lack of powers. Their mother was his next victim. Only she had hidden the tome. He dared not ask about the book, fearing that he would lose her and his access to her powers. Which he did anyway.

His mother had been a powerful woman. Very much like his sister, Harlow. Whom he had a strong suspicion that the prophecy was actually about her.

All of this came about because of their father's use of the portals. The very one they had all used to come here. The same one he had been using for years. But why had he stopped? Was he stuck here? Did he not have enough magick? Or was there more to it? He was thinking so.

To their mother, this man was Craven, and yet to Cormac, he was Garwyn. Curious. Routing around further, the truth shocked him. The two men were brothers, twins. Just like him. So if the man with two names was his father. That would make Cormac his uncle.

The very man who, at the age of five, had a premonition of a pretty lady who would save the world by saving all magick and magickal beings. She was the key.

This discovery had him falling back into the war room and stumbling back a few steps. His actions disconnected the entire chain of magick. Rubbing his hand down his face, he took a moment to breathe. Making eye contact with his twin, he informed her.

"Daddy dearest here was perpetually jealous of his powerful twin and his premonitions."

Pointing at Cormac.

Harlow's shocked words echoed off the walls.

"Holy Shit!"

This was messed up.

CHAPTER 41

This situation was a complete and utter mess! He was still dealing with all his new physical changes and urges. As well as hearing his mating call. He had yet to sniff her out. At least he knew where to look for her. But this, it just topped the cake.

He could not stay behind and heal while his mother and stepfather had gone to help his uncle rescue his True Mate. His aunt Honor was in some serious trouble and needed their help. Her former True Guard team leader and brother kidnapped her.

So he had snuck out of the palace and shifted, making his way to his family. It had been easy to follow them with his keen sense of smell. Even though they had traveled by magick to get here.

These past few days, or was it weeks? He wasn't even sure anymore. Long past caring about the amount of time that had gone by. Other things were on his mind. It wasn't the healing that was a challenge for him. Or the intensified senses he was having trouble adjusting to. It was the magnified urges.

Urges he had of a woman. His woman. One he had yet to meet. But was his all the same. The things he wanted to do to her and with her. Man, they were hot, kinky, and dirty. The worst of his thoughts and dreams had been when he had still been within Kieran's kingdom.

Well, he should get used to calling it Aidan's kingdom now.

Anyway, while he had been there, his skin had prickled and the urge to bite a specific someone was so strong. He could barely think. What embarrassed him the most was he was hard the entire time.

He wanted to fuck and fuck hard. The only one he had told was Aramis. He being a shifter as well; he understood. It was not something he had wanted to tell his mother about. She was at his bedside caring for him in between his bouts of conciseness.

The shifter king said it had likely been that his Mate was nearby. Since all the reactions were a normal part of the transition, they were not to last the duration. He was merely experiencing mating fever.

That had made him laugh. Not only was he now dealing with coming into a world of magick and being descended from a God race, but he was also a shifter, an alpha shifter likely experiencing his Mating heat.

His new friend had admitted he was jealous. He was still waiting to find his True Mate. Not that he didn't have his fun now and again. It would be nice to have that perfect partner.

Now he was in a room with his mother and her twin, their father, and both his great uncles. Oh, and his aunt. Then there was their found family. True Guard members who were like them magickal.

He was listening to his uncle Caden share what he had learned of his father and Cormac's brother. A real monster, torturing his grandmother for her power. A protector of the tome.

The very tome he had hidden when he arrived. Right before his grandfather's goons had captured him. Good thing too, he thought. If the man had had any idea, they wouldn't be standing here now.

It made him sick of the lengths this man had gone to gain even an ounce of more power. All because he was jealous of his twin. A man who had to hide his true gifts to survive. One who, as a small child, saw what could be.

Looking around the room, he watched the reactions of others to his uncle's words. Unanimous was their unwavering support for Caden and those he held dear.

When his uncle had ripped himself from the magickal connection and stumbled backward. His eyes and breathing were erratic. He had feared that something physically awful had occurred to him.

Instead, it was the knowledge of all the family connections that his mind pulled free. Sensing her Mate's distress, Honor had pulled free as well. Staring in silent support as he spoke. Even offering a reassuring smile to Harlow when she swore.

An eerie and hateful voice broke through.

"You all have it so easy. Unwilling to share just an ounce with those of us in need."

His grandfather sneered at them all in disgust.

His twin shook his head with a grim expression.

"It's never enough for you, brother. And never will be."

Taking a few steps backward, before he turned away. He spoke in an empty voice.

"Honor my dear, will you dole out justice? Harlow and I are too involved."

He watched as a single tear fell down the old man's face as moved and he watched as he embraced his mother. Harlow welcomed the loving hug from her uncle.

Hearing her whisper.

"Somehow I always knew."

He nodded, saying.

"Me too. My premonitions can be of those only related by blood. Now I know how."

As he turned his head to look at his brother.

Wow, what another revelation. They have been having way too many of those today. When his aunt Honor spoke, it was not in her usual voice. It was crystal clear and somewhat separated from her. His grandfather trembled in fear.

"You of the two names seek to cheat life and death. Forever in search of power. Your destiny shall be that which you desire."

His grandfather's eerie smile returned. He likely thought all would finally be his. However, he underestimated Honor. She was nice, yes, but wrong her, and look out she was devious and mean.

He also knew everything she had done to protect his mother and his uncle before they had disappeared. Sloan had later revealed all to him.

"I hear by grant your most inner wish. You will forevermore be a leech to feast, if only to survive. The blood you so richly desire shall be your blessing. The moon your sanctuary whilst the sun your enemy. So mote it be."

When she finished, he watched as she snapped her fingers and sparks flew. They swirled and surrounded his grandfather. His body lifted and jerked in the chair. The once scrawny man filled slightly, ashening in complexion.

At the same time, Honor, Caden and Garth all jerked in unison, gasping as if they shocked by an invisible force. All three of them looked at the palm of their right hand with a look of surprise and understanding.

His grandfather's once eerie voice was now velvety as he broke the spell and demanded.

"What have you done to me?"

To which Honor merely laughed.

"I told you. I granted your wish."

Smirking, she winked at him.

This angered him. Growling, he continued to fight the bond of his chair.

"You are what you wanted. A being able to suck the power needed to survive."

Placing her hands on her hips, she continued.

"I would be careful if I were you. As you now have more enemies than friends."

With that, she turned into the loving embrace of her True Mate.

In a shocking move, this newly created creature broke free of his bonds and lunged for Honor. Snapping and growling about revenge. He was almost on her when Jasper lunged in front of her, blocking the way.

In stunned silence, they all watched as his grandfather reared his teeth before sinking them into his neck. The echo of sucking reverberated around the room. His aunt had turned his grandfather into a vampire.

"Holly Shit."

Was all he could think to say. Well, it more or less just slipped out. When Aramis said.

"I've never seen anything like it."

He let slip again.

"Holy Shit."

The first ever vampire.

After finishing, he snapped his head up. Blood dripped from his chin. A smile crept across his face.

"I will see all again. With Duvessa at my side."

With that, he was gone. Only a cloud of dust plumed in the air where he had once been.

He was about to ask who Duvessa was when Kieran, Cormac, Aramis, and all the others from this time, in unison, said.

"No. It's not possible."

Confused, he looked at his mother, questionably. She had no clue either she was shaking her head with a scrunched nose.

It was Kieran who finally spoke.

"Duvessa is or was my mother."

Oh. Shit!

Enjoyed God Awakened, give it a review. It's appreciated & helpful

PLEASE JOIN!

Holly's Ravens Night Newsletter!

Stay up-to-date on what events are coming up, and how my writing is going. This is a good way to keep in touch and get release day links! I also share when I am running a sale on my books.
Oh, and let's not forget the free digital gifts I have for you.

MY BOOKS

Book 1 Goddess Kindled

Book 2 God Awakened

Book 3 God Bitten

TRIGGER CONTENT

God Awakened includes steamy sex, kidnapping, violence, sibling abuse, cruelty.

ABOUT THE AUTHOR

Holly MacGregor, the author of the magickal portal, spicy romance, and fantasy novels Ravens Night Saga. Which includes Goddess Kindled, and God Awakened, with God Bitten coming soon. I live in Canada with her husband, their son, and four furry friends.

Want to know more check out my website, hollymacgregor.com.

I am also on social media. Consider giving me a follow. I post frequently and enjoy interacting with my followers. I am Holly MacGregor on Facebook and Instagram I am @authourholly-macgregor.